ALSO BY FIONA MCFARLANE

The Sun Walks Down

The High Places

The Night Guest

HIGHWAY THIRTEEN

HIGHWAY THIRTEEN

STORIES

FIONA McFARLANE

FARRAR, STRAUS AND GIROUX

NEW YORK

Farrar, Straus and Giroux
120 Broadway, New York 10271

Printed in the United States of America
Originally published in 2024 by Allen and Unwin, Australia
Published in the United States by Farrar, Straus and Giroux
First American edition, 2024

Title-page image by MaxNadya / Shutterstock.com.

Grateful acknowledgment is made for permission to reprint lyrics by Walter Davis
from "13 Highway," 1938, courtesy of Berwick Music Corporation.

Library of Congress Cataloging-in-Publication Data
Names: McFarlane, Fiona, 1978– author.
Title: Highway thirteen : stories / Fiona McFarlane.
Description: First American edition. | New York : Farrar, Straus and Giroux, 2024.
Identifiers: LCCN 2024008114 | ISBN 9780374606268 (hardcover)
Subjects: LCSH: Serial murders—Fiction. | LCGFT: Thrillers (Fiction) | Linked
    stories.
Classification: LCC PR9619.4.M38355 H54 2024 | DDC 823/.92—dc23/
    eng/20240223
LC record available at https://lccn.loc.gov/2024008114

Designed by Gretchen Achilles

Our books may be purchased in bulk for promotional,
educational, or business use. Please contact your local bookseller
or the Macmillan Corporate and Premium Sales Department at
1-800-221-7945, extension 5442, or by email at
MacmillanSpecialMarkets@macmillan.com.

www.fsgbooks.com
Follow us on social media at @fsgbooks

1   3   5   7   9   10   8   6   4   2

For Michelle

Each substance of a grief hath twenty shadows.

—*Richard II*, 2.2.14

CONTENTS

HIGHWAY THIRTEEN

TOURISTS

(2008)

Lena Derwent had worked at Mason's for less than a week when they started making fun of her.

'Well hi there, handsome,' they said when she was out of sight. 'My name is Lena, and I come to you from the 1980s.'

'She looks like an art teacher,' said Gemma from Sales. 'Don't you think? Kind've over the top? Kinda demented?'

And Joe from Payroll laughed, as he often did when Gemma spoke, because he knew Gemma was unkind, but, but, what if she were to come unfurled, be private, open, alone with Joe— what then? So it embarrassed him to live on the same street as Lena Derwent and to have recognised her as soon as he saw her at Mason's, with her large, fuzzed hair, her slipped lipstick, her cleavage. She was the middle-aged woman in number twelve, who was out every Saturday working in her garden, whose large backside hung above her low front fence like the face of a sunflower. Sometimes she stood up from her gardening and said, 'Morning, sweetheart!' as he passed with his dog. Joe, smiling, polite, was never sure if the 'sweetheart' was aimed at him or the dog. And if she was still outside when he returned from his walk, he might smile again as she made an exaggerated motion: wiped her perspiring forehead with one arm, or pretended to bark at Groucho. She had a friendly bark—Groucho always replied, seeming to like it. Once she asked Joe in for a cool drink and some water for the 'pooch', and Joe stammered something out, said he had plans, tried not to walk that way again. So when Lena had arrived at Mason's and said right away to Joe, 'Hello, stranger!' it became necessary to laugh when Gemma spoke, when she was unkind.

'How do you know *her*?' Gemma had asked, and Joe explained that they were neighbours.

'Oh, out there in Murder Town?' she said, and he smiled; he disliked that name, but it was the only private joke they shared.

'Right in the heart of Murder Town,' he said.

A shudder passed through her: outsize, fastidious. 'Beats me how any of you can live out there.'

'Pure balls,' he said.

Gemma laughed, and someone called her name. So Gemma went.

Joe lived in Murder Town because his parents had lived there before they died not of murder but of natural causes, and now he lived in their house. This meant he had to drive to work and back each day along a highway that cut through a state forest. The trees of the forest rose up around his car: orderly pine plantations in some parts, and in others long, lean eucalypts with their loose leaves and their bark littering the greenish ground. The real name of Joe's town was Barrow. A man had lived in Barrow once, and in the 1990s this man used to drive the same highway—up and down for hours—to find a person, any person, who looked far from home, standing with a backpack at a junction or a bus stop or just walking along the road or waiting with a thumb out for a ride, and this man would offer them a ride, and if they accepted he would kill them and take their bodies to the forest. Or he'd take them to the forest and kill them there—Joe wasn't sure. The man had been caught and tried and had been in prison for several years. Joe drove daily through the forest, and there were no longer any hitch-hikers on that highway.

Not long after she'd started at Mason's, Lena approached Joe as he sat in the park eating lunch—seemed to appear before him, really; she was very stealthy for someone so large—and said, 'Mind if I sit?' She held a thin, stained sandwich.

Joe gave his Saturday smile.

Lena's sandwich, unwrapped, was spread with something green which he knew would get in her teeth and stay there.

'Now tell me,' she said. 'I've been thinking of getting a dog. You have that gorgeous, clever little guy. How old is he?'

'Around five or six, I think. I don't know for sure. He's from a shelter.'

'Aren't you a darling,' she said, biting into her green. 'Is he part bulldog? He looks it. That's what I'm after. What I want's a guard dog.'

'A guard dog,' said Joe. He ate the last of his own lunch with a conclusive flourish. The park was visible from Mason's.

'Can't be too careful, right?' said Lena, conspiratorial. 'Anything could happen. Considering where we live.' She licked her thumb. 'Pesto,' she said. 'I grow the basil myself. I'll bring you some.'

'No, no.' He raised his hands as if he were about to push a flat, heavy object away from his body. 'That's really nice of you, but please don't worry.'

Lena didn't look worried. She smiled as he stood up, lifting her face to him; but because she was looking into the sun, her eyes narrowed. Her smile was placid, drowsy, flecked with green. 'It's not for everyone, is it,' she said, and he assumed she was referring to the taste of pesto. She closed her lips and ran her tongue along her upper teeth.

'Bye,' said Joe, and Lena gave a happy shrug.

She never came to him at lunch again. Occasionally, he saw her sharing a bench with Jenny, the receptionist, who was having marital trouble and would talk to anyone. Gemma said Jenny cried in the toilets sometimes, poor thing. Lena made overtures to others without success. No one was rude, exactly, but she began to spend her lunch break reading at her desk. She was careful about her break, Joe noticed. She started it whenever Mason went out for lunch, and though he was always gone at least an hour—a fact of which his previous PAs had taken full advantage—Lena was back at work after exactly thirty minutes. No one wanted to drop things off for Mason while he was in his office, for fear that he would stir behind his desk, peer around the doorframe, and ask them in to 'have a word'. No one wanted to have a word with Mason, with his nicotine teeth and his 'call me Bob'. So they came when he was out, and they all saw how Lena spent her break.

'It's always true crime,' Gemma said, watching as Joe coaxed the coffee machine. 'The books she reads. Have you noticed?'

Joe hadn't. He preferred to go to Lena when Mason was present, despite the threat of being drawn into the office: its wood panelling, its yellow light, as if it were perpetually Sunday afternoon in there, in the 1970s. Joe risked all this so as not to seem as if he'd approached Lena herself, alone, with some neighbourly affinity.

Lena became part of the office soon enough. They just grew to expect her, cheerful in the mornings, reading out the horoscopes, watering the plants; behind her back they called her Luna, until one day they started saying it to her face, and she looked pleased to have a nickname. Joe's at first had been Josephine. He knew better than to resist, and when Josephine didn't appear to bother him they'd abandoned it—now they called him Jam for reasons no one could remember. There were theories that Lena and Mason were having a hot affair. Gemma acted it out once with Stuart from Distribution: lots of heavy breathing, faux buttons faux popped, rocking desks, and pumping legs. Joe found himself turned on. Until now, his attraction to Gemma had tended to dim outside the office—its full force seemed to steal up on him each morning as he drove north through the forest, and dissipate as he drove back south. If he'd thought of her while jerking off, she tended to blend and merge with someone else of roughly the same shape and colour. But after she and Stu panted on the desks he saw her clearly: her lifted legs, her head thrown back. That was harder to forget, even in Murder Town.

So things moved on at Mason's. They all went to the pub

on Friday nights, and there, one sticky evening, Gemma—
light on her weekend toes—kissed Joe in a dark corner, and
for weeks afterwards exhibited a sweet, surreptitious pity but
no further inclination; Mason went shouting to hospital with
a kidney stone and returned subdued; and, at home in Barrow,
Joe walked Groucho in any direction that wasn't Lena's.

One morning, Lena arrived at Mason's late, flustered,
raucous—her car, she announced, broken down, at the mechanic. Stranded! Indefinitely! Explained while flushed and
laughing, also teary—but then her eyes were always slightly
moist, as if she were poised to be moved by the world at any
moment. She spoke of this breakdown as a glorious event—
glorious in the sense that it was unusual, made her unusual, and
she seemed to believe that everyone should hear about it, even
Mason, who listened to the whole story and wanted to know
which mechanic the car was at so he could call and be insistent
with them. 'Relies on her car,' said Mason over the phone, 'lives
out of town,' and Lena bubbled and smiled, billowed with grati-
tude; but still, by the end of the workday the car wasn't ready,
and she really was stranded. Speculation began that Mason
would take Lena home with him, time to meet the wife, talk of
a threesome amid giggles and grimaces, and Joe—disliking this
but not brave enough to stop it, Joe who was reverent of bodies,
who valued kindness—went to Lena and offered her a ride.

'You darling!' she cried.

Joe didn't dare look to see Gemma's reaction. He tidied his
desk until Lena was ready to leave; then he walked out of the
office a step or two ahead of her, but surrounded by her bustle.

Lena in the car was larger than ever; she overflowed her seat by means of bag and hair and skirt. The skirt was a vivid yellow and got caught around the gearstick.

'Pure silk,' she said, gathering it in. 'Have a feel. It's lovely.'

Joe had no intention of having a feel. 'Sorry about the dog hair,' he said.

'I like a messy car,' Lena said. 'Shows personality.'

He imagined the interior of her car: zebra-print seat covers, scattered CDs, novelty dice. She looked like the kind of person who'd own many items to which the word *novelty* could be applied.

Joe drove carefully with Lena beside him, as if she were there to test him on his ability, and so they cruised out of town.

'I have a feeling,' she said, 'a teeny-weeny suspicion that you and I are the same. You feel things deeply, don't you? And you always know how other people are feeling.'

He considered the fact that he had no idea, ever, how Gemma was feeling, not even when she kissed him.

Lena, stroking the silk of her skirt, gave a small, hiccuping laugh. 'Anyone can see you're a sweetheart, but it's more than that. You knew just how I felt today about my car.'

Joe hummed noncommittally and peered ahead. Everyone in the office knew how Lena had felt that day: she'd told them.

They entered Barrow State Forest, and now the light flickered as it angled through the trees. The trees were all the same width and height, the same smooth, pale grey, and the sky was a narrow ribbon over the road.

Lena cleared her throat, as if the thing she had to say was viscous and deep and must be summoned. 'Tell me,' she said, 'do you know what an empath is?'

'Someone who feels empathy?'

'More than that,' said Lena, solemn, rummaging in her bag. She pulled out a tiny packet of tissues. 'More extreme. An empath feels other people's emotions exactly as if they were her own. It's a gift. I'm an empath.' She plucked a tissue from the pack. 'And you're an empath, too, Joe. I've known it since the minute I saw you with your precious dog, which— remember—is from a shelter. Classic empath.'

She turned her head towards the window and blew her nose with a discretion that seemed unlike her. Joe almost said, 'Bless you,' as if she'd sneezed.

'How old are you?' she asked.

'Old? Well, I'm twenty-nine. The big three-oh next month.'

'I was thirty-seven, maybe thirty-eight, before I really understood my gift. You have plenty of time.' She plunged the used tissue into the well of her bag.

They were now entirely enclosed in the white-green light of the eucalypts. On their right, there were still flashes of sun where paddocks had been cleared close to the forest's edge, but on their left, the bush lay in thick, bright shade. The gums were very straight until, near their tops, they branched and drooped with pale green leaves.

'Have you been in?' asked Lena, gesturing at the forest.

'All the time as a kid.'

'You grew up here!' she said, not asking a question so much as stating an agreeable fact. 'And what about since—you know?'

Since what? There were any number of events in Joe's life that might qualify: losing his virginity (in Barrow State, as it happened, on a Friday afternoon, with Philippa Kremp, in their sports uniforms; he was chewing gum and, lost to himself, swallowed it); leaving for uni; moving to London; his mother dying; moving back from London; his father dying. But he knew what Lena meant: since everyone found out that a serial killer was burying bodies in the forest.

'Not for years,' said Joe.

'I wonder,' wondered Lena, 'could we go in there?'

'Into the forest? I suppose so, if you like. Sometime.' Did he mean it? He didn't think he meant it.

'Why not now?'

She turned in her seat to face him. From the corner of his eye, he saw the white of her shirt and the yellow of her skirt, and thought, A cracked egg; then tried to unthink it.

'I know everything there is to know about the murders,' Lena said. 'I've read all the books.'

Joe looked with pronounced attention at the road ahead.

'I've never been brave enough to go in there alone, but I know just where I want to look.'

So she was a tourist. Joe's dad used to call them that, in the days after the arrest: all the people who drove to Barrow, rolled through the streets, asked for directions at the post office and the petrol station. Cruising through Murder Town. They had folders full of newspaper clippings, they marked things on maps in red pen. *Tourists* seemed a cruel word, considering many of the victims had, in fact, been tourists. Still, Joe understood his father's disgust, though Joe had just moved to London at the time, and this talk of murder in his home town seemed unreal. The killer's home had been demolished a few years ago, but diehards did still visit.

'What are you looking for?' he asked.

'Just around this corner, there's a fire trail. Do you know it?'

Of course he knew it. Fire trails were for teenagers: bored, bursting, smoking, fucking, spooking each other, showing off. Philippa Kremp lifting her green jersey over her head and handing it to him as if he'd understand what to do with it. God, what a golden mystery. She was married now and lived in Perth.

'Here, stop here,' said Lena, and Joe did, pulling over beside the entrance to the fire trail. He'd been startled into compliance, but there was also something in the mottled light that had the feel of adolescence, of being young and horny, and of wanting to prove to a girl that he wasn't frightened. Which was too simple a way of putting it, failing to account for the heavy burden of those teenage days, the demand for proof that the world wasn't terrible, he wasn't terrible, his parents weren't terrible, there was no such thing as terror; yet evidently there was and had to be, in order that life might be vast enough to include Philippa Kremp, who grunted gently on the forest floor, who bit her lip, who said afterwards, 'I knew you'd be nice about it,' and hadn't swallowed her gum.

Now Lena Derwent was flowing in her yellow from the car. She was plunging into the forest. It was simply a Thursday, and here he was—following her into the trees. He thought he should try to stop her, except that he didn't know what she was doing.

'Lena,' he called half-heartedly.

She turned to him, raised one hand to her ear, and said, 'Do you hear it?'

'Hear what?'

'Listen!'

Joe listened and heard the beat of insects, a clear, high bird, cars on the highway. 'What am I listening for?'

Lena shook her head, smiled fondly, turned away, and continued down the fire trail. It was wide and sandy at this point, unassuming, a practical channel into the scratchy green.

'Look out for snakes,' he said, which was what they'd said as teenagers. You conjured a snake by warning against it: reliably, the girls would press close and squeal, and Adam and Eve would stumble with their ciggies through the garden, the snake yawned and smiled, the fruit hung low, oh in the surging morning of the world.

Lena didn't stop or speak or acknowledge the warning in any way. She seemed to float down the fire trail, and when it grew narrower she pushed undaunted through the branches.

'What exactly are we looking for?' he asked, and she waved one forearm as if to say, Wait! Wait! Her head appeared enormous from behind, expanded by its fizzing curls, even as it ducked and weaved expertly through the tightening scrub. She'd gathered her skirt into a fist to stop it snagging. Joe resigned himself to being, yet again, a victim of his own politeness.

They walked in silence for another few minutes. It didn't matter how far they went—the forest was never dark. The light fell white through the slender trees. The low scrub became thicker, and they were heading downhill; soon they would reach a creek Joe knew, where the ferns grew huge and hairy along the banks.

But Lena stopped before they reached the creek. She gripped his arm. 'Here,' she said.

Joe felt an unravelling shame that he'd let things go so far. 'I think we should head back.'

'No, no,' she said, urgent. 'We're very close.'

'Close to what?'

'Listen.'

Joe listened to the thin, sharp pipe of hidden birds. 'It's just that I need to feed Groucho.'

'Fifteen minutes,' she said, and now she pivoted sideways, away from the track and into the scrub.

'Wait,' he said. 'You'll get lost in there.'

Lena stepped in one smooth motion out of her skirt and tossed it to Joe. She wore a petticoat underneath, in the same aggressive yellow, with lace along the hem; it was the kind of thing Gemma might wear as a skirt.

'Um,' Joe said, but Lena clicked her tongue.

'See that branch?' she said. 'Tie the skirt up there. We'll never miss it.'

And she moved off. Joe tied the skirt with some difficulty—the branch was high—and continued after her. Looking back, he saw the yellow in the tree, a limp flame.

Lena, ahead of him, called, 'Hansel and Gretel, baby!'

How was she moving so fast? He would put her age at fifty, minimum.

She called, 'The bark on the trees, so pale! A bit like flesh, isn't it?'

He was breathing hard, though the walk wasn't all that taxing.

She called, 'Nearly there, Joe, I can feel it!'

He thought of autumnal Saturdays he'd suffered as a kid, when his parents used to drag him into the piney parts of this very forest, hunting for the slimy mushrooms they called slippery jacks. The baskets would be full, Joe would be exhausted, but his parents, the thrifty optimists, always imagined another grove of mushrooms just ahead, plump and undiscovered. People had stopped foraging in Barrow State after the bodies were found by—Joe shuddered—mushroom pickers.

'Here!' Lena called.

She was waiting for him around a corner, drenched in yolky light, her face serious. How did she create corners in a forest?

'This is the place,' she said. 'This is where she is.'

'Where who is?'

Lena took a deep breath, like someone about to launch into a speech long suffered over. She said, 'There's another body. One they haven't found yet.'

Joe felt his heart behind his ears.

'Can't you sense it? Her final minutes? It's so powerful.' Lena, deferential, looked about her. 'The trees. Connect with the trees. They record intense emotion. Connect with the trees, and you'll connect with her.'

'I'm going back,' Joe said, but he already knew he would go nowhere without Lena.

She extended her arms as if balancing on a beam. She closed her eyes. 'We're here, honey. We're here. Help us find you.'

'This is crazy.'

Lena opened her eyes. Her mournful expression suggested that, of all her trials, Joe's betrayal was the least expected.

'There's nothing to be scared of,' she said.

'Seriously, Lena.'

'We can give her five more minutes, can't we? You don't have to do anything. You just stay right here and give me five more minutes to look around.'

Then Lena was moving away, though the yellow of her was always visible among the trees.

He recalled a painting he'd studied in an art class, sitting behind Tracey Rowe (Tracey, whom he'd thought of with a brief, deceitful spasm there among the leaves with Philippa Kremp): a painting of a woman in a blanched Victorian dress lost in the bush, and one of his classmates saying, 'It's weird in the bush how the trees seem really far apart but when you're inside them they're heaps thick,' and the trees were, yes, both far apart and thick. Joe was afraid even to glance into the spaces between them, so he watched a trail of ants ascend the nearest trunk. They made a busy line on the bark. They made the tree into a world, and the world was terrible and full of sourceless noise—at any moment, some active animal could run across his foot with a finger hanging out of its mouth. Or a snake would drop on him out of a tree, and looking up to ward it off he'd see a body in the branches. He felt heat in his face and knew the fear was making him blush. He knew, too, that Gemma, were she here, would laugh at him and join Lena on her stupid hunt.

'Joe!' Lena called, off to his left, detectable in her yellow but only just. 'Joe!'

What if I leave? he thought. Just go back, find the car, and drive away? Would she make it out of the forest? Would she stumble onto the road in the dusk; would a driver spot her frowzy hair and white face and think she was a ghost of the highway killer's?

'Joe!' she called again, and now she was coming for him,

heaving through the trees, erupting at his elbow. Her face was like an ecstatic saint's. 'You have to see this,' she said, and pulled at his arm and turned away, so he went with her—followed her—knowing all the while it was a mistake.

The forest tightened around them; Lena lost her way a little, then altered her path.

'It's right here, right here,' she said from behind her hair. Her arms groped at branches. Then she stopped and said once more, 'Right here,' and gestured to a tree ahead, an ordinary tree with the same smooth sides as all the others, the same pale bark, the same darker knots like navels in the naked trunk, and beneath them its roots curling and rotting and renewing, and far above them its branches moving in their own shade. But this tree—there was a length of reflective orange tape around it, quite low down. Lena put a hand beneath Joe's elbow and walked him towards it. He wanted to laugh.

'Police tape,' she said.

'Isn't police tape yellow? Or maybe it's blue?' He reached out to touch the tape. It had a honeycomb design and was iridescent in the way some flies are iridescent: beautiful, he observed, but for reasons that had nothing to do with him.

'Joe, Joe,' said Lena. She placed a palm against the tree and closed her eyes. 'Don't you see what this means? It means they found her and didn't tell us.'

'Found *who*, Lena?'

'I don't know her name yet.'

Joe was no longer frightened. 'This tape looks pretty recent,' he said. It was a relief to be rational.

Lena nodded. 'They must only have found her recently.'

'Why not tell us? And why just one piece of tape, around one tree?'

The tape was fastened with a knot, which Lena deftly untied, and then the tree became, again, like all the others. She held up the tape and studied it until Joe sighed; then she seemed to notice his impatience.

'You don't feel her?' she asked, with an encouraging shake of the tape.

'I really need to get home,' he said.

Lena nodded, turned, and began to walk. She led the way, and that seemed natural—this was her forest now—and also just as well, because Joe was unsure of the direction of the path. The tape fluttered in her fist. It occurred to him, walking behind her, that when the killer was here with the woman Lena had been looking for, he would have made her walk ahead of him. The killer behind and woman ahead. To keep her in his sight. And he'd have been saying something like Just walk, do what I say, go left now, hurry up, just walk. Maybe kicking at her if she stumbled or fell. The trees watching. And a fly at his face. Saying, Just walk. Also, laughing. And a growl spreading out, down his throat and spine, a rising from his gut and his legs burning, between his legs. Making noise the whole time, sometimes random things, songs,

I wandered around and finally found somebody who
and also talking, just to fill the spaces between the trees,

just to press back at the scum

that was the world saying, you're scum.

A raving in the trees.

Down came a jumbuck

Talking to the girl like,   you filthy, fucking cunt
you ugly bitch   you stupid whore

     you dead cunt   just walk

         She loves me, yeah

shut up shut up shut shut the fuck up

and walk, the trees watching, the world roaring

the girl ahead spilling over spilling out

   the world lurching up in green and white to say,

   yes, you're here

   the world saying, there she is now take it

   back and fuck you, fuck you,

                 on a bicycle built for two

and   telling her to stop here and she's   moaning

   like a bitch in heat   and her face is wet and

   she's wet and Joe

Joe bending at the waist his palm against a tree a fly at his face and throwing up a small puddle, yellow-green, which soaked immediately into the earth.

'Oh, honey!' said Lena. 'Oh no!'

Joe, still bent, tried to ward her off with a hand.

She crouched beside him. 'Can you stand?'

His throat gaped, but nothing more came up. He stood too fast, and the world tilted; he leaned against the tree. There were ants on this tree, too. They seemed attentive to something he was unable to detect. They retreated from him, but that was only natural. And Lena touched his arm, which she mustn't do; he pulled his arm away.

'I'm fine,' he said. The world righted itself. The green-white light stood back from him. But it watched.

Lena spoke to him gently, guided him through the scrub, and there was her skirt as promised, foaming golden on the branch; he untied it for her and, passing it over, enjoyed how soft and fine it felt, and then found that pleasure sickening, undeserved. But Lena was waiting. The path was waiting, then the car. In the car she gave him water to drink, tissues from her tiny pack, a rattling box of mints—all this from her bag, which seemed full of everything, of all he needed. She offered to drive, but he refused. He was embarrassed now and couldn't quite remember what had made him sick.

They were both quiet on the ride home. When he pulled up in front of her house, number twelve, the sky was close to dark, and in the final light the garden had a strange, wet, tossed look to it, as if it had just sailed up from somewhere far away. Joe saw how pretty it was, how much care she took with it.

'Come in for a minute,' Lena said. She had one foot outside the car already; she clutched her bag and smiled at him, showing big, round teeth. 'You've had a rough afternoon. I know I could do with a drink. Come in.'

Joe agreed, though what he wanted most was to be in his own house, alone with his dog. But something felt important about going in to Lena's, too. He'd imagined before what it would look like inside, and he needed to find out if he was right. He wanted to have been right, because that would mean the world was orderly, that people advertised their true selves, that they were knowable. That there were few surprises.

And yes: inside, the house was painted in warm colours, oranges and pinks, and there were plants everywhere in pots.

They curved and trailed in corners and along walls, and in the lounge room a lily on top of the television bore three waxy, red flowers. Lena turned on lamps—not overhead lights—and look, there was a novelty feather boa draped over a shade. Joe was grateful for its vehement purple. The furniture seemed heavy, overstuffed, burdened with cushions, and yet to float a millimetre off the floor. Every fabric surface glittered with secret mirrors. It was overwhelming to look at all at once.

In an awkward rush, he asked for the bathroom and found it clean and neat, with peach tiles and just one frothy fern on the windowsill. A Japanese print of a mountain hung above the toilet, as if placed to provide a serene view for a man of Joe's exact height. Something concealed in the toilet made it flush dark blue and release the violent smell of berries. He rubbed some toothpaste on his teeth.

When Joe came out of the bathroom, Lena had just finished lighting a number of candles. He thought of love scenes in movies and some of the blurrier porn he'd seen, which had always made him wonder, Who owns so many candles? Who takes the time to light them? They embarrassed him, their effort and their optimism embarrassed him, but Lena was practical as she shook the flame from the last match. She poured wine into glasses with chunky, coloured stems. She made him sit on the couch, and as she moved in front of a lamp and sat beside him, he could see the nice shape of her legs through the yellow silk skirt. And the wine was yellow, the room was yellow, and her hair—with the candles behind it—was golden at the edges.

She drank from her glass and said, 'I sometimes think there's a suspicion about people who live alone. That other people look at us and think we're all serial killers in waiting. Know what I mean?'

Joe nodded. He was unsure of what he knew.

Lena put her wineglass on the floor and, seeing this, Joe did the same. She was still talking, gesticulating with her hands. He leaned forward so that her face loomed up, her eyes half-closed as usual, a smell of something coming off her—a mix of summer and talcum powder—her trembling cleavage, the nervous volume of her hair, her mouth upturned, her hands upon his shoulders, and in the background candles, candles. He went to kiss her.

'Oh my god,' said Lena. 'Joe, honey, oh, oh no.'

The hands were on his shoulders to ward him off, the mouth upturned in disbelief to stop him, and now—God, she was laughing. The world swelled and spat and said,

      stupid bitch   old ugly fat   ugly.

'I'm sorry,' she said, one hand pressed against her chest. 'It isn't—I mean—you lovely thing.'

He smiled. What else was there to do? But he knew how he was floundering, how red his face was and his neck; his hands had never felt so empty.

'My god,' she said, more sober now, but merry. 'We've had a shock, haven't we? It's natural, when you think about it. You gorgeous thing, with all your eyelashes.'

Lena was standing up, and so was he. She patted down the front of her skirt. She bundled him towards the door and was still talking as she waved him down the path.

He walked home, shaking. Groucho greeted him, licked his fingers, his palms, up his forearms, and finally—as Joe lay upon the couch—his face.

The next morning, Joe went to where he'd parked in front of number twelve and found a note on his windscreen: *Car sorted, no need for lift, thanks!!! xo L.*

He drove slowly through the forest, and when he reached the fire trail he pulled over, without having planned to do so: just saw the trail opening in the scrub and slowed the car. But he didn't get out. He had the peculiar feeling that the trees didn't want him. He thought he saw, in two or three places, a scrap of orange. A magpie sang out of its wet throat. He drove back onto the highway.

At Mason's, Joe saw a gathering of people in the reception area but, conscious of being late, walked directly to his desk.

Gemma broke from the group to follow him. 'Jam!' she called.

He turned to her.

'You'll never believe this,' she said. 'Luna went into the forest on her own.'

'What forest?' he asked, and it was a genuine question—what forest had Lena been to on her own?

'"What forest?"!' said Gemma. 'Barrow State. What other forest *is* there?'

And because she pulled him back to reception—put one hand in his and kept it there—he went.

Lena, sitting in Jenny's chair at the front desk, seemed

unperturbed by his presence. Her voice was lowered, but it carried.

'I walked for hours,' she said, 'and I knew I was getting close to something big. You want to hear the strangest thing?'

The listeners nodded. Stuart from Distribution was there, with his rugby shoulders and his bully's face. He leaned closer to Lena with all the rest.

'The birds,' she said. 'No birdsong. Not a sound in that whole place. You know why? Birds know evil. They can sense it.'

The listeners inhaled.

'And look,' she said. From a pocket, she drew the orange tape. It surprised Joe with its brightness. 'Police tape,' said Lena.

The listeners extended their hands to it. 'No way,' said Stuart, as if pleading softly with an awful god.

Gemma let go of Joe's hand and put her arm around his shoulders, so that he felt one breast against his upper back. She spoke close to his ear. 'Hey, Jam?' she said.

She smelled of flowers, but not real ones. She wore her fair, straight hair in a knot on top of her head. She carried something with her, some future promise; it rattled with the thin, jewelled bangles on her wrists. If she had been with him in the forest, she would have laughed, and huddled close when he said 'snake', and stepped out of her skirt. But when she saw him leaning up against the tree with the green-white world spitting in his ear she would have hated him and been afraid, as she should. And then she, too, wouldn't let him kiss her.

'What about a drink tonight?' she said, with her breath behind his ear. 'Just you and me?'

He might have said no. But he didn't.

HUNTER ON THE HIGHWAY

(1996)

May asked Darcy if he had ever hitchhiked and he said he had, but not for a long time. When she wanted to know the best places to wait if you needed a ride, he told her never to do it, ever, because it was too dangerous for a girl.

'Just hypothetically,' said May, 'I mean I never would, but if I did?'

Then Darcy told her to wait just outside of town, somewhere cars can see you in plenty of time and there's a good place for them to pull over. You have to look neat and smile, but not too much. Another good place is at a service station.

So when May went out that Sunday, she started at a service station. She parked her car behind the servo and sat there for a while before she put on a baseball cap, went into the service station, bought a bottle of water, and used the toilet. Then she walked to the side of the road, held out her arm, and raised her thumb. Her backpack wasn't heavy—it was stuffed with a pillow—so she kept it on her back.

She'd been there a few minutes when a member of staff came out and said, 'Look, sorry, I have to say this, but technically you're trespassing and you can't do that here.' He seemed embarrassed; he was only a teenager, and his hair was gelled and combed as if he were about to star in a black-and-white movie. His shirt was also very smooth and she wondered if he ironed it himself. He looked like he went swing dancing every night. According to his name tag, his name was Jason.

'Sorry, sorry,' May said, and felt her face reddening.

'Honestly, if you just went about two metres down the road there's nothing I could do,' he said, and when May thanked him and hitched her backpack higher his face changed: became fatherly, which suited the hair somehow. 'But it's not a good idea,' Jason said. 'Look, where do you want to go? I finish work in a couple of hours and I can drive you to a train station.'

'That's okay,' May said.

'I mean, I have a girlfriend. I'm not trying to be sleazy. But haven't you seen the news? A girl was just attacked last week, just down the road.'

'I didn't know,' May said. But she did know.

'You need to be careful.' Jason looked like he might put a hand on her arm, but he stopped himself.

I *am* being careful, thought May. And she also thought: it was stupid to come here. He won't be back after last week— he'll try a different place.

'Thanks,' she said. 'Don't worry, it's fine.'

She went to her car and didn't look behind her and drove south until she reached another town. She parked near a playground but changed her mind and drove further towards the

edge of town, where she parked at a McDonald's, up in the far corner of the lot. From there she walked for about half an hour along
the side of the highway, passing businesses that sold things like
swimming pool pumps and garden sheds. She wore sunglasses
and carried her pack but didn't hold her hand out for a ride. Small
white flowers grew along the roadside and she picked a few and
held their stems in her fist. Her Blundstones began to rub at her
toes. Some cars honked but only one slowed and stopped ahead
of her. It was a bright green Camry, nothing to be afraid of, and
the driver was a woman. She opened her door, rose up out of the
driver's seat, and waited for May to get close. Her hair was dyed
the colour of plums. She was probably in her thirties.

'Hey,' said the woman, and May stopped and swung her pack
off her shoulders. The pillow inside it was stuffed with feathers,
and even feathers become heavy after a while. May rested the
pack on the tops of her feet to protect it from the ground.

'Hi,' May said.

'Do you need some help?'

'Me? No.'

'Are you hitchhiking?'

May shrugged.

'Oh my god,' said the woman. 'That's so dangerous.' She
elongated her 'oh' and her 'so' in a childish way. 'What are you,
sixteen? Seventeen?'

A white ute drove past. May, who was twenty-one, craned
her neck trying to see its numberplate, but it was moving too
quickly.

'You must know about the girl last week,' the woman said.
'That wasn't far from here. She's lucky to be alive.'

May didn't answer.

'Let me take you somewhere,' said the woman.

'No thanks,' May said. She hoisted the backpack onto her shoulders and took a drink from her water bottle, still holding her bundle of white flowers.

'Those are weeds,' said the woman. 'Onion weed. Can't you smell it?'

And May could, now, recognise a faint, damp onion smell that may have been emitted by the flowers or by the word 'onion'.

'Just, if they're a gift for someone, you should keep that in mind. The smell.'

'They're not,' said May, and she crouched down and laid the flowers on the roadside with a slowness that might have made them seem, to the woman, like a solemn tribute, but in fact arose from the effort of squatting and standing while wearing the backpack.

'Do you know her or something?' the woman asked. 'The girl who got attacked?'

'Why would I know her?' May said.

The woman dropped her forehead down onto the roof of the car for a moment, then lifted it again. 'I'm trying to help you,' she said, 'and if you don't come with me, I'm going to drive until I get to a payphone, and I'm going to call the police.'

'Why would you even do that?' May heard her sullen voice and was reminded of her teenage self: shaved head, chunky Docs, growling at her mother.

The woman shook her head. 'Because I'll never forgive myself if I see your picture in the paper next week.'

You won't, thought May. I'm safe. But it was as if the woman had entered into a transaction just by saying she would never forgive herself—had named a price, and May was in her debt. May was defenceless against this potential guilt. So she let the woman, whose name turned out to be Cherie, drive her back to the McDonald's, and in the car May found it hard to be impassive and unfriendly, wanted to remove her cap and sunglasses, to thank Cherie and smile. This was partly because the car was full of the definite life of Cherie—a baby seat in the back, orange peel, unopened mail—and also because Cherie, with her plum-coloured hair, was kind and credulous. She believed what May told her: that May's car was at McDonald's because she'd fought with her boyfriend, he'd wanted a thickshake though he was vegetarian—those shakes were full of pig fat, May said, and Cherie nodded sagely at the road—so she'd walked off with the keys and thought he would come after her. As proof, May took her car keys from her pocket and shook them like a rattle. By the time they reached McDonald's, May knew all about Cherie, her job, her daughter and boyfriend, her two-bedroom house with a buggered hot-water heater, her tree nut allergy, and May thought: the most effective killer would only need to act as if he expected people to be nice, to trust him, and they would.

That was enough for the first day. May was very tired, but she went to Franklins for milk on the way home and also bought the antihistamines Darcy took so he could smoke without his eyes itching. He would reimburse her for them later, just as he did everything she bought for him, and while at first she'd liked the careful way he counted out the cash or, if he was short, pinned his debt up on the kitchen noticeboard and always, always paid it, this tallying drove her crazy now. How scrupulous it was, how insistent, so that nothing could ever be a gift. Which meant he expected the same from her. For example, she paid for half the pot and smoked more than she would have (though still not half), thinking with every joint that she knew exactly what it cost. She would have liked the opportunity to be more generous.

He was home by seven. The white ute in the driveway; tall, thin Darcy in the doorway, his brown hair pulled back into a ponytail, dirt under his fingernails, his mouth open; talkative, horny, hungry, and high on something though he swore not. Just these last few months, and just on Sundays, he'd be gone all day and come back like this, bouncing on his toes, hands everywhere, cracking jokes. His energy was off—that's how May put it to herself: his energy is off—and only smoking would slow him down. So that by the very end of those Sundays he was so unhurried, so sleepy on the antihistamines, so dreamy on the pot and blissed out on the blues music he loved so much, that she could do or say almost anything and he would only smile.

Last Sunday night she was watching TV and when the late news came on he stayed and watched it with her, even though he hated watching the news. So they saw together that a young woman had, that very afternoon, been attacked on a highway south of Sydney, a girl of nineteen, English, and the man was white and tall and thin, tanned skin, brown shoulder-length hair, blue eyes, in his late twenties to mid-thirties, wearing jeans and a dark blue work shirt, driving a white ute, with dirt under his fingernails. The girl had been hitchhiking. The man pulled over, was very pleasant, then he hit her and tried to force her into his ute; the woman fought him off and ran into the

road, where a family in a van picked her up and drove her to a
police station.

Darcy had watched the news report about the attack in a
stoned, unfocused way and, when it was over, said, 'It's not
enough.' Then he stood up from the couch and went to bed.

May sat alone and watched the reporter on the news specu-
late that this man had some connection to all the people who'd
gone missing in the area over the past few years. She hadn't
realised there were so many, more than ten, or that they were
all so young, and as she looked at their pictures on the TV
screen—a cute girl in flannel with gappy front teeth; a skinny
guy in John Lennon glasses; a dark-haired couple posing in
front of the Harbour Bridge—she wondered, what part of it isn't
enough? Only kicking him, only bruising his fucking balls? Or
was the reporting itself not enough, with all its generalities? So
that any man of a certain age, a certain appearance, a certain
make of truck, a Sunday landscaping job south of Sydney, could
be accused by a news report; could, if he was paying attention, sense his girlfriend's breath hitch beside him; could feel
the need—perhaps unconsciously—to curl his fingers towards
his palms in order to hide the dirt beneath his nails.

That was a week ago. Now, this Sunday, after her own day
on the roads, May waited until Darcy was asleep and went to
look inside his truck.

Everything there was as it should be: the same equipment,
tools, the spades and tarpaulins, the chainsaw and edge trim-
mer, the brush cutter, the green wheelbarrow that said SHERLOCK
on the side as if to laugh at her amateur sleuthing, the crust
of dirt on everything but the tools themselves, so beautifully

cleaned as always. And in the cabin of the ute: nothing at all, so that the man who owned it might be a thousand different men. May thought of Cherie, the way she lived an apparent life even in the clutter of her car, and wondered what Darcy might be lacking, to have so anonymous a truck. Or was May only used to him? And would a stranger, sitting in his truck—or trying to stay out of it—see other things, definite and damning? So that they, in some ways, knew her boyfriend, and what he might be capable of, better than she did.

What was he capable of? He was capable of not eating meat at home because she was a vegetarian; of facilitating her first non-solo orgasm; of understanding a surprising amount of Japanese; of talking at length and in detail about American blues musicians; of introducing himself to any and every dog in yards and parks and on footpaths; of growing herbs on their balcony, although neither of them ever cooked with herbs. Yes, he was older than she was and his jobs shifted and he smoked a lot and talked about writing songs but never did. And May's parents didn't approve and spoke of him, with a churlish arrogance, as something she was only doing to cause them pain. But he was Darcy. He smelled of mint and dirt and weed and sometimes roses. He tanned so quickly in the sun.

May went to bed and slept beside him.

May had met Darcy when she was working part-time at a call centre in her first year at uni. Darcy was a full-timer at the centre, but really he played guitar in a band that May thought she might have seen a poster for once or twice in the toilets of her favourite cafe. The band played local pubs, had been on the radio, and were in the process of recording their first album. Would she like to check out their demo? Yeah, man, that'd be cool. Most of the women working at the call centre had crushes on Darcy. He had a way of making you feel singled out, even though you knew he was also asking Jess, Maria, and Cleo if they wanted to hear him play the guitar solo from 'Janie's Got a Gun'. May went to one of his gigs and was moved by how serious he looked on stage, like a boy absorbed in the construction of a particularly complicated Lego set. The band wasn't good, but he was: he was luminous when he played, grave and unpolluted. One moment his voice was a snarl; then it became a prayer. Afterwards, he swung down to the sticky pub floor and she bought him a drink and they grinned and leaned against each other until they were drunk enough, but not too drunk, to go to his place and fuck.

It may have been that, to begin with, May did want to scandalise her parents, who were conservative Christians— very kind, strict, and anxious, and perpetually puzzled by the world in which they found themselves living. Darcy was also a way of signalling that May wasn't a lesbian, despite her short hair and heavy boots. But within weeks it became clear that she liked Darcy for himself: liked how seriously he took the things he loved, and the optimism with which he believed his band would eventually succeed, simply because he was talented. Other bands followed, other jobs. He fell into landscape gardening and considered a solo music career; May graduated from her arts degree and was working as a receptionist in a medical centre while she figured out what to do next. They had been together for three years and lived together for seven months. It should not have been possible to suspect Darcy of doing anything truly terrible.

Once, during sex, he had put a hand to her throat and held it there for longer than she liked. She shook her head, tried to pull his hand off, but he held it there until he was finished. He was sorry afterwards.

It should have been totally unthinkable.

The next Sunday, May got up early to eat breakfast with Darcy. He wore jeans and boots and his dark blue shirt, because he was working today: when he finished breakfast, he would get in his ute and drive south to the town of Munnaburra, where lately he had been spending his Sundays working in the garden of some people his parents knew.

May ate a handful of cereal from the box and asked, 'What's this garden like, anyway?'

Darcy said, 'It's too big.'

'Can I see it?'

He shrugged and said, 'Why?'

'I could bring you lunch,' May said.

'They feed me. They feed me way too much food.'

'Just like they pay you too much.'

'Exactly,' said Darcy, and he went whistling out to his truck.

May waited fifteen minutes, then she got in her car and drove towards Munnaburra. The theory, according to the news reports, was that this man—the man in the white ute—had been picking up travellers who were hitchhiking or asking for rides in cafes or waiting for buses or whose cars had broken down, and once he picked them up he took them somewhere remote, somewhere rural, and killed them. Which made her think—she couldn't help it—of a song Darcy had, a few months ago, listened to repeatedly with passionate attention, in which a man called Muddy Waters sang along with an electric blues guitar and a slow drum about being alone on the highway after sunset, driving so fast he couldn't control his car. She had, with waning patience, suggested that the image of the lonesome highway was overused, and Darcy had objected, said it wasn't a cliché, because the song itself was from the 1930s, though *this* recording was from the sixties, it was Chicago style but recorded live in San Francisco, and it had only just been released. He'd urged her to listen, really *listen*, as if she hadn't already, and the song had begun once more with a slight whirr from the CD player, and there was Muddy Waters yet again, driving his brand-new Ford, lonesome on the highway with the sun gone down.

So now, driving out of the Sunday city, May sang the song in her head—the scraps of it, at least, that she remembered—and began to scan the sides of the road. Nobody stood out to her: no walkers, no breakdowns, no hitchhikers, no bus stops. No girls wearing backpacks. She had always thought of 'lonesome' as a lonelier word than 'lonely', maybe because no Australian would ever use it.

When May arrived, the town of Munnaburra looked like a fancy Sydney suburb that had been spirited from its natural home north of the harbour and deposited in the country. The houses were big, and their wide driveways were planted with avenues of trees; outside every fifth house, a white man in a polo shirt washed a four-wheel drive. Driving through the streets, May thought she knew the secret heart of each man in his polo shirt: his self-interested politics, his goofy way with children, his proud complaints about private school fees, his effortless handshake, his harmless winks at his wife's friends, his late-night terrors in soft pyjamas—is this it? Is it enough? I know you all, May thought, and believed it, and the men in polo shirts went on washing their cars, their calves spreading beneath their khaki pants, their hair thinning, the spray of their hoses curving like God's rainbow above their Land Rovers. The streets were named after native Australian flowers. Darcy's truck wasn't parked on any of them.

May pulled over to look at the street directory. She was stopped next to a park in which a boy flew a kite, and this was inevitable and sickeningly wholesome and also, yes, charming. The boy was about ten and very sweet and serious and also a redhead, and May had sympathy for redheads, as if they were an abandoned people and required extra kindness from the few, like May, who understood this. How could you sit by a pretty park on a Sunday and not be hopeful for the kite of this unsmiling child; how could you not want to see it soar? Although one day this boy, too, would coax his Land Rover to a burnished shine.

May got out of the car and stretched her limbs in the raw air of Munnaburra. The kite flew higher, but the boy still didn't smile; if anything, he seemed frightened of the sky. May walked in his direction. She would tell him what a good job he was doing, maybe suggest that he relax. She might ask him if he'd seen a white ute. But as May approached, a woman stepped onto the verandah of the house next to the park and called, 'Lachlan!' It was a completely ordinary way for a mother to call her child home, but May heard the hint of panic in the voice, and so did the boy, apparently, because he turned, looked at May, and began to run. The kite dipped and rose and plunged to the ground, and Lachlan, running, dragged it along behind him.

Don't worry, thought May. You're safe. And she thought, fuck Munnaburra, and got back into her car, and drove home.

Later that night, while they made dinner together, she asked Darcy what he'd had for lunch.

'Meat pie,' he said.

It seemed unlikely that anyone who lived in Munnaburra would feed their gardener a meat pie.

He was smiling, light on his feet, and he kept poking May in the ribs and waist as he passed her to get to the fridge or to the garbage bin; the ticklish pokes that little girls are told mean a little boy likes them. When she slapped his hands away, he found it funny. He cooked the tofu exactly the way she preferred it.

After dinner, they sat smoking on the balcony, and Darcy said he was onto a new supplier, that soon they'd have better stuff, and cheaper, because this guy was an old friend and would cut him a good deal. What guy? Where?

'Down south,' he said, but wouldn't reveal anything more.

She asked him about the Munnaburra garden again, and he

said, 'They're rich as fuck, they're putting in mature trees. You know how expensive mature trees are? They're too rich to wait for anything to grow.'

'Everyone's rich down there,' May said, and Darcy looked surprised.

'You've been?' he asked.

May inhaled, waited, exhaled. 'I've heard stuff about it.'

When they went inside, May turned on the late news. Darcy said, 'Jesus Christ,' and went to bed. Two more people were missing—a couple from Switzerland. A photograph appeared on screen: they were young, blond, tall, with uniform teeth; exactly how a couple from Switzerland should look. They wore life vests and stood in a boat and the sun shone on a lake behind them; they had their bronzed arms wrapped around each other in an effortless way that made you feel they had their whole joint future mapped out. They looked so healthy and strong that it was impossible to imagine them being forced to do anything they didn't want to, like get into a white ute with a stranger. The Swiss couple had been working at a farm about three hundred kilometres south of Sydney, and had set out to hitchhike back to the city. That was ten days ago. The police were asking anyone with any information to come forward, to call a dedicated hotline; even the smallest detail, apparently, could turn out to be significant. May ran to get a pen from beside the phone and wrote down the number on a page ripped out of the TV guide.

When she went into the bedroom, Darcy was still awake. 'Satisfied?' he asked.

'With what?'

'That the world is going to shit.'

May spent a long time cleaning her face and brushing her teeth in the hope that he would be asleep by the time she'd finished. He was, and this made it possible to get into bed beside him.

A few nights later, May's mother called to remind May that her cousin Steph's baby was being baptised on Sunday morning and that May and Darcy were expected at church and, afterwards, at Empress of China for lunch. May told her mother that Darcy worked on Sundays.

May's mother said, 'So he has a job.' Then she made May get a piece of paper and a pen ('You don't keep a pen beside the telephone?') and write down that the service on Sunday started at nine and that she should arrive at least half an hour early in order to get a good parking spot.

'What's on Sunday?' asked Darcy, who had been leaning against the kitchen counter drinking a beer while May spoke to her mother.

May explained about the baptism and lunch and said, 'But I know you have to work.'

Darcy held his beer bottle against the light, checking to see how much was left in it. Then he said, 'I could miss a Sunday. If you want me to come, I could get the day off.'

'They'd let you have the day off?' May asked, and she washed her hands although they weren't dirty, she hadn't done anything that would have made them dirty.

Darcy shrugged. 'I'll just say I'm sick.'

'Okay,' May said. She wasn't sure if his willingness to miss work was a good or bad sign. He came to her and put one hand on the back of her neck, stroking along the ridge of her spine with his big thumb. It felt nice. May tried to resist the awful hope that someone might be attacked while Darcy sat beside her in church, fully accounted for.

But on Saturday afternoon he said his parents' friends had called to let him know that the palm trees they'd ordered had arrived early, they needed to be planted asap, this just wasn't a week he could skip.

On Sunday, the day of the baptism, May got up early with Darcy and dressed in jeans and a silky top. Her mother would be horrified by the jeans and approve of the top, with the result that she would comment upon neither.

Darcy chewed his toast and said, 'You look fancy,' but his mind was on something else. He was already on the highway.

May watched him drive away in his ute. Then she slipped the piece of paper with the hotline number into the pocket of her jeans, got into her own car, and followed him. This was easy enough to do: Darcy was a careful driver, not likely to weave between lanes or indulge in unnecessary overtaking, and May's car was indistinguishable from a hundred others. The day was muggy with a bright white sky—just the sort of nothing day on which May's family would hold a baptism.

In the far southern suburbs of Sydney, Darcy pulled into a McDonald's and May waited in the car park, watching ibises squabble over a brimming bin. Darcy came out with a drink and a paper bag, got into the ute, and they set off again. May remained two cars behind him, and like this they followed the highway south under the stretched sky of the Royal National Park. Darcy took all the turn-offs he was supposed to if he were heading for Munnaburra.

Just north of Mittagong, they passed a teenage boy in large, low jeans, a Hawaiian shirt, and scruffy hair, standing by the side of the road with his thumb out. The boy looked as if his Saturday night had started out predictably enough and ended in hilarious disaster. He grinned at each passing car and wagged his phallic thumb. Darcy didn't stop for him; he didn't even slow down.

They drove into Munnaburra, which seemed to unfold along the sides of the road as if inked on a delicate screen. The same men washing Land Rovers, the same boys riding tricycles on sloping driveways. A sausage sizzle animated the park in which, last Sunday, the redhead had flown his kite. Darcy turned into Waratah Avenue, and May followed. There was no car between them now, but May no longer cared.

Waratah Avenue presented fences smothered in bougainvillea, jasmine, and great banks of gardenia, so that it felt to May like she was driving down the aisle of a church. She could almost see her parents' faces blinking up from among the flowers; there was pretty Steph with her pretty baby, and the minister smiling in his thick, square glasses and his long white robe, ready to baptise the baby into a world of inescapable sin. After a few blocks, the houses grew smaller, the fences lower, and the lawns less brilliantly green. Then the town stopped altogether, as if the street had got distracted and become, unexpectedly, a minor road through paddocks.

May dropped back—she didn't want to be right on Darcy's tail. Soon, the paddocks fell away and gum trees crowded up against the side of the road. May saw the white of Darcy's ute flickering ahead of her, around curves and up and down hills, and once over a bridge spanning a half-dry creek. Then, about ten minutes out of Munnaburra, May crested a hill and could see down into a broad, green valley. The road was visible a fair way ahead, and Darcy wasn't on it.

Her first thought was that he'd seen her and sped up. Her second was that, if he was taking this road any further, he'd been stretching the truth when he'd described himself as working 'in Munnaburra'. *Near* Munnaburra, maybe. *In* Munnaburra was a lie.

May pulled over and sat very still in her humming car. The ground rose up on either side of the road, so that it felt as if she were in a riverbed and anyone could be on the banks, looking down at her. The slopes were foamy with lantana, and the pale petals of the flowers made her think of the onion weed she'd picked by the highway two weeks before, and of Cherie saying, 'I'll never forgive myself if I see your picture in the paper.' She thought of the baby seat in Cherie's car, and of cousin Steph and her big, blank baby, and of how her whole family was, at that moment, sitting together in church. She imagined each of their faces upon hearing the news about her boyfriend, the pity and horror and disgust they would feel, her parents' shame and confusion, and their irresistible sense that they'd been right all along, that May should have married a nice Christian man and baptised a nice Christian baby. And the suspicion, too: Didn't you *know*? You must have *known*. We raised you to recognise evil.

She waited ten minutes, but there was no sign of Darcy's ute. Muddy Waters sang to her out of the sixties. '*Oh you know you're all alone by yourself*,' he sang. A taxi appeared on the road, heading into Munnaburra; strange to see a taxi all the way out here. It seemed to slow a fraction before passing.

May turned the car and drove back the way she'd come. She drove slowly, and now she noticed a few letterboxes on the sides of the road and, next to these, driveways disappearing into the green. Most of them had gates, some padlocked; the density of the bush formed its own fence. It was impossible to tell what sort of properties these drives led to, or whether or not anyone had used them recently, or which one Darcy might have gone down. There might be mansions, lavish with pools and gardens; or illegal cannabis plantations; or cult compounds ringing with the sounds of orgies and tambourines. She looked at each driveway she passed, expecting to see the glow of the white ute, or Darcy's tall, thin figure carrying a tall, thin palm tree. She never really considered driving beyond any of the letterboxes. The driveways seemed closed to her, and at the same time to offer a series of tantalising hopes. Darcy could, after all, have driven down any of them. He could be telling the truth. May drove, and the trees fell away, the paddocks opened out, and soon she was back in Munnaburra, which seemed to exist in its own sunlight.

The men of Munnaburra still attended to their Land Rovers,

or mowed their front lawns, or stood on their driveways teaching their sons how to hold cricket bats. But May was no longer sure that she knew their secret hearts. Each man she passed seemed more fatherly than the last: a little balder, and wearing a polo shirt in a slightly brighter white. The ones kneeling in flowerbeds, tugging at weeds, wouldn't allow dirt to lodge beneath their fingernails. She could buy things for them, and they would say thank you and not insist on paying her back. They would finish with their cars, or their lawns, or their sons, and they would step inside their houses and thank their wives for keeping a pen beside the telephone. Their wives, used to talking about their men in tones of doting exasperation with other wives, might suspect them of adultery, or gambling, or embezzlement, but never of trying to gag a girl by the side of a road.

May pulled over by the kite-flying park. She looked for red-haired Lachlan among the children at the play equipment, but couldn't see him. When she shifted in her seat, she felt the crackle of the paper with the hotline number on it. She would call, even though he was probably just planting baby palms down one of those driveways. She'd call because it was the right thing to do; because the smallest detail could turn out to be significant. She'd call, and it wouldn't be him, and then she'd be doubly glad she'd called. She'd drive back to Sydney first, would go to lunch with her family first; then she really would, she'd call.

May drove back to Sydney and across the city to Empress of China, the restaurant at which her family celebrated every milestone. The waitresses pushing the steaming dumpling carts all knew her name; the head waiter had been a guest at Steph's wedding. It was possible to track May's growth in her mother's photo albums by comparing her height to that of the gem tree in the restaurant lobby, with its hard apricot petals.

She found her family at their usual tables. Her mother looked her outfit over without comment, took the handbag from off the seat she'd been saving, and scolded May for not being at the church. Steph's baby, newly entered into covenant with God, blinked and hiccupped in the arms of its relatives. Whenever anyone asked May where Darcy was, she said he worked on Sundays. When they asked where, she didn't mention Munnaburra; instead, she gave them the name of a posh North Shore suburb and told them about the rich clients who planted mature trees because they were too impatient to wait for their gardens to grow. She talked about the baby palms as if she believed in them. They smiled at Darcy's gardening job and glanced, in clear comparison, at Steph's husband, who was ten years older and worked for a management consultant, whatever that might be; his parents and Steph's were lifelong friends. He earned the kind of salary that meant he'd probably never have to wait for a garden to grow. He was a perfectly nice baby-faced guy who May happened to know had been in AA since Steph got pregnant.

After lunch, she drove behind her parents' car to Steph's mother's house. Aunt Helen had invited them, and it would be rude not to go. Afterwards, she would call the hotline. She stayed at Aunt Helen's into the evening, and finally she agreed to hold Steph's baby, which had woken up crying and now fell into a drooling sleep against May's right shoulder. For minutes at a time she didn't think of Darcy, but when she did May felt her heart drop. It was a very physical feeling, and it reminded her of falling in love with him, in those early days when her nerve had often failed, when he seemed distant, or she undeserving, or both of them unsure of what they wanted. She sat in an arm-chair with the baby's head very warm against her neck. A moth had flown into the house and now bounced between the many lamps. May pretended she couldn't go home because the baby was sleeping, and her mother and Aunt Helen smiled at her and at each other, and Steph passed between the lamps, chasing the moth and laughing, but quietly. Then May's mother was leaving, and Steph and her husband were leaving—the baby snuffled as May laid him in the travel cot—and there was nothing to do but go home. It was too late, now, to call the hotline. She would call in the morning.

May parked her car behind Darcy's ute and saw that mud had flicked up from his tyres onto its white sides. She sat for a moment, imagining she could still smell the milky warmth of Steph's baby's head. When May finally went inside, Darcy was already in bed, asleep. Her reading lamp had been left on for her.

In the kitchen, May found a large glass jar full of plump, dried cannabis buds. She also found a tray of glossy cherries; there was a flowery card tucked in among them, on which someone had written: *For Mister Darcy, Grazie mille for going above and beyond. Love, Gloria, Dave & all the little bitty baby palms.*

May looked at this note for a long time. Then she ate three cherries, spitting the pits into the sink. She undressed, throwing her jeans in the laundry basket, and got into the shower, where she noticed the water pooling around her feet. May hooked a finger into the drain and pulled up a fine net of brown hair. She looked at the hair looped on the end of her finger—Darcy's hair, matted and soapy—and was filled with tenderness, with love, as if she'd never doubted him, and never been afraid.

ABROAD

(2011)

The witch rings the doorbell at nine thirty, a full hour after the last trick-or-treater, and she appears to be alone. When Simon opens the door to her, she frightens him a little. She's so small, and imperfectly green, as if someone began the job of colouring her face with gusto and then grew bored. Her hat is regulation—tall and conical, with a broad brim and a yellow buckle—but she wears a black T-shirt, black trousers, and a pair of purple high-top Converse. An off-duty witch, a witch on casual Friday, carrying a broom and one of those orange plastic baskets shaped like a pumpkin. She looks up at Simon without saying 'trick or treat'—without saying anything—and Simon looks back at her, unsure of how to proceed. He's English and doesn't understand American Halloween, but he's married to an American and lives in America and finds, now, that he has no choice: the souls of the dead have risen, and he must, for one night, live among them.

'Hello,' says Simon.

Behind him, in the house, he can hear Sunny on the phone, arguing with her mother. The night is mild because this is Texas, and its late October climate is gloriously hospitable.

The witch adjusts her grip on the broom. She looks about ten years old, and someone has drawn a large wart on the tip of her nose. She says, 'I know you probably don't have any good candy left.'

Simon glances at her pumpkin, which looks to be fairly full of shiny wrappers, but he doesn't know enough about American candy to interpret the quality of what he sees. He does know—now—that Peanut Butter Kisses are not the same thing as Reese's Peanut Butter Cups, because when he brought the former home from H-E-B, Sunny laughed at him and said she should have known better than to send an Englishman out to buy Halloween candy. To Sunny, Simon had defended himself by pointing out that American Halloween was a commercial bastardisation of an ancient Celtic festival, something much darker and older than the constitution of this fanatical country, and that the day he understood Halloween candy would be the day he gave up on being British.

To the witch, he says, 'I'll bring the candy bowl, shall I, and let you be the judge?'

When he steps into the dining room to fetch the bowl— Sunny, in her American way, would say 'grab' the bowl, which seems to him unnecessarily violent—Sunny comes to the door of the kitchen, dressed as a pirate in white ruffles, a tight vest, and a long skirt. Her shoulders are bare and brown. She muffles her cell phone against one hand and says, 'It's so late. Who is it? Teens? Teens are the worst.'

Then she returns the phone to her ear and says, 'Okay, Mommy, but you need to look at it from his point of view. He works for an airline.'

They're arguing about Sunny's brother, who for the third year in a row has disappointed his mother by claiming he's too busy at work to come home to Sacramento for Thanksgiving. Sunny, too, is annoyed with Anil, but she's justifying his decision in order to spare her mother's feelings. She strides back into the kitchen with bare feet, her pirate skirt hitched up and tucked rakishly into her wide belt so that she's showing most of one leg. She's magnificent, and the only thing in the world that could possibly have convinced Simon to move to Texas.

Simon returns to the front door carrying the mostly empty bowl, which is shaped like a cauldron. 'What do you think?' he asks. 'Anything pass muster?'

The witch stands on her toes in order to peer into the bowl, even though Simon has held it low enough for her easy inspection. Perhaps this is a witch thing: this narrowing of the eyes, these tiptoes; perhaps it's witch etiquette around a cauldron.

'Okay, so, it's kind of dark in there,' she says. 'Can we tip it out? I want to make sure I pick the best one.'

'Why not?' says Simon, who in most situations also prefers to pick the best one.

He takes unexpected pleasure in pouring the contents of the cauldron onto the front porch. When his older sister was going through her early-adolescent Pre-Raphaelite phase, she'd had a poster on her bedroom wall of a beautiful witch standing on a sea monster and pouring a glowing liquid into the waves from a wide, shallow bowl. Simon, much younger, had been frightened by it: by the pale bulge of the witch's breast as much as the domesticated sea monster. He remembers this image now as the little witch crouches to inspect the candy. It feels menacing to loom above her, so Simon also lowers himself into a squat—carefully, because he's dressed in the kilt he wore as a groomsman at his best friend's wedding, which is the closest he's willing to come to a Halloween costume.

'These are pretty good,' says the witch, poking with one contemplative green finger at the bright packages on the porch. She's let her broom fall against the railings, but grips the handle of her pumpkin bucket as if she's afraid it might be snatched from her at any moment. A group of teenagers goes careening by. They're each dressed as a different condiment. Hot Sauce has taken a clump of Spanish moss—probably from the boughs of one of Carol West's beloved magnolias, three houses down— and is wearing it as a crown, like a Dickensian Christmas ghost.

'It's quite late,' Simon says to the witch. 'Are you out on your own?'

The witch, bending over the candy—her hat, still atop her head, must be held on by elastic—sighs as if she's disappointed in him for asking such a tiresome question. 'I live one street over. You can hear my house.'

Simon listens. He can hear a low, thumping bass, and only now realises that it's provided a steady heartbeat to the entire evening.

'They're having a party?' Simon asks.

'Uh-huh,' says the witch. Her small hand hovers above a miniature Snickers. She shifts her weight from one folded leg to another, then looks up at Simon. Her green eyes are startling in her green face. She says, 'Some people give out full-size candy bars.'

Simon nods. 'So my wife tells me.'

'But you have to be early, before the other kids. Did you have full-size ones?'

Simon shakes his head. 'My wife thinks they're excessive.'

The witch thinks this over, then shrugs. 'It's only once a year,' she says.

Simon hears Sunny's high, barking laugh—the one that signals both incredulity and an almost regretful dismay. She often resorts to this laugh while on the phone with her mother.

'How about,' says Simon, 'you choose a chocolate bar, and I'll get my wife, and we'll walk you home.' I'll *grab* my wife, he thinks.

The witch's eyes return to the pile of candy glittering at her feet. 'How about,' she says, reproducing Simon's exact tone and inflection, 'I get two of these, since they're not full size.'

Simon considers resisting these terms—until he hears a scream in the night, a pitchy, garbled shriek of what appears to be genuine fright, which may have come from two blocks away or from the shuttered attic of the house next door, and he's reminded, again, that the dead are abroad, whether he likes it or not. Then it seems to him unwise to try to bargain for anything on this particular night, in case he binds himself or the witch to some devilish contract.

Sunny, he knows, would be shocked to learn that he entertained such a superstition; she might say, 'You don't really believe that, do you? You're a software developer.' And Simon might have to say that 'belief' wasn't the right word for what he felt when it came to the world of the dead, because belief suggested faith, which implied a lack of certainty; whereas his was a profound, certain knowledge of which he would rather be ignorant. 'A knowledge of what?' Sunny would ask, because Sunny always asks—she's unabashed in her curiosity. And it would be difficult to answer her. What *does* he know? That the dead are close? That they're only waiting for us to acknowledge them? That they would speak to us if we asked them to?

What nonsense. But Sunny wouldn't laugh at him; very quickly she would connect his superstition to what she called the 'psychological trauma of his sister's disappearance'. She would say—with conviction, although she was in grad school at UT for architecture, not psychology—that he was haunted by ambiguous loss, because twenty-one years ago, when he was only twelve years old, his sister went on vacation to Australia and disappeared. Was certainly dead, but where, and how? And then Sunny would pity him, which he couldn't bear. So Simon won't tell her about his superstitions, and he'll allow this min-iature witch her two bars of chocolate. He hands them over and the shriek comes again; this time he recognises it as the cry of a late-to-bed grackle.

'Stay there a minute,' Simon says, 'and I'll get my wife. Stay right there.'

He hurries through the living room, through the dining room, and into the kitchen, where Sunny is saying, 'Okay, I know what you mean, but also, climate change.' Seeing Simon, she rolls her eyes and mouths, 'She's crying.'

Simon holds up one finger in the private semaphore that means 'Can I have one minute of your time? Can I *grab* one minute? Can I step for one minute into the miracle that is you beholding me and still saying *yes*?'

'Hold on, Mommy,' Sunny says, and flattens her phone against her chest.

Simon knows to speak fast. 'There's a little girl out there, without her parents—without anybody—and we need to get her home. She lives in the next street.'

Sunny's face gathers into surprise, pity, and, finally, entreaty. She has beautifully expressive eyebrows. 'I can't leave my mother like this,' she says, indicating the phone. 'Can't you just take her?'

He raises his own, less forthcoming eyebrows. 'Wouldn't it be better to, you know, have a woman?'

'People will just think she's your kid.' Sunny beams at him: sure, as always, that Simon's undeniable goodness will be as evident to other people as it is to her.

The witch's exact ethnicity is concealed by her patchily green skin and hair-encompassing hat; nevertheless, Simon suspects that, even if she were wiped clean to reveal his specific shade of pink, no one would ever mistake them for father and daughter. The witch is assured and fearless, whereas he would never, as a child, have gone out alone at night—at any time, least of all Halloween. Even now, as an adult, as a married software developer, he doesn't like the idea of being out alone at night on Halloween; especially here, where the dead are summoned by lawn decorations. Simon knows himself to have inherited his parents' latent Methodist terror of the wicked world. His sister had been eight years older than him, he'd watched her live through an entire adolescence without him, and she in her glamorous privacy had seemed unafraid of anything.

When Sunny draws the phone away from her chest, Simon hears the high wail of his mother-in-law calling, 'Sunita? Sunita?'

'Please?' Sunny asks, nodding as if he's already agreed; she does this often, this pre-emptive nodding, as if she thinks that performing the response she hopes for will produce it. It almost always does.

Simon makes use of a loud, emphatic sigh: a largely ineffectual weapon, but one he tends to fall back on. He takes his keys from where they sit on the kitchen counter and returns to the front door.

The witch is gone, and all of the candy with her.

'Fuck,' says Simon. The crisp, definite, English way in which he says 'fuck' is another one of his weapons; Sunny finds it both sexy and adorable.

He runs down the path and into the street, which appears to be empty. It's hard to tell, though; this Austin neighbourhood is famous for its gardens, which tumble over fences and onto sidewalks, turning them into dark, leafy tunnels. The streets are lined with old live oaks, which spill drifts of pollen in the spring; tonight, their branches are hung with fake spiderwebs, floating in the breeze like slow smoke. There are cars parked in every available space—so many cars, cluttering the street. And in the front gardens—yards—of those houses that aren't screened by foliage, Simon can see humanoid figures, which he knows to be dangling skeletons, rotating witches, solar-powered ghosts, and mannequin zombies. If the Bristol of his childhood had been decorated like this every Halloween, he wouldn't have left the house for the entirety of October.

No little witch to the left or to the right. No little witch knocking at his neighbours' doors or crouching between cars with her candy haul. No little witch on this block at all. Simon runs along the street, feeling the strange movement of the kilt against his legs; he heads towards the nearest corner, thinking to follow the sound of the party. The mild air moves gently, insinuatingly, as he runs, as if guiding him from one place to another. It feels thin and permeable.

The Queen Anne mansion on the corner has planted its lawn with resin headstones, each spotlit; some of the graves stir with the mechanical hands of the uneasy dead. One of the stones reads: *Bone Voyage*. On the porch, which is unlit, two shadowy figures mutter above a large cauldron bubbling with dry ice. Simon calls to them, almost but not entirely sure they're figurines. 'Hello? Excuse me?' he calls, and they answer. Or someone answers, but not the weird sisters at the cauldron, who remain motionless. The voice comes from deeper within the dark porch, and probably belongs to a man, but also possibly to a vampire, a ghoul, or Frankenstein's melancholy monster.

'Can I help you?' says the voice. It sounds affable enough— but then, so do those canny wizards who stop travellers in the woods, ask pleasant questions, then demand the answers to deadly riddles.

'Have you seen a little girl come past, a little witch girl, with a pointy hat and a pumpkin?'

'Seen a lot of witches tonight,' says the voice.

'In the last few minutes.'

'Nope,' comes the voice. 'Afraid not.'

Simon calls, 'Thanks!' and runs on, turning the corner. As

he runs, the phrase 'afraid not' returns to him over and over again as a kind of pulse, so that he wonders if he's just had an encounter with an angel, the sort who says 'Be not afraid' while flaunting the holy horror of its radiant-eyed wings. Which is, of course, nonsense.

Simon would call the witch's name, but he doesn't know it. His sister's name was Angie, and it's impossible not to think of that now; impossible, also, not to think of how, for years, his father would go walking alone immediately after supper, leaving the house with an air of apology and returning half an hour later with the same air, as if he knew his walk was farcical and inconvenient, meant leaving his wife and son to clear the table and wash the dishes and carry on the business of every-day life without him, but that the walk was necessary all the same, a way of honouring his daughter, or looking for her, or just acknowledging that he had let her leave the safety of his house in the first place. The walks began after his very private parents returned from their first trip to Australia, which had been full of very public pleas, and they continued every night for nearly five years, no matter the weather. And Simon, even at age twelve, fifteen, seventeen, had known not to question this nightly routine, or to comment on it, or even to wonder what it was for. Sunny, if she knew about the walks, would be sure she understood what they were for. She'd conclude that Simon's father spent his days full of rage and fear at his own helplessness; that these feelings built in him like a storm front as he worked and talked and ate; and that he walked at night to ensure that the clouds, bursting, didn't soak Simon and his mother. But Sunny has never met that version of his parents, the first-five-years version: the fright, the shame, the waiting. She only knows the thick sorrow that runs beneath all the ways in which they are perfectly ordinary.

Around the corner and halfway down the block, Simon comes upon the party, which is taking place in a heaving 1920s bungalow. Most of the guests seem to be in the yard behind the house, which can be accessed from the front by an open gate in a tall fence. The fence is covered with chalk warnings: *Beware*; *Enter If You Dare*; *Trespassers Will Be Mummified*. The house, like most of the others in the neighbourhood, has a large porch, and on the porch a swing. Sitting on the swing are a kid in a full Spider-Man costume and a girl, probably in her early twenties, holding a bottle of Dos Equis. She's wearing jeans and a cropped shirt and looks damp, as if she's just run through a light shower of rain.

Simon walks up the path towards them.

'Hey!' calls Spider-Man. 'You're wearing a skirt.'

'It's called a kilt,' says the girl, and she looks at Simon with wide eyes, as if to say, 'Can you believe what I have to put up with?'

'I know that,' says Spider-Man. 'Hey, look.' He pulls his mask down around his neck and reveals that his face is almost entirely covered in temporary tattoos, also of Spider-Man.

'That's brilliant,' says Simon.

'I'm a toe,' says the girl, and tilts her head towards a large, beige papier-mâché structure sitting beside the swing. It's toe-shaped, and appears to involve a red toenail. Simon can see how the girl might have worn it over her body and become, indeed, a toe.

'Her boyfriend's a camel,' says Spider-Man. He's about the same age as the missing witch.

'It's a couple's costume,' says the girl. 'Get it? Camel toe.'

'I get it,' says Spider-Man.

'You don't,' says the girl. 'You just think you do.'

'Listen,' says Simon, and he feels himself marshalling his accent, which rarely fails to charm Americans. 'I don't want to bother you,' he continues, 'but is there a little girl at this party, dressed as a witch? With a green face and purple shoes?'

He half-expects them to turn to each other and exclaim, in old-timey film accents, 'A girl like that hasn't been seen in these parts for fifty years.' But they both nod and say in tandem, 'Sophia.'

'My cousin,' says the girl, and takes a swig of her beer.

'*My* cousin,' says Spider-Man.

'Well,' says Simon, 'have you seen her recently? Because she was just at my house in the next street, trick-or-treating on her own, but she ran off.'

The girl frowns. She's pretty, Latina, with her hair pulled back into a ponytail; damp wisps of it curl around her face. She must have been hot.

'Didn't we just see her?' she asks Spider-Man.

Spider-Man nods. 'She threw that at me,' he says, and kicks one spider-stockinged leg out at a scrunched-up Kit Kat wrapper.

'How long ago was that?' Simon asks.

'A couple minutes?' says the girl. Spider-Man shrugs.

'Ah,' says Simon, on the verge of feeling enormous relief. He's so ready to turn back down the path, go home, kiss Sunny's bare piratical shoulders. But he says, 'Are you sure? I'd really feel much better if I could just see her with my own eyes. If I could just be absolutely certain that she's safe.'

'Go find Sophia,' the girl orders Spider-Man, and he obeys without question, leaping up from the seat, jumping down from the porch without using the steps, and trotting around to the gate. His costume gapes open in the back.

'It's nice that you're so worried about her,' says the girl. 'Want a drink?' She gestures towards the seat Spider-Man has just vacated.

'Oh, thanks very much, I'm fine,' says Simon. He sits on the porch swing because it seems rude not to, and she immediately sets it in gentle motion with one pointed foot.

'I don't know if that means yes or no,' says the girl, and passes him her bottle. He takes a drink and passes it back. The chains of the swing creak; looking up, he sees a festive flutter of police tape. A chill runs down his spine, but it's only minor— a local chill.

'Are you from England?' the girl asks. 'I love your accent.'

Is she hitting on him? The thought makes him nervous; it makes him want a cigarette, though he hasn't smoked since uni. Just so that he has something to do with his hands. As the swing rocks, his kilt shifts back and forth over his knees—sometimes more flesh on display, sometimes less. There are moments at which he properly understands that he is physically in a strange land among strange people; this is one of those moments. He has made decisions that have led him to this porch, this girl, this Texas. Anything might happen. She might reach up to his face, take his glasses off, and say, with surprise, 'Oh, but you're beautiful!' She might invite him to prom. Someone might shoot at them from a passing car. She might say—does, in fact, say, 'Halloween is my favourite holiday, and I always make, like, a big deal out of it, and every year I get kinda depressed. You know what I mean?'

'Huh,' says Simon. 'Why is it your favourite?'

The girl shrugs and passes him the bottle of beer. 'It's spooky, I guess. And silly, you know? Fun.'

The silliness and fun, Simon thinks, are the problem. They're an invitation to mischief—old mischief, which is nasty, sly, and not entirely human. He feels these superstitions as deep ancestral wells upon which he rarely draws, and resents that this American fun has forced him to acknowledge them. He is, after all, a software developer.

'And why do you get depressed?' he asks.

'It's always better in my imagination.'

'The toe is great,' he says. 'It's a great idea.'

The girl holds her hand out for the beer, and he gives it to her. She sighs, and he wonders where her camel boyfriend is.

She says, 'I should have gone with something slutty.'

This might shock Simon, except that he knows about the cheerfully provocative Halloween costumes of young American women: sexy nurse, sexy nun, sexy UPS driver. He knows because, last year, he and Sunny attended the Halloween party of one of her grad school friends, and Sunny went as an Ethical Slut. Simon wore his kilt. They didn't enjoy themselves, though Simon isn't entirely sure why. He thinks Sunny would have had fun without him, and that she thought the same thing and felt bad about it. This year, she insisted on staying home to hand out candy.

The girl finishes the beer, stills the swing with her foot, and places the empty bottle beside the toe. Then she turns to him. Simon feels that he must extricate himself as soon as possible— from the girl, the swing, perhaps from Texas.

As if in answered prayer, Spider-Man appears at the bottom of the porch stairs. 'She won't come,' he announces.

'Oh?' says Simon.

'She's shy,' says Spider-Man.

The girl snorts. 'She's not shy.'

'Well,' says Simon, 'her shyness may have something to do with the fact that she ran off with all our chocolate.'

The girl laughs, and Spider-Man grins through his temporary tattoos. The mask of his costume is still a wrinkled cowl around his neck.

Simon says, 'Please tell Sophia that all is forgiven, that all I want is to see that she's safe, and then I'll go home.'

Spider-Man leaps away towards the gate.

Simon and the girl sit in silence for a moment on the swing, which begins to rock again, apparently of its own accord. He almost asks her name, but feels with a sudden dreadful certainty that it will be Angie, and that to hear her say so would be unbearable. Or perhaps her name won't be Angie, but she'll answer 'Angie' all the same, because by leaving his house alone at Halloween he has asked for an encounter of some kind, long delayed but at the same time premature. If she were to say her name, if she were to say 'Angie', he would have to ask questions:

'Where are you? What happened? Did it hurt? Do I love you? Are you real?' And he would have to learn the answers, then live with them.

So he won't ask the girl's name. He looks at her and she's looking at him; they begin to speak simultaneously, which Simon finds both awkward and useful, because he's not entirely sure what he was going to say. They laugh.

'You go,' says the girl.

'No, please,' says Simon.

The girl smiles. 'I was going to ask you to tell me a scary story.'

But Simon only knows one scary story, and he won't tell it. If he were to try tonight, when the dead are abroad, he's afraid he'd become trapped in the telling. It's an odd phrase, thinking about it—'the dead are abroad': like they're on holiday. The dead in Mallorca, in Benidorm. His parents go every summer to the Costa del Sol, as if by doctor's orders.

He finds himself saying, 'What about you? I've never heard a Texan ghost story.'

The girl leans closer.

'So my friend used to live out on this old ranch,' she says, 'way, way out in the Hill Country, no one else around, and this one night she's in bed and she hears someone walking outside, underneath her window. Crunch, crunch, crunch, crunch.'

The girl accompanies each 'crunch' with a sinuous movement of her hands—left, right, left, right—as if they're sneaking feet.

'So she thinks it's her dad outside checking something, or whatever. But she keeps hearing it. Like, she hears the steps under her window, they go away, they come back under her window again. Like her dad's walking around and around the house in a big circle.'

Here she moves her right forearm in a tornado motion, her index finger extended. Simon notices that she's wearing red nail polish, like her toe.

'And she can't sleep, you know, she can't relax, because she keeps waiting for the noise: crunch, crunch, crunch, crunch. And it's really annoying. She counts how many times he comes around: four, five, six.'

She holds up her left thumb, her index finger, and her middle finger in turn, as if counting to three.

'On the sixth time she's had it. Crunch, crunch—so she yells: *Dad, would you stop that!* And the steps stop'—she claps, then holds her hands up towards him, palms out—'just for a second, then they walk off again. A minute later, her dad comes into her room and says, *What're you yelling about?* So she tells him, you know, *Quit walking around outside, I can't sleep.*'

When she's saying the friend's lines, the girl raises her voice into a breathless silliness; when she's the father, she lowers her chin to her chest and produces a bass drawl.

'And he says, *I wasn't outside.* And she's like, *Tell Mom, then. It's really bugging me.* And he says, *Your mom's not outside. There's nothing there.* She says, *I keep hearing someone outside my window*, and he says, *You heard a coyote, go to sleep.* But right at that moment?'

The girl lifts her hands: crunch, crunch, crunch, crunch.

'Her dad hears it too. And he goes real white and she says, *See? Like someone's walking around the house.* And he says, *How many times have you heard it?* She tells him this is number seven.

Her dad says, *Seven? Are you sure?* He's obviously freaking out. Then he tells her to turn on her bedside lamp and stay away from the window and he runs out and she hears him calling her mom. He's saying, *She's back, she's back, check the doors, are the doors locked*, and her mom's saying, *How long do we have, how many times*, and he's saying, *Seven, seven.* And my friend hears them running around checking windows and doors and turning on all the lights.'

Her eyes are wide. Simon feels himself sway, just slightly.

'Then it comes again: crunch, crunch, crunch, crunch.'

Simon is in bed, his feet are near the window and so far from his head and so vulnerable, his arm is incapable of reaching out to turn on the lamp, his parents are trying to keep their voices down, trying not to scare him, but he hears them panicking, they're whispering horrors to one another, there are crucial steps they need to take and not enough time in which to take them, and he hears the footsteps: crunch, crunch, crunch, crunch.

The girl takes a breath. Before she can speak, she's interrupted by a sudden scream—close at hand, terrifying, as if in answer to something.

Both he and the girl jump, rattling the chains of the swing; they look towards the sound, and there is Sophia at the bottom of the porch steps, his little green witch, with mischief on her face, in her face, crackling about her like bad weather. She's lost her hat, and brown hair erupts in a ponytail from the top of her head. She stands for a moment, glorying in the effect of her scream, then gives a wild laugh and runs away, back through the gate.

'Oh my god,' says the girl.

Simon is laughing without finding anything funny. He knows he's laughed just a fraction too long when he sees the girl's face stiffen from friendly warmth into wary politeness; so he stops.

'I'm glad she's all right,' he says. He stands up, stopping the swing with the backs of his knees. His heart beats very fast.

The girl looks up at him. 'Don't you want to hear the rest of the story?'

'I have to get back,' he says. 'Thanks for the beer!'

He jogs down the stairs and hurries into the street. He needs to be home at once. He has the feeling—urgent, perverse—that unless he gets home immediately, he'll be forced to leave the house after supper every evening, to leave Sunny with the business of everyday life and walk for half an hour, and that what he'll be doing—and sees now that his father was doing—is going out to find Angie, meeting her, and leading her away, so that theirs might be something approaching an ordinary house, and Simon's might be something approaching an ordinary adolescence; so that he might be able to forget, for minutes at a time, that he ever had a sister, and would never lie awake listening for her footsteps beneath his window.

Simon runs past the cars and the gardens, past the Queen Anne witches and their speaking porch, past the live oaks strung with webbing and Mardi Gras beads in black and orange, past a middle-aged couple dressed as Gomez and Morticia, past Carol West's magnolias, and then he's home, where he's acutely aware of the crunch of his feet on the gravel of the path, and where he sees to his horror that the front door is open, though he's almost sure he closed it when he went after his witch.

He runs into the house calling, 'Sunny! Sunny! Sunita!'

She answers almost immediately. 'In here!' she calls, and he knows she's in the kitchen, and that she's safe.

But the door is open. Anyone could have snuck in while he was gone, anyone could be in the house with her. Anything. He begins to search the rooms, frantic—behind curtains, inside closets, underneath the couch.

Sunny appears beside him. 'What is it?' she's saying. 'What's wrong?'

But there's no time to tell her. He pushes past her and on into the next room. It's empty, but that makes no difference. The dead are abroad. The dead are everywhere.

DEMOLITION

(2003)

T he Biga house is coming down,' Gerald said. 'Finally.' He
took the tray from Eva's lap.

'That lovely house,' Eva said.

Gerald held the tray in one hand and, with a finger of the
other, lifted a slat of the venetian blinds. He peered out the window. 'What's lovely about it?' he asked, and the tray tilted.

'Gerald!' Eva called, and he righted his hand without looking at her. 'The Japanese maple with the crimson leaves.'

'They dug it up already,' Gerald said. 'Worth a fortune, a tree
like that.'

Eva wheeled herself to the window.

'I'll open the blinds,' Gerald said, but he went away first, into
the kitchen with the tray. Until he came back, she studied the
dust on the edges of the blinds—the very thin rim of it. But who
could fault Gerald, who was tremendous with the housework
and had said, 'What's wrong with curtains? Blinds'll only catch

the dust,' and still let her have them installed? Now he came back and leaned over the couch the way you had to and fiddled with the cords of the blinds until Eva could see the Biga house.

'So many cars,' she said, and Gerald snorted.

A man approached the Biga house and stopped at the front gate. He said something to the workmen inside the fence and, when they answered him, he turned to the letterbox—an ordinary metal letterbox—and, with one sure movement, wrenched it off its post. Then he cradled it against his stomach the way you might a heavy watermelon and carried it to a car parked down the street.

'Souvenir,' Gerald said. 'Sickos.'

But he stayed at the window to watch for the excavator. When it came around the corner, the doors of the cars parked on the street all opened up and people rose out of them. They held cameras and camcorders, and they wore clothes in muted colours—like the ones you see on TV journalists in war zones, Eva thought. As if they wanted to hide themselves. And all there to watch that little house come down. Eva had been a girl inside that house, visiting the Laineys. And after the Laineys moved to Sydney, she had seen tenants come and go, the shutters loosen and tighten, the maple tree's red turn on and off each year. Some tenants had raked the leaves and others hadn't. Some of her students had lived there with their families, and there had been nights when the windows were lit and music came out of them, and fatty smoke from grilling lamb chops. Christmas trees in the front window. So many women standing at the gate, calling children's names. And sometimes pets—the

Bigas themselves had had a dog, and later Paul Biga had birds. All of that, today, would go.

The street was getting crowded now. Workers in hard hats called out for people to stay back, and along came Jim Grant who, in his police uniform, still looked like a big, red-cheeked tenth-grader. Behind him was a woman Eva thought she knew, a short woman in a navy suit, who seemed almost superstitiously to avoid looking towards the Biga house—and, yes, it was their house, Eva and Gerald's, that she was looking at, their gate she opened, their path she stepped onto.

'Who's this then?' Gerald said. He liked to get to the door before a visitor. He was so large he filled the entire doorway—Eva knew how wonderful it was to see him waiting there, with his big voice calling, 'Welcome!', and how imposing he was if the welcome didn't come. She went back across the room to her usual place and listened to him say hello, and he was gracious as he said it; his tone was affable. So he approved of the short woman, and would admit her.

'You've got a visitor,' he said, coming back in from the hallway.

The woman was the type who put her head around the door before she entered a room: here was her head, light hair, sharp nose, and now here was her body. Was it to conceal her shortness? Eva understood these strategies; she didn't like people to see her wheelchair first.

'Hello, Mrs Forsythe,' the woman said, bending to kiss Eva's cheek, perhaps because Eva had lifted her face.

'This is a Miss Kate Hawkins,' Gerald said. 'Says you're old mates.'

'Oh no!' the woman said. She wore a bag across her body; it flattened one breast. 'I mean—I wonder if you remember me?'

'One of your old students, love?' Gerald said.

But Eva knew now who she was: she was the woman who'd written the book about Paul Biga. Her hair was lighter, but otherwise she looked the same. Eva nodded.

'I might pop out,' Gerald said, 'if you ladies are all right. See how old Terry's getting on.'

Eva could imagine Terry—next-door neighbour Terry, with whom Gerald was at war but only on Monday evenings, garbage night—standing on his lawn to watch the Biga house come down. Gerald went and joined him, and Eva knew exactly how they would look: Gerald Forsythe and Terry Jarrett, feet planted firmly apart, arms crossed high on their chests, as if they were supervising the demolition. Which could now proceed.

The short woman said, 'Perhaps you don't remember, Mrs Forsythe. We spoke five years ago, here in this room, about Paul Biga.'

'Yes, I remember,' Eva said. 'But was that really five years ago?'

'It was 1998. October. Just after the federal election.'

'Well, goodness, years!' Eva said.

'I was writing a book. Did you ever receive a copy? I gave the publisher your address.'

'You know, I think we did.' Eva gestured at the bookshelf.

Kate Hawkins walked towards it, and there, as if by magic, was the book. Kate pulled it off the shelf and handed it to Eva: a black jacket, red letters, and that lurid title. *Hunter on the Highway: The True Story of a Monster Among Us*. The cover was a close-up of Paul's adult face, most of it in shadow, except for the bland blue of his eyes.

Kate Hawkins said, 'It's all right if you never read it. I wouldn't blame you.' She seemed uncertain, standing there in stripes of light—the blinds. 'And now I'm working on an article—five years later, looking back, and the house coming down. How have people coped? How has the town changed? Or not? Where are we now? That type of thing. Because it was all so raw back then.'

Eva remembered, now, how much this woman talked at first—how tentative it made her seem, how apologetic, until, in putting her at ease, you found that you had talked too much yourself. Eva recognised this trick because she'd used it many times—not so much on her students as on their parents.

'How about some tea?' Eva said, moving towards the kitchen so that Kate Hawkins couldn't ask or make some gesture that would mean 'can you manage?' or 'let me do that for you'. Eva was handy in the kitchen; she could make a pot of tea and set some biscuits on a plate. Gerald put everything she needed in the lower cupboards.

'What have you been up to since I saw you last?' Eva asked, deliberately chatty among the mugs and teabags.

'Oh, this and that,' Kate Hawkins said. 'A lot of articles, another book.'

'More murders?' Still in her brisk, deliberately oblivious voice.

'Yes, a matricide,' Kate said, quite casual, and then, 'It's shocking, really, that murder pays my bills.'

'I wouldn't say "shocking". Could you carry the tray, dear?'

Kate Hawkins, with the tray, followed Eva back into the lounge room. She set the tray on the coffee table and perched on the edge of the couch, exactly as she had five years ago. 'What I wanted to do first of all,' she said, 'was apologise for coming so soon after Paul's arrest.'

'You did come rather swiftly,' Eva said.

'It had to be the first book out—payment was double if I was first.'

'And was it quite a lot?'

'It was,' Kate said. She didn't seem ashamed now. 'Down payment on a house.'

'Good,' Eva said. And it *was* good—to turn a murderer into a house. What a clever thing. She picked up Kate's book, with Paul's face on it.

Kate blew at the steam above her tea. 'Journalists get so used to barging in. To be honest, I saw you as an opportunity—his neighbour, school principal, employer. Your garden's looking lovely, by the way.'

'That's all Gerald, now that he's retired,' Eva said. 'No need to pay anyone to do it for us.'

'I wanted to say—I wanted to apologise, but also to say that, actually, you made an enormous impression when we spoke, Mrs Forsythe.'

'You must call me Eva. You did before.'

'Thank you. Perhaps you won't remember, but I asked if you had children and you said no. A few minutes later, you wanted to change your answer. Do you remember?'

Eva shook her head. What had she said to anybody, years ago?

'You said, "I was a teacher and a principal. That's how I had my children."'

'Oh, yes,' Eva said. She'd made this statement a number of times, to different people. Maybe it had seemed clever at first, or sincere, or simply dutiful—it didn't surprise her to hear that she'd said it to this journalist.

'I wanted you to know how much that moved me,' Kate Hawkins said. 'I think of it often. My daughter is in second grade.'

Eva was reminded, then, that Kate had asked a lot of questions about Paul's mother. That was why she'd wanted to know if Eva had children: it was a way into asking about Lucinda Biga. And Eva had thought, at the time, how unfair it was that mothers are so often blamed for their children's sins.

A fearsome noise began outside.

'Goodness, what a racket,' Eva said. She noticed that she was rubbing her thumb against Paul's shiny face on the book jacket.

Kate glanced at the window. 'You're not interested in watching?' she asked.

Eva took a sip of her tea. 'I'm not the one writing an article,' she said. 'Shouldn't *you* be watching?'

Kate Hawkins laughed. 'I have someone outside recording it. I'd much rather talk to you. What does it mean to you that the Biga house is finally being demolished?'

'Are we on to the official interview now?'

Kate laughed again. 'May I record our conversation?' She produced a Dictaphone from her bag.

Gerald would disapprove of this, just as he'd disapproved

of *Hunter on the Highway* and of all the people who had come to gawk, even years after Paul's arrest, at the Biga house; who'd taken photos and plant cuttings, who'd knocked on doors, who'd left tributes to the people he'd killed, and who'd parked badly in the street. Gerald would have had the Biga house demolished just to get some peace; he'd threatened, once, to set it on fire, and got annoyed when she started crying as if he'd meant it. Gerald had called her sentimental, but Eva didn't think she was. Maybe she would feel differently if Paul had brought his victims to the house; maybe she wouldn't. There was something in that house, quite aside from Paul, that should persist.

'Yes,' Eva said. 'You can record. What was the question?'

'How do you feel about the Biga house being demolished?'

Eva placed *Hunter on the Highway* facedown on the coffee table next to her mug of tea. There was a photo of Kate on the back cover, looking approachably pretty in a pastel shirt.

'Well, first of all,' Eva said, 'it isn't the Biga house. It's the Lainey house.'

'Lainey?'

'The Lainey family. L-a-i-n-e-y. Mr Lainey built it in the early twenties, a year or so before my father built this place. They've rented it out for decades—since, let me think, 1946. Yes, I was sixteen when they left. The Bigas came in the late seventies. They were the Lainey's longest tenants—more than twenty years.'

'They moved to Barrow in 1976,' Kate said. 'And Biga's father moved out in early 1999, a few months after the arrest.'

Eva supposed this must be right. 'You know,' she said, 'this isn't a tenant sort of town. It's a town where people die and then their children live in their houses. So people were funny about that house, about everyone who lived there, though by the end most people forgot that the Bigas didn't own. They took good care of it, the Lainey house.'

Maybe no one else in town still referred to it as the Lainey house; Gerald certainly didn't. But when Jan Biga and his wife, Lucinda, and their teenage son, Paul, had moved in, it was to the Lainey house. 'I hear there's a Pole moved in to Lainey's,' Gerald said, and Eva thought at first he meant a pole, a post. He meant, of course, a Polish man. How literal she was about the Lainey house. It was as if she couldn't absorb the changes that had taken place there: the Laineys leaving, Josie Lainey waving goodbye from the back window of their car; the tenants moving in and out; the Japanese maple turning its intricate red; the Bigas arriving, and teenage Paul crossing the road to work in the Forsythes' garden for seven dollars an hour. Last time Kate Hawkins had come, just after Paul's arrest, she'd asked about those gardening days. Had Eva ever noticed anything unusual about him—anything that might have given an indication of the monster he turned out to be? 'Oh no,' Eva had said, 'a quiet boy, and so polite you'd never dream'—that sort of thing. She remembered later that when Paul had come to do the garden the first time, she'd noticed the length of his fingernails. He used to pinch caterpillars out of the gardenias with those long nails. Was that a sign of anything? But Paul was only ever a sign of himself.

'It's hard to think of it as a family home,' Kate said.

'Not for me,' Eva said.

Mrs Lainey at the gate calling, 'Josie! Josie!', her hands caught up in her apron; ham on the Lainey table; hands swatting at flies all through the saying of grace—the laziness of lunchtime flies, the slowness of hands during grace, and Josie's foot pressing Eva's under the table; the organ in the front room with its odd, resisting pedals, Mr Lainey playing it with a bottle of beer beside him on the stool and Josie turning the pages of the music; Eva holding the baby while Mrs Lainey hung the washing, white drool staining Eva's arm and her never minding, Josie sulking at how much Eva loved the baby; Josie asking, 'Would you save Harry Cox if his house was on fire? Would you save Norman Monk?', running through all the boys in their class: 'Would you save John McInnes, Gerald Forsythe? Would you save Michael Byrne?'; Josie walking the brick fence wearing a yellow dress and red lipstick; Josie, Josie, Josie.

Kate waited for a particularly loud burst of noise to pass. Then she said, 'And how do the Laineys feel about having had Paul Biga as a tenant? Do you know?'

Josie Lainey throwing a cricket ball at her brother, missing, laughing, dodging when he threw it back.

'No idea,' Eva said. 'We lost touch. I can't imagine they like it. Of course, Mr and Mrs Lainey were gone well before—well, everything.'

'When did they pass?'

Eva disliked the euphemistic use of 'pass', especially from a woman who had earned a lot of money describing death in vivid detail. She said, 'They died in the early eighties, I believe.'

Mrs Lainey and Josie sitting on the stuffy sofa in the front room—the formal room, which no one ever used. They were holding hands, their faces pale. Mr Lainey guiding Eva into the hallway, saying, 'All right, Evelyn, you'd better go on home now,' and closing the door to the front room.

Eva left in the hallway, sobbing without making any sound.

Kate Hawkins asked, 'How many children in the Lainey family?'

'Three.'

'Their names?'

Josephine, Michael, Margaret.

'Oh,' Eva said, 'I wouldn't be comfortable. They won't want their names associated.'

'I understand,' Kate said, and wrote a few words in her notebook.

I suppose, Eva thought, she'll simply look it up or ask someone else. If she were my student, I'd want her to be canny and resourceful; I'd insist that she go on until she'd found her answers.

Kate took a sip of her tea. 'So, they built the house in the early twenties, and they left in—did you say 1946? Just after the war. They'd lived there for at least twenty years. Why did they move?'

There had never been a face, or lips, or arms more beautiful to Eva than Josie Lainey's. Not even Gerald, whom she had loved and desired for years, had ever lain like Josie in a bed, as if there were no clear distinction between her body and the warmth, the softness, the sweetness of the sheets.

'Mr Lainey got a job in Sydney.'

'What kind of work did he do?'

The front door opened and the noise of the demolition

increased, then was muffled again. Gerald arrived in the lounge room, rubbing his hands.

'Just getting my camera,' he said. 'Might take a photo or two.'

'Is it already down?' Eva asked.

'Front rooms are down,' Gerald said, hurrying through to his study. 'Bedrooms to go. They certainly know how to get the job done, once they've put their minds to it.'

Josie Lainey's bedroom, done all in pink (Josie eventually too old for this, rolling her eyes, not a *baby* anymore), had become Paul's. And Eva wondered, sometimes, if there had been some residue left in that room, some trace of Eva and Josie. It wasn't the sort of thing she ordinarily considered. But it would be one way to explain, wouldn't it, the letter Paul had sent?

'Are you tired, Eva?' Kate asked. Her face was creased with concern; Eva didn't trust it.

'Not at all,' Eva said. But she *was* tired. 'What was your last question?'

'What kind of job did Mr Lainey move to Sydney for?'

Gerald erupted from his study carrying his chunky camera. 'He didn't move for a job, did he?' he said. 'Wasn't there some family drama? That's what I heard. They certainly left pretty quick smart.'

'A drama?' Kate asked, sitting up straighter on the edge of the couch.

'It was definitely a job,' Eva said. 'He worked in agricultural machinery. He'd been a salesman, and he was promoted to a larger district.'

Gerald shrugged. 'Evie would know,' he said, then launched

into the hallway and out the front door. The sound of the de-molition rose with the opened door, then receded again.

'You were close to the Laineys?' Kate asked.

Eva said, 'The older daughter was in my class at school.'

'The same school you went on to become principal of?'

'The high school, yes, but we started kindergarten together.'

'The same school Paul Biga attended,' Kate said.

'The high school, yes,' Eva said. 'Eventually.'

'Paul was a student at your school for years ten, eleven, and twelve,' Kate said, and Eva nodded. 'Did you often hire your students to work for you?'

Eva looked at the photo of Kate on the back of *Hunter on the Highway*. Her chin was resting on her left hand, and she wore a wedding ring. She wasn't wearing one now. Eva had only skimmed the book, looking for any mention of her name or Gerald's. She'd seen snatches here and there—Paul's 'prowl-ing taxi' and 'the sinister underbelly of Barrow's storybook appeal' and 'the mute silence of all his victims, known and unknown'—before finally finding herself. She occupied two sentences, in which the implication was that she, in her provin-cial naivety, had been hoodwinked by Paul's calculated charm. To live opposite a monster without recognising his evil might, Eva supposed, require a special variety of delusion. Others in town had been quick to say that there was always something off about him.

'My students?' Eva said. 'No. We hired Paul as a neighbour more than as a student. A neighbourhood boy.'

'He was seventeen when he started,' Kate said, as if riffling through mental files. 'And he came every day?'

'I thought we were talking about the Lainey house,' Eva said. She wanted Gerald to come back now, to fill the door-frame, to recognise her distress and drive the woman away with his forceful conviviality.

'We are,' Kate said. 'Did Paul work in his parents' garden, too?'

'He spent a lot of time out at the aviary,' Eva said. 'The Laineys built the aviary.'

Josie with a cockatoo on her head, the cockatoo screaming, 'Give us a kiss! Give us a kiss!'

'The Laineys kept birds?'

'Yes. A sulphur-crested cockatoo.'

'Just the one? Did they take it with them when they moved to Sydney?'

'No,' Eva said. 'They set it free. It lived in the garden for months, then eventually it was gone.'

'And did any of the other tenants keep birds in the aviary?'

'No,' Eva said. 'Only Paul.'

Paul bringing her a glossy offering of magpie feathers; Eva saying, 'Oh, my mother would have used these to trim a hat,' and then not knowing what to do with them, so they lived in a mug beside the telephone for more than a year. Black-and-white pennants.

'It was still in good shape, then?' Kate asked. 'If the Bigas came in seventy-six, the aviary hadn't been used for nearly thirty years.'

'Paul repaired it,' Eva said. Gerald had helped him. Gerald had always been handy. He'd wanted children.

'So, gardening at your house but birds at home,' Kate said. 'Did he come every day?'

'We couldn't have afforded for him to come every day.'

'Your neighbours,' Kate said, 'on this side'—she pointed in the direction of the Jarrett house, Terry Jarrett of the sloppy garbage bins—'remember him coming nearly every day.'

Well, yes, there had been those few weeks one summer when he came most days, without asking for extra payment. You would look out a window and see him deadheading the daisies, or you'd hear a sound and it would be Paul sweeping the front path. If you opened the door and offered him a cup of tea, he always said no. There was only one task he refused, and that was killing stink bugs. It was Eva who had picked the stink bugs off the kumquats by hand and dropped them in a jar of methylated spirits. Gerald had wanted to spray, but she didn't want chemicals on the fruit trees, and Paul was too disgusted to touch them, even with gloves on (Paul, who would allow spiders to crawl on his bare palms and throw snails hard against the fence to crack their shells and keep them out of her irises). But Eva had been fascinated, had noted the frantic waving of the stink bugs' striped antennae, had made herself dizzy with the fumes of metho and stink that rose from the jar, had watched as valiant bugs pulled themselves to apparent safety on rafts made of other bugs until she tilted the jar, creating terrible tsunamis. The jar, full of clinging death, gave her considerable satisfaction. The kumquat tree, no longer under attack, put forth fruit and blossom and was visited by bees; the marmalade Gerald made from it (an excellent maker of jams, Gerald) was delicious spread on toast or on thick slices of cheddar cheese. She had dumped the bodies of the bugs in one corner of the garden and, after the alcohol evaporated, the ants had made feasts of the softer flesh.

'He came three hours a week,' Eva said. 'Usually on Saturday mornings. That's what we paid him for. But haven't I already told you everything I can about Paul? I didn't know him well, especially once he finished school. The Bigas moved in their own circle.'

By which Eva meant they had kept to themselves. Jan Biga was invariably polite, but there had been a chill to it, a sort of distrustful reserve, as if his ramrod posture and faultless manners advertised how little he wanted you to know his business. He never took to Gerald; but then, Gerald never made much effort with him.

'Their own circle,' Kate said. 'Of course. But living across the road . . .' She gestured towards the window.

Eva imagined a yellow machine clambering over the rubble that used to be the front room of the Lainey house. The windows in that room had been set with squares of stained glass; she and Josie used to find it funny, in the afternoons, to lie on the floor so that the squares of blue and red light fell on their chests, exactly where their breasts would one day be. The tender pucker of Josie's breasts. Looking back on that last year with Josie—1945 and into 1946—Eva marvelled at how chaste they'd been, how pure. Even their kisses, full of heat, had been wholesome. The stained-glass windows had been removed before the demolition. By whom? Eva wondered.

What Kate meant, of course, was that you learn things about people when you live so close to them, even if you don't spend time together. That you notice things without meaning to—surely you notice things. Nobody wanted to believe Eva when she said that Paul Biga had seemed like a perfectly ordinary boy. And he had, although one of the things Eva had learned as a teacher and a principal was that there are no perfectly ordinary adolescents, that each of them is strange, and bewildered, and in mourning, because they're all in exile from their childhoods, just as they always longed to be. There had been only one thing that marked Paul Biga as unusual, and Eva had never told it to anyone—not even Gerald. At the end of that summer when he'd come to the garden every day, Paul had written Eva a letter on those thin sheets of paper—so thin that if your hands were even a little damp the paper became translucent or tore, the paper that people used when they were sending letters overseas and wanted to keep the weight down. The things he said he'd planned for the two of them: a farm, and horses, an aviary, of course, and because he knew she loved the maple tree in his front garden, he would dig it up to bring with them, he would plant it outside their bedroom window and every night he would, and she would, and then he would, and would, and would—

How detailed he was—her pussy, her arse, her tits—how well he spelled when he spelled her body out, and how lonely that seemed, to spell 'cunnilingus' right and 'specific' wrong. In what film, what TV show, had he seen the farm with the gentle, sexual, older wife, or learned about love letters, so that he could approximate one now, for her? And what was the sign he'd wanted her to give him? A candle in the window, or something just as ludicrous—as if Gerald wouldn't have noticed a candle!

As if a candle in the window wouldn't set the curtains on fire and burn down the house; as if people walking along the street wouldn't see a candle in the Forsythe window with the lights all off and think, I'd better knock on the door. They've gone to bed with a candle burning. And the terror, then, lying in bed, that he would come anyway, would be a candle himself waiting at the door, coming into the house, standing over her in the bedroom. Would you save Eva Forsythe if her house was on fire?

She could have told someone, told Gerald or spoken to Paul or to his father, but she hadn't. Which had probably been irresponsible of her, but Paul had just graduated from school, his mother was very ill with the cancer that went on to kill her, and the letter was so passionate, so precise, that she was afraid of anyone reading it and assuming she'd encouraged him. She convinced Gerald that they no longer needed Paul in the garden; she pretended not to see Paul if she passed him in the supermarket, though she still waved at Jan Biga if they were both out on the street. Glancing into their windows, she saw the blue TV, the yellow wallpaper, the paintings crooked on the wall after Lucinda died. The maple tree dressed and undressed, blazing up and down again, while Paul—quiet behind the curtains—grew older, stronger, better-looking, began spending time with girls his own age, bought his truck, got his taxi licence, and acted civil behind his father's lawnmower, as if there had never been a letter, as if she had imagined it. Then he moved away to marry, and she was pleased for him, and pleased to have him gone. By the time he moved back—the marriage over, presumably—he was a complete stranger. She'd never hired his taxi; but then, she'd never needed to.

As for the letter, she had torn it immediately into hundreds of pieces, placed those pieces in an envelope, taped the envelope shut, and concealed it in a box of cereal, which went into the bin and was collected early the following Tuesday morning. She'd lain in bed listening to the garbage truck trundle up and down the street, Gerald snoring, Terry carrying out his bin in a last-minute frenzy, and all the birds in Paul's aviary greeting the pretty dawn.

Kate, on the couch, her hand still pointing at the window, waited with a look of expectation on her face, as if she had offered an extra serving of cake and was hoping Eva would be greedy enough to accept it. Imagine her glee if Eva were to say, 'There *was* one strange thing. Paul wrote me a letter.' Imagine Kate looking at her second-grade daughter and remembering Eva saying, 'I had my children,' and thinking, then, of the letter.

'I know it's dull of me,' Eva said. 'But really, they were a very quiet family.'

Outside, the people watching the demolition began to applaud—not the way they might at the end of a football match but as they did when one of the Sydney orchestras visited on a regional tour and the townspeople felt obliged to attend the concert. There was liberation in the applause, joy that the thing was finally over, but also deflation—as if the spectators had expected rapture and, once again, been disappointed.

'That must be the last wall down,' Kate said.

It felt to Eva as if the whole life of the Lainey house would now be on display to the world; as if everyone who had ever lived in it would be visible there, all at once, going about their intimate business, completely unaware that the walls were

missing. A sort of doll's house. And in the room that everyone knew had been Paul's, they would see him—what? Making
his plans? Dreaming his violent dreams? And they would see
Josie and Eva in Josie's bed, loving each other, very gentle, very
pure; they would see Mrs Lainey opening the bedroom door
(if there were still doors in the Lainey house) and crying out,
the two girls sitting up; and, oh, would they watch as the girls
pulled on their summer dresses, as Mrs Lainey took Josie's hand
and led her into the front room, as Mr Lainey said, 'All right,
Evelyn, you'd better go on home now'?

'You really don't want to see?' Kate asked.

'Oh no,' Eva said.

'Are you sure?' Kate stood and went to the window.

Eva looked again at the photo on the back of the book.
Kate's hand was positioned under her chin in a way that made
it look as if her head had been impaled on a fleshy spike. That
was unkind; then again, Kate had written page after page describing each murder, and the positions of all the bodies when
they were found. Eva hadn't read any of those pages, but she
knew, from the talk around town, that they were there.

'Reduced to rubble,' Kate said. 'How does it feel to know it's
down?'

Eva regarded the actual Kate, who had propped one knee on
the arm of the couch in order to get closer to the window. Her
hair was pulled back into a girlish ponytail and, from behind,
her creased navy jacket looked like a school blazer. 'Would you
be pleased? If you were me?' Eva asked, in the voice she had
refined over years of teaching: affectionately stern, lightly curi-
ous, and prepared at all times for disappointment.

'God, yes,' Kate said. Then she turned to look at Eva and gave a short, graceless laugh. 'Of course I would.'

Now a new house would be built: larger, uglier, and filled with the inexplicable lives of other people.

'You won't have to look at it every day,' Kate said.

Josie lying in the heat under the maple tree, balancing an apple on her forehead, saying, 'Never getting married, never never.' Every freckle like a small, warm sun.

'Anyone would be relieved,' Kate said. She laughed a second time and said, 'But I can't quote myself. Let me ask you again, how do *you* feel about the Biga house coming down?'

'The Lainey house,' Eva said.

'The Lainey house.'

'I feel,' Eva said, 'completely indifferent.'

The front door opened and closed. Gerald and Terry came staggering in, each carrying a milk crate full of bricks that were the russet colour of the Lainey house.

'I'm going to build you an outdoor bread oven,' Gerald said.

Kate turned off her Dictaphone.

Terry grinned above his crate, as if he could already feel the oven's heat. Eva looked at him and thought she wouldn't save him, Terry Jarrett—not even if his house were on fire.

HOSTESS

(1986)

met Jill in 1982. We were working the Sydney to LA route, and she looked exactly the way an air hostess was supposed to: like Marilyn Monroe on stilts, playing the part of a firm, friendly nurse with a naughty inner life. None of the passengers would have guessed she spent every flight half-fucked on champagne and orange juice, which she would down in the galley from take-off to landing. By the time I rented a room from her—1986, in a remote beach town on the north coast of Western Australia—she had retired. Her hair was short and brown, she never wore make-up or shaved her armpits, and she looked better than ever. But she was nearing forty, and our airline encouraged its hostesses to make a graceful exit by the age of thirty-five.

My own retirement made less sense: I was only twenty-six, and anyway, being a man, I could have held on until at least fifty. But I had believed all those handsy husbands in business class who, assuming I was gay, liked to tell me I was good-looking enough to be on TV. So, I left—not long after Jill did—to be on TV. When that didn't pan out and I wanted to lick my wounds for a while, the only idea I had was to head north-west: to follow Jill to her feral little township, which was, by the way, chock-full of retired flight attendants.

Well, where else were we hosties going to go when we got too old, too tired, when our voices gave out from all those smoky flights? When we'd spent years in the air, crossing the Pacific, crossing the Nullarbor, half-imagining that, because time seems to slow during plane travel, the years weren't passing below us, killing our parents, burying our friends in marriages and the wrecks of marriages, driving up the price of city real estate? So that when we retired, the single place we could afford to live was a tropical town so remote you could justify flying there only if you had an ex-employee's airline discount. Mid-sized cruise ships stopped in all the time: for the sunsets, the seafood platters, the Japanese cemetery, the quaint pearling boats. But by car, the town was twenty-two hours from the nearest city.

No one stayed long. You bought a cheap house or you rented a room off someone you knew; then you either drank yourself to death, or you figured yourself out and moved on to your second, grounded life, the one you'd been trying to dodge by taking to the skies in the first place. Before retirement, Jill had been good at saving her airline salary and living off the allowance they gave us for stopovers; she'd also run a lucrative side business buying cigarettes in Singapore and selling them in London. She'd saved enough to buy a house in a place like this. I spent nearly everything on having a good time, so, when I reached town in late November of '86, I rented her spare bedroom.

Jill met me at the airport. She was wearing white shorts and a pale pink blouse, her face was bare and her hair was spiky, and the first thing she said was 'Recognise me without my glad rags?'

I did, of course; whatever she wore, she was unmistakable. I want to explain why, and won't be able to, but here goes: she looked like luck. Jill had this open, mobile face, and a megawatt smile, and there was an intense vitality to her, a kind of giving-off of energy, like life was electric and she was at the very middle of it, even up there in that town on the shitty rim of nowhere. It was all irresistible. And what made it so irresistible was that while she hummed in the charged centre of life she also seemed relaxed, unbothered, like a goddess operating on a different timescale from everyone around her. She walked with a kind of serene shimmy. She never moved or spoke or smiled quickly; she let it all unfold with a slight reserve that felt luxurious because it seemed so unnecessary. I couldn't have said any of this back then, when I walked into that airport—which was basically a shed in the middle of a paddock—and saw Jill waiting for me. I just thought she was the most desirable thing I'd ever seen. I wanted to sleep with her, obviously. Who wouldn't? But I also felt, walking towards her, that my life would be better, easier, for her proximity; that she'd always be able to tell me what to do, and she'd always be right. She had a dishevelled dog with her, sitting obediently at her feet—a standard poodle the colour of toast.

We drove to her place in an old Jeep Cherokee: Jill and I in the front, the dog in the back with my one measly suitcase. As we pulled into the driveway of the house—long, squat, with a sloping tin roof, huddling beneath a tropical mass of messy trees—she said, 'I'm glad you're here.'

I wanted to believe that this was something she'd say only to me, not just to any colleague with whom she'd been reasonably friendly. I had recently made the discovery that I was interchangeable with almost any other good-looking young man, so I wanted Jill to be glad that I, specifically, was there. Really, she was glad because her sister was getting married in early February. Jill would be flying to Sydney for the wedding, she'd be away for about a week, and she needed a house-sitter. She'd teach me how to feed the chickens and water the garden, and, most important, how to take care of the dog, which had been sniffing without conviction at the back of my neck; now he looked across at Jill with a doubtful tilt of the head. Even then, on my first day with her, I sensed that there was something off about the sister's wedding: that Jill didn't approve, or didn't want to go. Her speech was usually ample and unhurried, but her voice had been pinched when she said 'my sister's wedding'.

For the next couple of months, we spent our days sitting under the fruit trees in the backyard, playing dominoes and drinking beer. I'd wake every morning vaguely surprised that a tidal wave hadn't come roaring in over the mudflats to bury the whole town overnight: the grid of red roads, the palm trees, the Surf Life Saving Club, both churches, Komodo's Bar and Bistro, all the low sprawling houses with their deep verandahs and their roofs full of possums and pythons. I'd head outside, where Jill would already be in her spot: a hammock under the custard apple tree. My spot was a wobbly cane chair by the avocado. The house did have a covered patio—cavernous, with a high, winged roof that made you think of an airport—but we never sat beneath it: the roof was tin and stinking hot as soon as the sun came up. Nothing's cooler than tree shade, anyway.

Jill drank strong black tea, I drank instant coffee. Jill smoked Bensons, I smoked weed. We'd sit watching the black clouds pile up in the north-east until they crowded overhead; then we went inside while they drenched the town. After the rain, which never lasted long, we'd return to the steaming garden. The beer came out, the dominoes, and we sat in plastic chairs at a flaking picnic table: Jill braless in a dress like a long singlet and me in the microscopic shorts we all wore back then, ball-squeakingly tight. When her chickens got too noisy, Jill reprimanded them by name: Lotto, Pigeon, America's Cup, Lady Di, and Ginger Meggs. Her poodle would lie stretched beside her chair with his chin to the ground, one paw on either side of his long nose, sighing.

We ate eggs from Jill's chooks and fruit from Jill's trees, and tin after tin of smoked oysters. We didn't talk about ourselves much; instead, we invented an intricate, ongoing story about the property over the road, which we decided housed a cult because of its high fence and the weird things they'd put out for rubbish pick-up. Often, we just played dominoes in silence. Every now and then you'd hear the ripe fall of a fig onto the patio roof. The shuffling of the radio in the background: Madonna, Pseudo Echo, ads for the new shopping plaza, reports of oil prices and nuclear tests in the Pacific. The click of the domino tiles and the periodically tizzy chickens and getting up for more beer and pissing lazily against the side fence and those long, scorching afternoons in that town on the edge of the gleaming sea.

Which you couldn't swim in, by the way—the sea. Not in summer. It was crawling with deadly jellyfish, and sometimes you saw crocodiles, big prehistoric salties, hauling themselves up onto the beach. The mozzies descended towards sunset, which was how we knew it was time to go inside, to shower, to dress, and to climb into Jill's old Jeep. When she'd coaxed its wheezy engine to a start, she'd say, 'Hear me roar.' Then she'd drive us to Komodo's, where we both worked—she as a waitress, me at the bar.

The poodle came with us. If she left him alone in the house, he would literally batter his way through the fibro walls to get outside. If she left him in the yard, he would burrow or climb or magic his way out and roam the streets, yapping and howling, searching for Jill. I understood completely. Like I said, Jill was a goddess. Everyone in town assumed we were sleeping together—and we were, sometimes. The sex was friendly. Don't get me wrong: if she'd loved me, I would have considered myself lucky to have been swept, even if by shipwreck, onto the shores of that particular life. But I was ten years younger than she was, and aware of how little a woman like Jill needed from a man like me. I knew that anyone could have rented that room, and then he would have been the one to feel her hand tug at his shoulder in the heavy afternoon, to follow her into her dark bedroom, to taste the smoky mango of her mouth. Her filthy, lovesick poodle would come too, and settle, still sighing, into the armchair beside her bed. She'd stolen him from a boyfriend in Rome, where apparently dogs are trained with German commands, and as I moved above her in the bed and she gave me firm, friendly instructions—faster, slower, stop, more, here—

I couldn't help but translate: *schnell*, *ja*, *stopp*, *hier*, *braver Hund*. To this day, the only German I know.

At Komodo's, the dog stayed in the staffroom, where Jill would go every now and then to hand-feed him a scrap of ham or an oily crouton from an abandoned plate. Then she'd take a swig of vodka from a flask she kept in her purse, or accept the offer of something pharmaceutical from one of the burly Scandinavian chefs. When she re-emerged on the bistro floor, gliding between the tables with a steady swivel as if down a narrow aisle, I swear the customers—tourists, cruise ship crews, pearl corporates—would sit noticeably straighter in their chairs.

But every one of the waitresses at Komodo's was stunning—of course they were; they were all retired hosties. They all carried prawn cocktails like Communion cups. They drank and got high and went on dates with the customers. At some point during most of my shifts, a guy would stand up from a table where he sat with his family or his colleagues, approach the bar, and lean against it with his palms pressed to its smoothed edge, like he was about to perform a spontaneous press-up. He'd order a martini and, when I served it to him, pass me his business card and ask me to get it to his waitress. Then he'd down his drink and head back to the table. If he left the olive in the glass, I'd fish it out, rinse it off, and set it aside in a small bowl.

As Jill and I drove home from work—usually at around one or two in the morning, and me driving the Jeep, because I never drank on the clock—she fed those olives to the poodle, passing them to him in the back seat, and that's when she would get more confidential and talk about her sister, the one who was getting married in February. Just as I'd suspected, she was against the marriage. The sister was twenty years younger than Jill—only sixteen, though not a half-sister, as you'd expect with that kind of age difference. Her name was Cheryl, and she was about to marry some taxi driver she'd met in a pub. Jill had herself been married at a young age—briefly, disastrously—to an older man. She rarely talked about her ex-husband, whom she described vaguely as being 'in import-export', but she did tell me more than once that he'd proposed at Brisbane Airport. He was waiting at arrivals to meet her at the end of her shift, and he asked her right there, in front of all the other hosties. Went down on one well-dressed knee and said, 'Baby, will you marry me?' He didn't even have a ring. When Jill said yes, he lifted her into a Hollywood twirl. Romantic, yes? But she'd ended up helpless in his arms, flashing her backside at the applauding crowd.

'If he'd just thought for two seconds,' Jill would say. 'If he'd just thought to lift me above the hips, so my skirt wouldn't ride up.'

But even at this she would shake her head and smile slowly, as if it wasn't worth the bother of complaining about.

It certainly bothered Jill that her sister was so young, and that the fiancé was nearly ten years older; that Jill had never met him; that he kept pet birds; that one of his favourite jokes was, apparently, to fake epileptic fits in public places; and that Cheryl now spent all her time with his friends and not her own. She'd even given up table tennis, despite her trophies.

These conversations happened almost every night, and in

my memory tend to blend together. There was a specific one, though, which took place on a night in late January of 1987, a few days before Jill was due to leave for the wedding. She was at the height of her objection to the marriage, and I'd never heard her speak with such vehemence.

'He's twenty-five. He's an adult. What does an adult man want with a teenage girl?' She lifted her arm as she leaned into the back seat, offering an olive to her poodle, offering me the musky privacy of her armpit. 'Control. That's all he can possibly want from her. Total control.'

I agreed, and said so. I also suggested that Cheryl should be allowed to make up her own mind—to 'learn from her own mistakes', or something like that.

'Your problem,' Jill said, with an uncharacteristic bitterness in her voice, a quality that felt like it devoured energy rather than giving it out, 'your problem is you think all mistakes are created equal. But some mistakes don't build character—they destroy it. If someone had locked me up so I couldn't make those kinds of mistakes, I'd be eternally grateful.'

'You wouldn't,' I argued. 'You'd be pissed off. You wouldn't know to be eternally grateful, because you'd never have made the mistakes.'

Jill said, 'I'll lock her up anyway.' It was the only time I ever heard Jill's voice approach what I'd call shrill. The poodle whined and she leaned towards him with one more olive.

'That's what parents are for,' I said. 'But you're her sister. Your job is to be a shoulder to cry on when things go wrong.'

Jill went to speak, then leaned her head back against her

seat. A few moments passed in silence. Then she said, in a low, hesitant voice, 'Mum and Dad were too strict with her. Worried she'd turn out like me.'

We'd reached the house and pulled into the driveway, but I kept the car running for a moment with the headlights on. A flying fox froze, bright-eyed, on the patio roof, caught in the act of stealing figs.

'Worried she'd turn out like you?' I said. 'What, perfect?'

Jill laughed. Her slow, lucky smile returned. She kissed me on the cheek in the way that meant I was dismissed for the night, and said, 'Thanks, honey.' She called everyone 'honey': everyone on a crew, everyone at Komodo's, every passenger or diner no matter their age or gender or general disposition. Also her dog, which now followed her out to her hammock. Being called 'honey' meant nothing, but I was greedy for it anyway. I took it to bed with me and slept beside it all night.

When I went to use the toilet early the next morning, I saw that Jill was outside in her hammock, still in her black work clothes, smoking her Bensons. The sun was just rising, and a slight breeze carried the sour smell of the mangroves. I would have liked to go to her, to stand beside her hammock and ask her how I could help, but I was afraid she'd look at me as if I were a perfect stranger who had nothing to do with her and never would. I went back to bed.

Jill woke me a few hours later to say she was going to ring her sister and beg her to call off the wedding. If she'd said it in the clipped, angry tones of last night's conversation, I might have suggested she reconsider, but she'd washed and changed since then, she wasn't the woman I'd seen out at the hammock, and she seemed so sure of herself, in her usual unhurried way, that I didn't argue. She said she couldn't call with me in the house, so she shooed me outside to walk the dog.

It was muggy as hell. The morning rains had passed; two dripping, discarded half-mannequins stood on the verge outside the cult house. Shirtless and shoeless, I followed the dog down the hot streets, letting him lead me, letting him eat or piss on anything he encountered, and whenever we reached a corner he rolled his eyes towards me as if, having been given the freedom to do exactly as he liked, he was willing to consult me on important decisions, such as turning left or right. By the time the dog and I returned to the house, Jill was back out in the hammock, smoking, and she sat up and looked at me with an immaculate, guarded readiness, as though I had taxed her patience innumerable times that day, was about to do so again, and had already been forgiven for it. The pivoting look, in fact, of flight attendants when you disturb them while they relax in the galley between services. The dog, trembling with delight, leaped into her lap.

She'd spoken to her sister, and then to her parents, and then again to her sister. She didn't tell me much, only that everyone was angry at her: Cheryl had cried and eventually refused to talk; her mother had accused her of 'butting in where she had no business'; her father had suggested she not come to the wedding, which only made her more determined to go. He'd described the taxi driver as a 'quiet, reliable sort of bloke', and I wondered aloud what was quiet and reliable about faking a fit on the floor of a Wollongong pub.

Jill lay back in her hammock. 'I said to Dad, better if he was the life of the party. It's the quiet ones you have to keep your eye on.'

'What did your dad think of that?' I asked, wondering if I might ever have been considered a quiet one.

Jill smiled. She tapped her cigarette and a fine sprinkling of ash settled on the dog's coat. 'He said I was jealous because I'll never have a normal family of my own.'

Then she requested a piña colada, the first of many, and we spent a subdued afternoon playing dominoes and hardly speaking, in a way that felt more intimate than sex. Jill called in sick to work that night, and when I left for Komodo's she was back beneath the custard apple tree, smoking and swatting mosquitoes. She had one flawless leg hanging out of the hammock; the poodle lay on the ground beside her, and she was scratching his belly with her big toe.

My shift was ordinary enough: there was a spectacular electric storm out at sea, which thrilled the customers, and a new waitress, ex-Ansett, who winked at me over a plate of barramundi, then floated away like a pearl lugger in full sail. Her name was something like Debbie or Tracey. At the end of the shift, she asked me back to her place for a drink, but I was worried about Jill and, like a bloody idiot, I took a raincheck. I probably assumed, at the time, that I had a whole life of those invitations ahead of me; that the Debbies and Traceys of the world would never stop offering me drinks.

When I got home, I found Jill in the hallway outside my bedroom door, her arms full of my dirty sheets.

'The wedding's off,' she announced. She was vibrating with something: joy, or fury, or both. 'Cheryl rang me in private.

She'll be here tomorrow night—I got her a ticket on the evening flight. I need you packed up and out of the room.'

The sudden lurching terror of eviction, of an empty, earth-bound life full of decisions and their consequences.

Then she said, 'You can sleep in with me.'

And now the relief that someone older, better, with their shit more together, had made a decision for me: immense grati-tude, the slightest contrarian hint of resistance, one more lazy step towards a lifetime of humdrum discontent.

I packed up my room while Jill vacuumed. I listened to her tell me that the fiancé had just this afternoon called Cheryl a stupid bitch for some trivial reason, like overcooking sausages or smiling at a stranger. I listened as Jill told me that her sister had never flown before, and also that, when she was a little girl, Cheryl had waved at every plane she saw, believing Jill to be on it. For each of Cheryl's birthdays and at Christmas, Jill had sent dolls in national dress, bought from airports around the world; there was a glass cabinet full of these dolls in her par-ents' house, some of them slim-hipped women in hula skirts or dirndls, others fat-cheeked toddlers with enormous eyes, wear-ing kilts or kimonos. Jill sent them with notes that said: *You mean the world to me.*

We stayed up until five or so, cleaning and making prepara-tions, Jill telling me more about Cheryl as a baby (the soft red pudge of her hands), as a kindergartener (the cutest lisp), as an eight-year-old (crying over a bike-broken arm because she thought it meant she'd never be an air hostess like her sister). I'd never heard Jill talk so much and so personally. At one point, she asked almost shyly if I thought she would make a good mother, and I realised that she had, in fact, spent very little time with Cheryl; that they'd never even lived in the same house.

Finally, we went to bed—to her bed, where Jill fell asleep immediately, her right arm flung across the top of my pillow as if indicating an exit. The dog, splayed at our feet, was dreaming in snorts and twitches. We all slept for most of the day.

Neither of us had work that night, so I drove Jill to the airport. The dog came with us, even though he was in disgrace: made anxious by the changes in the house, he'd pissed on the barbecue, which was *verboten*. Jill had put on make-up, and she wore a dress I'd never seen before, light green with a Chinese collar. She'd been drinking. She smoked in the Jeep, and she smoked in the airport. She wanted to go out onto the tarmac to meet the plane, but the staff wouldn't let her take the dog, so he and I stayed inside. He was quaking with misery, watching intently through the windows, his eyes fixed on the spot where Jill stood looking eastwards. She couldn't smoke out there, but I saw her lift an invisible cigarette to her lips multiple times as she waited for her first glimpse of the plane. At least once, she pressed her palms against her eyes, as if crying or trying not to. From where I stood, her dress looked white.

I can still see her standing there, which is something people say when time has passed, but I mean it. Just as, on summer nights up there in our gritty little pearl of a town, you'd watch an electrical storm and then, when you closed your eyes, your eyelids would be veined with lightning—when I close my eyes now I see the dark runway, the square of window light in which Jill stands, the shape of my own reflection in the glass, and, finally, the blinking of the plane as it emerges from a scattering of stars. I see Jill throw her arms into the air as if in greeting, then fold them on top of her head, each hand holding an elbow as she rises on her tiptoes. Beside me, the poodle whimpers with his nose against the window. And the plane, an old twenty-one-passenger DC-3, one pilot, one cabin attendant, descends upon our sleazy paradise.

The landing takes a year; the taxiing takes a century. Finally, the rear door opens like a clamshell, revealing stairs. After the usual fuss, a passenger appears: a bosomy matron carrying a basket. Then two men in business suits, one of whom is shaking out a reviving leg. A family in holiday wear, with cameras strung around their necks. A honeymooning couple, maybe, in a haze of self-congratulation. I don't remember them all, not really, so I'm making them up. I do remember scrutinising every new arrival, auditioning them for Cherylness, and at some point I realised I was counting: eight passengers, thirteen passengers, nineteen.

The twentieth passenger was a slight teenage girl in a turquoise dress, with matching bag, earrings, and court shoes. She looked like someone who'd never been on a plane before and had dressed up for the flight, maybe in the going-away outfit she'd bought for a wedding that had since been cancelled. She walked with uncertainty across the tarmac, looking back at the plane as if she was worried she'd left something on it. I saw Jill make a rapid forward movement. The girl passed her with a shy smile. She entered the terminal and was swept up by a grandmotherly type, who walked around her in a slow, approving circle, examining her clothes.

Finally, the pilot and hostess disembarked, each carrying an overnight bag. I knew their types exactly: he was handsome, ageing, sheepishly charming, married to an ex-hostie; she was a determined people-pleaser, quick-witted and on the verge of dangerously thin. There was no desire between them, but they flirted in a rote way as they walked across the tarmac, as if that were part of what they were being paid to do. They were both tired, probably dreading a night spent at the arse-end of the world, but they still produced impeccable smiles when Jill approached them. I saw them listen attentively to what she had to say, then shake their heads with what looked like genuine regret. The hostess put a hand on Jill's upper arm; she may have squeezed it. Then she and the pilot walked away.

We found out later, when Jill rang her parents, that Cheryl hadn't come because she was already married: the taxi driver had talked her into a registry wedding that morning, and they'd left for a honeymoon on the south coast. Jill heard all this from her dad; her mother wouldn't speak to her, blamed Jill for the abandoned wedding, and thought she'd caused the trouble out of spite, just so they wouldn't get their one chance to enjoy a decent celebration with a decent child. Her father warned Jill, in no uncertain terms, to stay out of Cheryl's life. He was shouting, and I heard him. He said, 'She's better off without you, always has been.'

But that came later. First, Jill had to walk into the terminal, and I had to meet her. She stood on the tarmac for a good two or three minutes, arms crossed, her back to me and her chin tilted upward, so that I could see the top of her head but not her face. I assumed she was crying, mostly because the dog was, with whinging yelps. When he saw her turn and begin to move, he towed me over to the door she'd have to come through, his tail beating against my leg. I wondered, not for the first time, what it would be like if humans were as demonstrative as dogs: how Jill might react if, thrown by her sister's absence, she came through the door and saw me standing there, mouth open, tongue out, full of admiration and endless, dumb, euphoric faith in her goodness.

Maybe that's why, in those moments, I formed a crazy plan. I would walk towards her, the dog by my side; I would go down on one knee right there in arrivals and ask Jill to marry me. Not because she was in love with me, or even because I was in love with her, although probably I was, but because I was beginning to see life as a series of losses—that have already happened and are happening and will inevitably happen—and no one should have to endure that alone. I sure as hell didn't want to. This could be something permanent, I thought, me and Jill and the dog. Some family. Some luck.

I didn't, of course. I didn't even lift her in my arms and twirl her so carefully that her dress wouldn't ride up and expose her backside. What did I expect to come through that door? A tear-stained face, a broken woman, a damsel in distress? What came was Jill. Her face, as usual, seemed to promise access to something fundamental, some deep source of beauty and generosity that had always been just outside my reach. No one would ever have guessed at the disappointment she'd just suffered. I had some sense, then, of the energy she must have expended every minute of every day, sustaining the myth of herself.

The dog lurched out of my grasp, flew to her, jumped so that its front paws were on her shoulders and the lead trailed with a tinkle on the floor. Jill laughed and let him lick her face, and the men in business suits gaped like puppets. She approached me with a smile and didn't mention Cheryl. I drove us home and stayed with her while she rang her parents, but I wasn't necessary. After the call, she made us scrambled eggs, and I went without asking to sleep in my old bed.

Not long after, I made plans to leave town: I would fly back east, enrol in a hospitality course, and become particular to someone. These were the first of many thought-out, definite decisions I went on to make for myself; I'm almost sure they were the right ones. In those last few weeks I spent at Jill's house, she was her usual self. She didn't seem to mind that I was going, and she never talked about Cheryl. But I did see her one early morning in her hammock, when she thought I was asleep. It was just bright enough that if you'd switched on a light, no moths would have flocked to it. There'd been rain overnight, and the air was already stifling; the dripping garden stank of lush rot, but Jill was dry beneath her custard apple tree. The first green, scaly fruits were beginning to form on its branches. She was sitting up in the hammock with her legs crossed like a schoolgirl, and the poodle was in her lap. It was years, and I'd become a parent myself, before I understood that the grief on her face was a mother's grief. Back then, as I watched the slight swing of the hammock, all I could feel was envy, because she held that dog like he was all she had.

HOSTEL

(1995)

've never told my husband this story, but I suppose I will eventually, on some sticky night in, say, February, as we lie naked in bed with the ceiling fan set at its highest speed. We'll be waiting for a storm to bluster in from the south, and I'll see the relevant part of him lying flushed and heavy against his thigh, and I'll think about how I'd consider taking it in my mouth if the room were cooler by as little as two degrees. That will remind me of Roy and his wife, and I'll feel like talking about them. And I'll start by telling my husband that I used to know this couple who, on learning they were going to have a baby, began taking long walks together in the evening.

I might not use their real names. It would be hard, though, not to reveal Roy's, which seemed almost to have shaped his personality. His given name—much to his embarrassment— was Royal, and in defiance of his parents' grandiosity, he'd cultivated an un-royal persona. He was a humble guy, self-effacing. He lived his life—at least, his public, social life—as if he were answering a survey about it. If someone asked, 'How was your trip to Fiji, Roy?,' his answer might be 'I'd describe myself as having enjoyed it.' The trouble was that he took his humility to such lengths that he actually came across, in the end, as kingly: detached, benevolent, devoid of individuality. His opinions and tastes and desires were as carefully bland as a king's must be. A polite king, I mean, who coexists with a constitution, and whose irrelevance now and then sparks a complicated optimism about the possibility of a republic. Or, of course, a queen.

There's no need to use Roy's wife's real name; in fact, she's no longer his wife. I'll call her Mandy. A name like this reveals nothing about her except, perhaps, that she was pretty and athletic. The evening walks were a response to Mandy's fear that pregnancy might change her body. It's not that Mandy was vain; she just liked to be good at everything she did. So she liked to be good at having a body.

At the time, Roy and Mandy lived in Newtown—which, I'll explain to my husband, is a crowded inner-city Sydney neighbourhood that, back in the nineties, was grimy but beginning to gentrify. They were part of that gentrification: they'd bought a tall Victorian terrace house in north Newtown and fitted it with many skylights, so that sunlight filtered down like incandescent smoke through the stairwells, and woke them each morning from a gleaming square above their bed. You could sit on their guest toilet and see the undersides of aeroplanes. They'd added an extension, too, to open out the kitchen, and painted the front door an intrepid red, as if to advertise their plucky personalities. They were both lawyers with good salaries, and the timing of the pregnancy was part of a long-term plan that took into account the rising property values in their neighbourhood. Each night, they strolled hand in hand through the streets of Newtown, Mandy's belly beginning to show, while Sydney Uni students rolled joints in the tiled front gardens of their share houses, and the employees of Thai restaurants ferried bags of fragrant rubbish out into narrow alleyways.

Sometimes Roy and Mandy walked down one particular street that had a backpacker hostel on it. The hostel was shabby and loud, but Roy and Mandy claimed to like it: they said it reminded them of their own student travels through Europe, of being nineteen and crawling into each other's beds in crowded dorms. There was the time at a hostel on Mykonos when, apparently, Roy sat on a top bunk, his legs dangling while Mandy stood between them sucking him off, and some raucous Croatian girls burst into the dorm. I heard Roy and Mandy tell this story multiple times, separately and together. Roy told it as if someone had informed him that, if he didn't tell a slightly risqué story at least once every year or two, he'd be considered terminally unadventurous. Mandy told it with genuine relish, as if she were astonished at herself for living a life in which an incident like this had taken place. The details changed over the years; eventually, the girls' nationality became Czech, and they ran from the room shouting, 'God save the Queen!'

Roy and Mandy had had other backpacking adventures, but hasn't every middle-class Australian? Weren't we all once sweet, oblivious amateurs? There was a night on the roof of a hostel in Marrakech that I've told my husband about; another in Penang, in a hotel full of Belgian doctors, that I haven't; a full-moon party on Kuta Beach that explains the negligible scar beneath my left ear. Everywhere I travelled in the eighties, I found Australians in short shorts carrying treasured copies of *Southeast Asia on a Shoestring*. We all stank and thought we were poor, and none of the sex we had was interesting enough to talk about within two years of coming home. But Roy and Mandy continued to recount their escapades. They spoke with such partiality for their very young selves, as if they had some-how been especially sweet and especially amateurish, that I was always vaguely annoyed by their stories of those times.

The backpacker hostel in their gentrifying neighbour-hood was made up of three connected terrace houses, leprous with pink paint and festooned with Tibetan prayer flags. It was being slowly devoured by one or more enormous night-blooming jasmines, which clotted the street with their creamy smell. No matter the time of day, there were always lights in the windows; there was always music playing and laundry hanging from the balconies. The street wasn't well lit, and the hostel reared up so suddenly from the footpath and was so tall and bright that walking past it in the dark felt a little like being in a tugboat bumping along the edge of an ocean liner. The hostel was next to a park, which in turn was next to a church, and on warm nights backpackers usually occupied both the park and the churchyard in more or less furtive stages of drunkenness, sex, or both. In my experience, it was impossible to walk past that hostel without thinking of all the fumblings and unzip-pings of your own youth, the stubborn grass stains, the greedy crevices, the rueful grimaces when someone's wrist seized up at an awkward angle. In the vicinity of that hostel, I'd remember even the most pedestrian local encounters as if they'd taken place in an impossibly remote country.

These are my own impressions, of course. I don't really know how Mandy and Roy felt about the hostel, only that they walked past it one night and heard someone crying in the park next door. According to Roy, he knew at once that the person crying was a girl, but Mandy was less sure: there was a depth to the weeping that seemed masculine to her, or may even have been the growl of a possum. Anyway, something about the sound unsettled her enough that when Roy stopped walking, she squeezed his hand and shook her head, as if to say that they shouldn't get involved. But Roy—noble, kingly Roy—squeezed back, gave a reassuring smile, and called out, 'Hello? Hello? Is anybody there?'

The weeper took some time to emerge, but when she did she was a tall blonde girl in cut-off denim shorts and a baggy tie-dyed T-shirt. Apparently, she'd been crouching against the wall of the hostel, not far from the footpath but concealed by a bushy bottlebrush, and the first things Mandy noticed about her were that her braided hair was dotted with thin red fibres— the stamens of bottlebrush flowers—and that she was barefoot. When Roy told the story, he never mentioned what he'd first noticed about the girl. Mandy was always quick to say how pretty she was. I heard her compare the girl to assorted actresses, all of whom had been blonde in at least one major role but otherwise looked nothing alike.

The girl came sobbing up from the bottlebrush, wiping her nose with the back of her wrist. For several minutes, she was able only to apologise, and to weep. According to Roy, Mandy flew to the girl and took both her hands, asked her what was wrong, while the girl just stood with her streaming face and her gulping mouth, saying, 'Sorry.'

Roy asked if she was hurt, and I can imagine this—Roy stepping up to her and asking, gravely, 'Would you describe yourself as having been hurt?' There would be some urgency in his voice, but also some restraint, and the effect would be that of a member of the royal family pausing in a receiving line to speak to a retired Olympian.

The girl shook her head to say that no, she wasn't hurt. Roy asked if there was anyone they could find for her—a friend? A boyfriend? Someone inside? Because it was obvious that she had come from the hostel: her fair hair was twisted in Balinese braids, her neck was noticeably dirty, and she seemed to cry with a European accent. The girl only shook her head again and cried louder.

'Can we take you to your room? Can we get you anything?' asked Mandy, asked Roy, and the whole time the little life they'd created together was floating inside Mandy, preparing itself to be part of the world.

But the girl didn't want to go to her room, or to be brought anything. Mandy felt that there was nothing to do but to take the girl in her arms, so she did. This seemed to be the right thing: the girl collapsed against Mandy's neck in relief and sorrow. Since they could get nothing more intelligible from her, Mandy and Roy decided to take her home with them.

It was one of those decisions a couple makes without discussion, but in full knowledge that they're in agreement. Roy nodded, stepped away from Mandy and the girl, and gestured down the street; Mandy, with her arm around the girl's shaking shoulders, led her away from the park and the hostel. The girl came without hesitation. Five minutes later, they were safe behind the red front door. Roy filled the kettle for tea and Mandy guided the girl to one of the chrome bar stools at the kitchen island. When she was shopping for the stools, Mandy had imagined her children sitting at them, crayons gripped in chunky fists while she made dinner. Roy, in Mandy's vision, would arrive home from work, enter the kitchen rolling up his shirtsleeves, kiss everybody hello, and open a bottle of merlot. It would all be very ordinary, very lovely, and as she described the scene I could see it too, and the safety it represented: a safety I had always associated with Roy. In fact, I always found those stools perilous—and I spun back and forth on them many times, confessional and unhappy, my hands pushing off from the Corian countertop, while Roy leaned towards me over the island with a look of concern on his reassuring face. Mandy told me about the kids and crayons later, after the divorce, when they'd just sold the house and she was offering me the bar stools. I had no use for bar stools, but it seemed important to accept them.

So Mandy guided the girl to one of those stools, and this was the point at which they learned that the girl was Swiss and eighteen; but her name was unusual enough, or her accent heavy enough, that all they could be sure of was the letter it started with, 'S.' She was no longer crying, although her body was still racked occasionally by dry, soundless sobs; in order to subdue these, she buried her chin against her chest in such a way that Roy and Mandy could see every bit of the wincing scalp exposed by her braids. She explained that she was backpacking around Asia and Australia with her boyfriend, Daniel—his name brought a quaver to her voice, but she didn't give in to it. She and Daniel had another six months of travel planned, and were due to leave Sydney in two days, hitchhiking to southern New South Wales, where they'd lined up a season of work picking fruit. After that, their plan was to head north to the Great Barrier Reef for a final, tropical hurrah, then return to Basel in time to start at university. S wanted to study psychology. Daniel was supposed to become a doctor. S looked sceptical at the idea of Daniel as a doctor, and the wry face she pulled made Roy and Mandy laugh. S joined in this laughter and relaxed visibly. She curled her bare feet around the legs of the stool, shook her tight, greasy braids behind her shoulders, and tugged at the neckline of her T-shirt as if to cool herself down. She wore a halter bikini top beneath the shirt—Roy and Mandy now noticed the withered bikini strings pressed into the back of her pinkish neck.

The whole sad story came out as she drank her tea: there had been a barbecue at the hostel that evening. Daniel had been drinking all afternoon, he was flirting with an Irish girl, had been flirting all week, and when the Irish girl sat in Daniel's lap and S objected, Daniel made a joke at her expense—at S's expense—and everyone at the barbecue had laughed. S told the story as if she saw, now, how trivial it must sound—but there was still dignity to the way she seemed to look back on it, with sorrow and wisdom, as if it had happened to a much younger person. Mandy and Roy, listening, must have thought of their passionate, brave young selves in those filthy backpacker hostels across Europe. They must have felt protective towards S, and much older.

Now Mandy suggested that a glass of wine might be in order—something stronger than tea—although, naturally, she wouldn't have any herself. (I can see the way she would have stroked her rounding stomach as she said this.) When Roy told the story, he always made it clear that the wine had been Mandy's idea, that he would never have suggested it, and, of course, that he would never have drunk wine alone with the girl, who was after all only eighteen and in a vulnerable state. Mandy would nod in agreement as he said this. I once saw them tell the story while Mandy was breastfeeding, and she nodded so vehemently that the baby's mouth detached from Mandy's purple nipple.

So Roy opened a bottle of shiraz and he and the girl drank—only a glass or two each—as they all sat talking together in the kitchen. Mandy and Roy told stories of their travels and their university days; S talked about her parents, who had divorced a few years earlier and were both now seeing much older partners. It was as if, S said, the divorce had aged them, and she shook her head in wonder and disbelief, because she was at just the right age to start pitying her parents. They talked about the baby and somehow got around to looking at childhood photos of Roy and Mandy, and S said that if the baby was a girl they should name it after her. She was joking, of course, but the familiarity of this made it doubly impossible to ask for her name again.

Finally, Mandy yawned and said she thought it was time to

get some sleep, and she suggested that Roy walk S back to the hostel—or, of course, S was very welcome to stay the night, although they had already converted the guest room into a nursery and she would need to sleep in the lounge room, on the couch, which folded out into a bed and was apparently fairly comfortable. I slept on that couch a few times myself—always heartbroken or drunk, usually both, absolutely sure that my life would never improve, that loneliness was everlasting, that no man with forearms like Roy's would ever turn to me with love—and I can confirm that it was, indeed, fairly comfortable.

S, of course, chose to stay the night. Why do I say 'of course'? I'm not sure—only that it's so easy to imagine the intimacy of the three of them as they giggled at baby albums in that varnished kitchen, and how much nicer a stay in this pristine house must have seemed than a sheepish return to the hostel. Also, S said, she liked the idea of Daniel wondering where she was. She wanted him to suffer.

Roy made up the fold-out bed, as he'd done for me so many times, and told S to help herself to anything in the kitchen. Then he withdrew. Mandy found the girl some pyjamas and issued warnings about the delicate temperament of the downstairs shower; then she and S hugged in such a genuine way that Mandy, apparently, felt they might have been sisters.

At this point in the story, someone in Mandy and Roy's audience would usually ask if it had occurred to them that the girl might rob them, and Mandy and Roy would always say no, absolutely not. And Mandy would say that she had only done what she hoped some stranger might one day do, if necessary, for her own daughter. When she said this, she would lean down to kiss the baby's head; or she and Roy would look at each other as if to say, 'Don't worry, we'll never actually let her out of our sight—there will never be any need for the kindness of strangers.'

Both Roy and Mandy insisted that they'd felt perfectly safe with S in their house, and that they had slept long and deep through the night. But surely Mandy must have spent some time, during that night, gazing at the dim square of the bedroom skylight and thinking about the girl sleeping in the lounge room, who had been so unabashed about changing that Mandy had seen her young, buoyant breasts. And Roy must have thought about how he'd gone around making sure the windows and doors were locked, and all the time there was a stranger inside the house with them, a girl who might have been anyone, whose name they didn't even know.

I've also imagined them having giddy, hushed sex, knowing the girl was sleeping downstairs—of course I've imagined that, though I probably won't mention it to my husband. And I've imagined the girl coming into their room in the early light, slipping into their bed with her long blonde limbs. Or maybe Mandy spent the night awake, rigid, waiting to see if Roy would get up as if to use the bathroom, say her name in a loud whisper, and then, on receiving no response, creep trembling down the stairs towards the fold-out bed. I don't know what it was really like, but I do know that every unhappy night I slept in that fairly comfortable bed, I wondered if Roy would come down those stairs. I listened for his step and thought at some length about what he would say or do, and how I'd respond. When he didn't come, not once, I cursed the effortless happiness of married people.

In the morning, the girl was gone. She'd stripped the bed,

turned it back into a couch, drunk a mug of instant coffee, and left a note that said, *Thank you very much*, with *very* underlined three times. She signed it 'S'. She hadn't stolen or damaged anything, and had even closed the gate on her way out. I imagine the house feeling strangely empty that day, both Roy and Mandy looking in at the spotless nursery even more than usual, reminding themselves that they were awaiting a joyous arrival, not mourning a departure.

Mandy and Roy walked by the hostel again that night. They considered going in and asking after S, but because they didn't know her name, they decided against it. Their baby was born three months later. She was the first of many babies of my acquaintance to be named Isabella.

When Isabella was a few weeks old, Mandy read a newspaper article about a couple of Swiss backpackers who had been picking fruit in southern New South Wales. At the end of the harvest, these backpackers had left for Sydney—they were planning to hitchhike—and hadn't been heard from since. Their names were Daniel and Sabina. Mandy studied the photo of the couple in the newspaper. Sabina didn't look like S, but she also didn't *not* look like S. Mandy showed the picture to Roy, who agreed that she *might* have been S. Every time I heard them tell this story, they always looked a little apologetic at this point, as if they knew it would have been improved by a positive identification of S—but of course it had to be her, she was the right age, she was reported as being from Basel, her boyfriend's name was Daniel, and, like S, the couple had spent time in Vietnam, Thailand, and Indonesia before their arrival in

Australia. Sabina's hair wasn't in braids in the newspaper photo, which may have been why she looked different.

At first, Roy and Mandy ended their story here, with this ambiguous thrill.

The story was enriched a few months later when a group of mushroom foragers found Daniel and Sabina's bodies in Barrow State Forest. They had been shot; Daniel had also been stabbed. Until then, I had never taken seriously the concept of evil. It was too abstract, I thought, and too convenient. Of course there was no power that moved in darkness through the world, recruiting some people and striking others. But I remember watching the news that day: the screen showed police tape across a bush track, officers walking with black Labradors, helicopters hovering above treetops. Nothing graphic, but all of it horrifying: the tautness of the tape, the businesslike trot of the dogs, the way the crowns of the trees thrashed with the force of the helicopter blades. I felt the presence of something then, quite suddenly, in my stomach and at the roots of my hair. I watched the helicopters rise from the treetops as if hauling a vast net full of a heavy, invisible substance that seemed to want to drag them back down; but they broke away.

Isabella was nine months old when the bodies were found, able to sit up on her own in a tottering way. At barbecues and lunches and catch-ups and cafes, Roy and Mandy were asked to tell the story of S, the murdered girl who stayed the night. They always complied. As we leaned towards them to listen, I would look at Mandy, and at Roy, and at everyone else present, to see which of us might be willing to suggest that by being kind to S that night, Roy and Mandy had made her so trusting of Australian strangers that she might, for example, have been less careful if a man approached her on a highway, offering her a ride in his truck. Maybe no one else ever thought about this. Maybe only I pictured S on a lonely road with her tight braids and her boyfriend, backpack at her feet, one thumb raised, hoping for hospitality and thinking, when the white truck pulled up, that she had found it.

My husband, when I tell him about S, will recognise this part of the story, because Sabina and Daniel were only the first of the bodies found at Barrow State, and what came next—the capture of the man who had chosen his victims at random, the media circus, the trashy books and TV movies—was spread out like a wicked feast for anyone to pick at. But S was something private, a connection. She was Roy and Mandy's. She was mine.

Years passed, despite the existence of evil. None of our friends would admit to being surprised when Roy and Mandy broke up, but I was. I had been so sure of the red door, the skylights, the way they looked at each other as they told the story of S. I had been sure that marriage to a man like Roy—so reliable, so benevolent—would be like stepping onto a throne from which there could be no abdication. But apparently, they had found themselves in different places, wanting different things. Isabella was just starting high school at the time. Property values in their neighbourhood were soaring and the house sold for a record price. Mandy inherited me in the divorce, but we lost touch when I married and moved out of state.

Yesterday, I was back in Sydney and ran into Roy on a street in Paddington. He looked good: older, leaner, like a man who would no longer talk about his backpacking days. There was no ring on his finger. He suggested a drink, and I liked the idea and was going to say yes. I wanted to ask him about the divorce, hoping he might say, 'I wouldn't describe myself as having enjoyed it.' I wanted to hear the story of S one more time, as told by Roy. It felt as though this might be my last chance to get close to the largeness of life, its terror and mystery, while remaining perfectly safe.

And I wanted to ask if he'd ever thought about me as I lay in the fold-out bed. I already knew he'd thought about me, and I also knew that, if I did go for a drink with him, we would find ourselves in a bed together sooner or later. But as he stood with me in the street, his hand on my elbow, suggesting this drink, I was reminded of a member of the royal family showing concern for patients on a hospital visit. It hurt just to look at him. I still might have gone, but then I remembered that I was married now, and that married people are happy.

DEMOCRACY SAUSAGE

(1998)

Because Australians are incapable of fulfilling their legal obligation to participate in the democratic process without also being given the opportunity to purchase and consume a sausage sandwich, this woman has asked me, politely but with conviction, to burn a sausage for her—burn it black, she said—so that's what I'm doing, carefully and affably, here at the barbecue on election day in the school grounds, wearing my apron that reads *What's the Biga Idea?*, and which I thought, up until approximately two hours ago, I might have to wear backwards, because the name 'Biga' has, in the last four days, become an appalling liability, the kind of one-in-a-million piece of bad luck that not even the sharpest campaign manager could plan for, not even Celeste, but she's come through, as she tends to, in her pointy way, and I'm wearing the apron as God and Celeste intended, slogan visible, and also a badge in campaign colours that says NO RELATION, which is true, as far as I know—as far as it's possible to know exactly who might or might not be related to, for example, a grandfather who emigrated from Poland but never spoke about it, preferred to keep quiet about any brothers or cousins or uncles, preferred in fact to keep quiet about almost everything and just sit in a stained velour armchair inhaling incessant smoke into his lungs, which were already scarred by the pneumonia he contracted while building dams in midwinter in the Murray–Darling Basin, and who is now more tight-lipped than ever, being dead—so yes, this Biga that everyone's talking about, this Biga who's just been arrested for multiple horrific murders, could possibly be a distant cousin, but as far as I know, and my parents know, and Celeste knows, and my wife and children know, he truly is NO RELATION, although something about this woman's tapping foot suggests that she isn't entirely convinced, this woman in the sixty-plus age bracket who's asked for the burnt sausage, which I think she's planning to feed to the dog she has with her, itself a low sausage, name of Roger, whose eyes are so framed by oversized ears that he must see the world as if peeping through hanging laundry, and who I imagine would prefer a nice, plump, pink snag, though obviously I won't say so, because the customer is always right, just as the voter is always right, unless they're voting for the other party, which she may be, this woman—voting for another party, I mean, since with her undyed hair and hippie sandals she doesn't look like what Celeste calls a 'core vote', the ones who are mine to lose, whose simple needs feed the simple themes of a strong campaign, who all shop in the same two places and drive all-terrain vehicles in suburbia, whereas this woman looks like a greenie, but I probably only think so because the chain on her glasses reminds me of Mum, who in retirement has joined Greenpeace and gets herself in newspapers as SENATE CANDIDATE'S MOTHER CHAINED TO BULLDOZERS IN TASMANIAN RAINFOREST, who keeps threatening to join one of those boats whose crews berate Japanese whaling ships through megaphones, and who has, to the delight of my daughter, gone vegetarian, which means she wouldn't order a sausage, not even from me, her son, and certainly not for a chance to gawk because SENATE CANDIDATE SHARES NAME WITH SE-RIAL KILLER, though the more this particular sausage sizzles on the barbecue, forming its carcinogenic crust in the same grad-ual way an oyster produces a pearl, the less I feel like I'll ever eat a sausage again, keeping in mind that I've said exactly this before, three or four years ago, when my wife's dog—bigger than Roger, smarter, a lovable border collie with a hundred-word vocabulary, may he rest in peace—came springing out from the underbrush of a local riverside path with, between his teeth, a large rubber dildo, the colour of fair flesh but streaked with silty mud, resembling nothing so much as a poorly barbe-cued sausage, and I vowed, my wife vowed, never to eat a sau-sage again, although of course we have, most weekends in summer, when our vegetarian youngest is likely to be out with her vegetarian friends, and our eldest, who'll eat basically any-thing, is likely to be snowboarding in Canada, where he lives on instant noodles for six months of the year in houses full of other snowboarding young men, Aussies and Kiwis mostly, friends who have no idea his dad is in politics, that his dad feels with a pang every day the long impossible distance to Canada, friends who wouldn't care even if they did know, but who might, in the last few days, have started teasing my son about his name, just gentle digs, a new nickname maybe, so that he'll be introduced to girls in bars as 'Killer', this boy who still cries at the scene where the horse drowns in *The NeverEnding Story* and has never given the collection of syllables that is his surname a second thought, unlike our daughter, who did a project on Poland in year five—at this very school, in fact, where both my children received their primary education—and on completing this project became the official Pole in our family, full of national factoids, like a tiny officer sent to re-educate us about our heritage, and is now a masterful maker of pierogi, and who's taking it hard, poor passionate sweetheart, that there should be this correlation between our name—of all the names in all the world—and that man—of all the men in Australia— so that this one thing that's always been slightly special about her, the weird name no one knows how to pronounce, which I foisted on her without thought but which she's since embraced and made her own, has now been infected by something so repulsive she can't stand to think of it, since horror for her is something that happens only when Polish soldiers on horseback charge German tanks, say, or when Polish Jews die in Auschwitz, things that happen far away and in the past, to which she has a sympathetic but abstract connection, whereas horror should have no relation to girls just a few years older than she is, girls who walked along a highway she's familiar with because my parents live at one end of it and probably always will, even though Dad claims they'll move closer to us once he retires, but like all family doctors he'll never retire, will never be willing to surrender the pleasure of being a kindly expert among grateful women, will never know that the thought of him misremembering something medical or blowing his nose in the midst of his old-man's dignity brings tears to my eyes, which are naturally watery anyway, an unfortunate trait in a politician, and also in a dog like Roger, whose eyes are watering right now as if, like me, he's sensitive to raw onion, which has been a real problem at the barbecue today, this tendency to look like I'm crying and having to blame, conveniently, the onions I'm cooking, since Celeste is worried voters will find it off-putting, that they'll glimpse me across the asphalt—exactly the required six metres away from the polling station—and will proceed into the assembly hall thinking they'll never vote for a weeper with the name of a murderer, though either way they'll come straight over here after voting, just as this woman in her greenie sandals did, and order a sausage sandwich, because, un-like the campaign flyers people are refusing at the school gates, the sandwich doesn't have the name 'Biga' on it, and is therefore safe to associate with, to carry around, exhilarating even, be-cause there's a touch of celebrity to any name that's been in the paper, even if for a disgusting reason, and it occurs to me, as I turn the woman's sausage for the last time, so as to make sure all of its surface is equitably burned, that my wife, who is now fully justified in her long-time insistence on retaining her maiden name in professional contexts, might in the future be hesitant to introduce me to colleagues or clients, or might begin to place noticeable stress on my first name, which isn't the first name of the murderer, so that I'll become, over time, monony-mous, simply Chris, like Prince or Cher—Chris the surname-less, Chris the not-murderer—and that she might, while showing houses to clients, even pretend to be divorced, or married to another man entirely, some other Chris whose sur-name has no grimace behind it, no need to say NO RELATION, and that this man might become a third party in our marriage, and that our marriage—which on the whole has been success-ful, having survived miscarriages and mortgages, having sur-vived hypercritical vegetarian daughters and sons who drop out of uni to go snowboarding in Canada, having survived the day-to-day embarrassment of bumping clumsily about in the world, and having survived all this with friendship intact, with respect and good humour intact, with sex life more or less intact—that our marriage might become a shameful secret, and my wife might even begin to feel that she's cheating on that third man, that not-murderer Chris, by keeping her vows to me, and that the fear of this and other things might mean that she's hoping, right now—while she stands at the school gates, smile on, try-ing to distribute flyers no one will take—that I don't win my seat today, might even mean that she considers it selfish of me, in fact, not to have pulled out of the race, to still want to take office, to stand before my fellow Australians and to participate in such an egotistical way in the democratic process, when I share my name with a murderer and, more importantly, with my children, because I suspect she believes I'm actually capable of curbing these ambitions of mine, of damming up all the boundless hungers and humiliations that have led me here, all that vanity and optimism and altruism and envy, and since she believes that I'm capable of curbing all this, it follows that she also believes I must be choosing not to, that I'm choosing to condemn my children with their tainted name to additional scrutiny, knowing they'll have to bump clumsily about in a hostile world, which is difficult and boring and complicated enough without fluke coincidences and attention-seeking fathers, but is also beautiful, full of wonder and surprise, though this is the sort of wishy-washy sentimentality I've been coached to steer clear of—been ordered, frankly, to avoid, by Celeste, who is already disappointed in me and my idiot name, who was hoping for a 'clean campaign', by which she means an easy win, a landslide, and who even now is coming up behind me, looking important and confidential in her sleek suit, leaning in to say that it's time to take off the NO RELATION badge, it's not polling well, there's no effective way to polish that particular turd and the last thing we want is to seem like you're joking about this, and both Roger and the woman are straining forward now as if they'd like to hear what a lady who wears a suit on a Saturday might be saying into the ear of the candidate who has just at this moment finished burning them a sausage, who is amenably placing that sausage in a piece of square white buttered bread, where it leaves an obscenely sooty smear, and is passing this delicacy over in its flimsy napkin, and it seems they've both caught what Celeste said, I could swear they have, which is why the woman is now staying put, taking a bite off the protruding end of the burnt sausage and rolling it around in her mouth, extracting it, and dropping it to the asphalt in front of tense, baited, quivering Roger, who immediately after snatching it up in his low little mouth looks back at me, just as the woman looks across at me, both of them intent now on watching me as I'm putting down the tongs, wiping my hands on the apron, and removing the badge, both of them noting that by doing all of this, as instructed and with careful nonchalance, I seem to be—I feel myself to be, as my big blunt thumb struggles with the pin before handing the badge over to Celeste, who disappears it into her suit—admitting to a relation between this monster and myself, announcing A RELATION, and making right now, for my own self-interested purposes, a place for this stray Biga in my household, where he will forever be a danger to the family I love so deeply and who may one day become ashamed of me, who perhaps already are, and this woman in her glasses knows it, Roger knows it, I certainly know it, just as I know that despite all this—the sausages, the apron, the campaign manager, the snowboarding son, the devastated daughter, the loyal wife with her gutsy smile—I may still lose the election, and that if and when I do he'll still be there, this other Biga, living strangely in our house, spitting in our milk and grinning in our wardrobes and leaving his imprint on the blankets of our beds, and exercising at all times his right to participate in the process of my name, the democratic process, my blackened name.

CHAPERONE

(1995)

E ven if Sister Mary Placid had known this trip was going to go wrong, that this would be the last time she'd
take a sixth form Ancient History class to Rome, she
couldn't have prayed over it more than she already had. Prayer
was simply the medium in which she moved. So she prayed to
the Virgin over every preparation, and she prayed to the Virgin on the early bus to Heathrow as the girls slept in the seats
around her. She prayed—*mirror of justice, seat of wisdom*—at
the airport as the girls, who had well and truly woken up, ran
about screaming with the joy and fright of the trip: four days in
Rome with only one teacher and one mother as chaperones. The
girls bought vast quantities of chocolate, they went continually
to the bathrooms in shifting groups of two or three, and there
were so many of them! Only nine, in reality, but they seemed to
multiply once they were out of uniform, so that every sixteen-
or seventeen-year-old girl Mary Placid spied might be a member of her class, and therefore her concern.

The chaperoning mother, Charlotte Gibson, occupied herself before the flight by sniffing every perfume in the duty-free shop beside the gate. She had volunteered for the trip because she and her husband were in the process of divorcing, and Charlotte thought it best to keep ahead of any disapproval from the school. According to Tess, Charlotte's daughter, the nuns had been known to penalise girls with divorced parents, and Tess's offer from Cambridge required an A in history. Charlotte, browsing the perfumes, had always thought of herself as preferring a light, floral scent; now, as she raised each bottle to her nose, she wondered if she might in fact enjoy something spicy, which would sit waiting on her skin and intrude at unpredictable moments, welling up to announce the rich existence of her body.

Tess Gibson sat in the part of the gate that was furthest from her mother's duty-free browsing. She hunched over her Discman, which she was sharing with her friend Grace Reed: one bud of a headphone in Tess's left ear, one in Grace's right, tethered by wire to a song with which Tess felt, each time she heard it, reunited, as if her body was the song's beloved instrument. Her blood surged with the singer's exhausted gasps, the unexpected silences, the sudden distorted explosions of guitar. Tess smiled at Grace, a little shy in her ecstasy. Grace smiled back, but she was bored with the song, which seemed fuzzy to her, shapeless and imprecise, like stars seen without glasses, and the androgynous voice of the singer wailed with self-pity. Grace, too, was full of self-pity, not least because she didn't own a Discman; but Grace would never sing about it.

Mary Placid prayed—*cause of our joy, spiritual vessel*—on

the plane while the girls threw objects at one another across the narrow aisles and screamed with laughter at senseless repeated phrases. They requested, from the flight attendants, endless cups of warm Diet Coke, which careless Rosie Delahunt managed to spill all over her jeans. Mary Placid rose from her seat every now and then, a dark column, and said, 'Girls, please!' The girls giggled and quieted, but never for long.

Whenever a flurry of noise began, Charlotte Gibson looked across the aisle at Mary Placid with curiosity, her eyes half-closed, waiting to see what the nun would do. Eventually, Charlotte plugged her ears with pink foam, allowed her sunglasses to drop from the top of her head to cover her eyes, and pretended to be asleep for the remainder of the flight. Her daughter, at least, was behaving herself. Tess was tucked up in her window seat, no doubt singing along silently with whatever urgent, unprecedented music was currently playing on her Discman. Charlotte experienced a now-familiar throb of worry about the way Tess had withdrawn from her since learning about the divorce; but, in terms of her role as chaperone, she felt that her daughter's current good conduct absolved her of any responsibility.

The music stopped, momentarily, for Tess Gibson—a song had just finished in a reverberant growl of longing. In this brief silence, she looked down at France and understood it to be something larger than the campgrounds she'd stayed in every summer as a child, when her parents still loved one another and would, every morning, send Tess and her older brothers to buy bread from the campground's shop, so that they might have some privacy. Then the music began again, claiming her.

Beside her, in the middle seat, Grace Reed pushed her knees

up against the seat in front, in which Jenny Jessop cackled and squirmed. Grace would have liked the window seat but hadn't said so; had pretended, when Tess asked, not to care, because to care might mean admitting that this was her first time on a plane. On Grace's other side, Monica Alvares was describing in detail how sick she'd once been on a flight from Gatwick to Bahrain; Amy Diouf threw an empty cup across the aisle in an attempt to shut her up.

Mary Placid prayed—*Virgin most prudent, Virgin most venerable*—when they touched down in Rome and no one had lost their passport—not even Laura Barr, who tended to confuse her elder and younger Plinys—and all of the bags had arrived. The girls pressed close to one another and to their teacher as they boarded the train to Rome, and Charlotte Gibson, despite her age, became one of them: showing her ticket when Sister Mary Placid called, '*Biglietti*, girls, have them ready!'; trotting behind Mary Placid as she led them through the chaos of Termini and argued with taxi drivers about fares; and, finally, giggling with relief as they arrived at their *pensione* in the historical centre of the city. Mary Placid brought her sixth form Ancient History students to this *pensione* every year, but this visit was different: old Andrea and Gianna had retired to a seaside town in the Maremma, and their son Davide was now in charge. Davide was nowhere to be seen, however, and where Mary Placid would usually have been greeted as an old friend, the group was checked in by an unsmiling young woman who refused to respond to Mary Placid's Italian with anything but English.

What a shame! It had been a pleasure for Mary Placid to be welcomed every year with familiarity, to exchange warm greetings in rapid Italian, and then to turn to her students, clap her hands, and slip with ease back into English. It was one of the reasons she insisted on staying here and not in a convent, although some of the other nuns objected. The *pensione* always raised her in the girls' esteem: here was their teacher, who seemed only to exist within the boundaries of the school, the chapel, and the convent, turning out to have made her mark in the wider world and to be intimate with another style of life.

Once checked in, the girls were shown to a large dormitory equipped with eight single beds. A fold-out bed—low, on wheels—was positioned below one of the windows. It was understood by everyone that this cot would be occupied by Grace Reed, who was on a scholarship and had paid less than full price for the trip. How much less was a secret between Sister Mary Placid and Grace's parents; Mary Placid, keeper of this confidence, stood in the doorway of the room to make sure Grace knew her place. Grace, more aware of her place than anyone, sat on the cot, coursing with rage and shame and gratitude. When Mary Placid left the room, Grace made a stiff salute, said, 'Bless *you*,' and winked at Tess, who lay back smiling on her full-sized bed.

Down the corridor, Mrs Gibson was already in her room, hanging her linen trousers in the wardrobe, fluffing her hair, applying lipstick, and leaning from the window to inspect the street below. It was a narrow, paved street and there were two young priests walking down it, talking animatedly to one another in what sounded like German; a Vespa sped towards the priests, who moved against the wall, still talking; as the Vespa passed, Charlotte heard the young man who drove it say, 'Julia

Roberts?' while his passenger, a girl in tight jeans, spoke into his ear, shaking her head. The girl looked to be about twenty-two years old, which was the length of time Charlotte had been married before her husband told her he was leaving her for another woman.

When Mary Placid reached her room, she sat on her single bed, paddled her white travel trainers against the terracotta floor, and listened to the sirens and scooters and car horns that meant she was in Rome. She was exhausted. Her room was small and stuffy, the shutters were half-open, and through them she could see a peeling ochre wall. Of course, she continued to pray. She had been requesting the Virgin Mother's intercession for more than fifty years. The continual nature of the plea was a form of armour to her, and a form of cradle, and also one hand held out in the dark in case of danger. But whenever she had one of her atrocious sleepless nights, the only thing that calmed her was to lie in a bed as neat and narrow as this one and walk the streets of Rome: back and forth, in her mind, between Piazza Navona and Piazza Colonna, following a specific route she had memorised long ago, on her very first visit as an undergraduate reading Classics. And this had little to do with God, because Rome, to Sister Mary Placid, remained obstinately and beautifully pagan, and arrested in the particular period of history—late Republic, early Empire—that she most enjoyed teaching. She would, of course, take the girls to the Vatican for Wednesday's papal audience, but they would see the Forum first.

Now, sitting in her room, she closed her eyes and reminded herself that, not far from this building—perhaps even beneath it—Julius Caesar had died in the Curia of Pompey. This was enough to energise her. She sat up and shook out her feet in their white trainers. 'We'll eat,' she said aloud—perhaps to God, perhaps to Caesar, possibly to both—'and then I'll show them Rome.' And it was high time: she could hear steps thundering down the corridor and the distinctive snort of Jenny Jessop's laugh. Then Bridget Thomas, who'd become especially arrogant since her parents had agreed to finance a gap year in Australia, burst into Mary Placid's room without knocking and announced, 'Sister, Jenny wants you to show us how to use a bidet.'

Mary Placid didn't wear a habit, but Rome saw her high white collar, her dark vest and trousers, and the unfashionable cut of her undyed hair, and knew her for a nun. The difference this made in a city full of nuns was negligible; nevertheless, Mary Placid appreciated the way mothers snatched their errant toddlers from her path and hawkers of cheap sunglasses kept their distance. The girls, sensing this rote respect for their teacher, fell in behind her. The better-behaved ones hovered right at her back: Monica Alvares, Laura Barr, and of course Amanda Norton and Rosie Delahunt, who were inseparable. The bolder ones dawdled: Jenny Jessop, Amy Diouf, and their ringleader, Bridget Thomas. Grace Reed alternated between the groups in her usual capricious way. Behind them all, Tess Gibson walked with her mother. Tess had been made to leave her Discman at the hotel and now needed to focus all of her attention on enduring the violent clamour of Rome. For this reason, she didn't notice her mother stopping at a kiosk to flick through a calendar of sexy priests. When Charlotte, smiling affectionately to herself, full of both craving and disdain, turned to ask Tess if she should buy a calendar, she saw her daughter's bobbed hair disappearing into the crowd and had to run in order to catch up.

The group managed to stay together as they walked to Mary Placid's favourite trattoria in the via del Gesù, where ceiling fans ticked above tiled floors and the girls refused to order anything but pasta, despite being told the chicken was the best in Rome. Charlotte drank wine, even in the face of Mary Placid's evident disapproval. After lunch, during which nothing had gone wrong, they marched to the Trevi Fountain and the Spanish Steps. The girls posed for photos in both locations, and blushed as they refused offers of single roses from smiling men; Mary Placid had warned them in advance that, having taken a rose, they would be expected to pay for it. Then they ate gelato in front of the Pantheon, where Mary Placid delivered a brief lecture on Marcus Agrippa.

'Can we go inside?' Amanda Norton asked, and Mary Placid pursed her lips and said they would come back first thing in the morning, when the queues were shorter. The girls were delighted to discover a McDonald's across the piazza from the Pantheon, and several of them ran in to use its toilet. While the others waited, Mrs Gibson asked if she might take Tess, and anyone else who was interested, to see the Bernini elephant, which was just around the corner.

'You know Rome, then?' asked Mary Placid, clearly taken aback, and Charlotte Gibson found herself colouring as if she'd been caught doing something unseemly. She'd last been in

Rome twenty-one years ago, when she was young and newly married, childless, in love, and what she remembered most vividly was climbing the broad, white stairs to the Capitoline Museums while her husband walked behind her, commenting like a sportscaster on the shapeliness of her backside. He'd had so much hair then, he'd worn peacock-blue trousers, and when they reached the top of the stairs he'd kissed her while all the bells in Rome rang out for noon. It had been July, so hot that the tar of the pavements stuck to their shoes, and she'd had ghastly allergies. She remembered blowing her nose in front of the Bernini elephant.

Laura Barr, wide-eyed, with a smudge of chocolate gelato on her cheek, asked, 'Is it a real elephant?'

Sister Mary Placid said no, of course not, it was a statue of an elephant carrying an obelisk on its back, it was by a very famous and important sculptor called Bernini, and they would all go to see it together—no separating from the group, thank you, not in these crowds.

When Bridget Thomas and her disciples returned, without incident, from McDonald's, everyone went to look at Bernini's elephant, with its pert trunk and miniature obelisk. Beneath it, a busker sat on a folding chair, playing a cello.

'Bach!' proclaimed Mary Placid. Then she led them into a vast, dark church with a blue ceiling full of gold stars. Tess stayed near the door of the church in order to hear the cello, the measured sound of which was so calming that she forgot she was in Rome, that her parents were divorcing, that whenever she walked in the world she felt raw and open. Only music could protect her from the ragged, heaving despair of other people.

Grace ran up to her and asked, 'Do you have any coins? I've only got notes. I need coins for the lights.'

Tess dug in her pocket for change, which Grace used to illuminate several chapels. Grace didn't look long at any one of them; once a chapel was lit, she ran on to the next one, eager to hear the chunky clink of the coin falling into the box. She liked to see the sudden brightening of the Virgin's face, pious and gentle under electric light, and then she was impatient for the next chapel, where another Virgin or saint awaited their illumination. It seemed to Grace that her life was like this: brief moments of pleasure, a coin dropped in a box, a burst of sumptuous light, then on to the next shadowy room, the beauty of which she might glimpse but never enter.

Finished with the church, Mary Placid took them to see the Column of Marcus Aurelius; then back to the Pantheon via the Temple of Hadrian; then on to Piazza Navona. Although they didn't know it, the girls were being trooped through their teacher's most intimate self, the one she occupied while drifting on the edge of sleep. But they were tired, and they grumbled when Mary Placid told them that they couldn't rest yet, and that they all (including, or perhaps especially, Charlotte Gibson) should have worn trainers as comfortable as her own.

And still, nothing went wrong. She took them to Chiesa del Gesù, where they attended mass by special arrangement in a private chapel, and Mary Placid tried to interest an indifferent Monica Alvares in the sacred arm of St Francis Xavier by explaining that the rest of him was entombed in Goa, where Monica's family was from. Then an early supper, eaten beneath the umbrellas of an empty pizzeria while its bemused staff were still laying its tables in readiness for the later crowds; then back to the *pensione*, where Davide was finally in residence behind the check-in desk, handsome, wholesome, short and stocky in a well-made shirt, speaking extravagant Italian with Mary Placid, making gestures of absurd chivalry to the girls, and managing, in a period of approximately four minutes—during which Mary Placid was reminding her charges of the rules, the most important of which was *do not under any circumstances leave the hotel*— to invite Charlotte Gibson for a drink, before sending them all off to their rooms with cries of *buona notte! buona notte!*, insisting that each girl—including Charlotte—repeat the words until he was satisfied with their pronunciation.

And that was their first day in Rome. No one had got lost, been robbed or injured, cried, or thrown up; the November weather was mild; and Mary Placid, safe in her room, prayed— *tower of David, tower of ivory*—in thanks and relief. She pushed her comfy trainers off her feet, stretched her toes, and closed her shutters on the city.

In the girls' dormitory, Tess Gibson reached immediately for her Discman and curled up on her bed, a Roman tadpole. She ignored the whisperings of the other girls, whose plans and schemes were of no interest to her. Among them, it was Grace who objected most to being shut up in a poky hotel when the city was on the verge of waking up; she imagined its streets full of beautiful men and women, as if the loveliest saints had stepped down from their niches and paintings in order to smoke in bars or go to the cinema. If Tess had shown any inclination to explore, Grace might have planned an escape for just the two of them. As it was, she turned to the other girls with her suggestion of sneaking out of the hotel, and the foolproof plan she'd devised for getting them all past the front desk. Of course, only Bridget Thomas had the power to convince all hushed, skittish eight of them into the streets, which she did by saying, 'Yeah, I guess.'

In her room, Charlotte Gibson changed into a burgundy blouse with the slightest shimmer running through its threads, fluffed her hair, applied a deep plum lipstick, and lifted her face into the fine, ripe mist of her new perfume. While waiting until it was time to go downstairs and meet Davide at the bar on the corner, she examined herself in the mirror: slim, stylish, attractive. None of it had been enough. Every half-hour or so, from somewhere in the city, came a volley of fireworks.

Sister Mary Placid couldn't sleep. So she did what she would have done had she been in England: still in her bed, she went out into the streets of Rome to walk between Piazza Navona and Piazza Colonna. Just as the girls were leaving the hotel, she was on via dei Sediari, a short street containing hotels and a workshop that made wicker baskets. Mary Placid's night-time routine usually included a pause in order to look at these baskets, and she often placed a woman in a chair in front of the shop—a wicker chair, of course—working at the cane. Weaving, weaving the cane. The motion was soothing. Mary Placid inspected the baskets as she walked one way, towards the Pantheon and on to Piazza Colonna, and she inspected them as she walked back the other way, towards Piazza Navona. Back and forth she went—for hours, it seemed, but it may only have been minutes—until finally sleep came to her.

Tess Gibson had fallen asleep almost immediately after the other girls had left, but that wasn't surprising: the passage from music into sleep into dream wasn't difficult for Tess, and didn't always happen in that exact order. She was so inclined to sleep that her father often called her Dozy Daisy. Her father was in love with a woman called Delia, whom Tess had met when she'd done her week of fourth-form work experience at her father's office in the City; who'd seemed severe in her business suit; who'd opened a drawer in her office to show Tess a framed photo of her dog; who looked older than Tess's mother, and not as pretty. Tess had existed, since learning about her father's love for Delia, in a walking dream of disbelief. The music came from and spoke to her heartsickness, but also promised to obliterate it. Even now, the music was part of her sleep, and she clutched the Discman, where the CD spun on repeat, close to her chest.

The bar on the corner was only small, and most of its patrons had spilled into the street. Charlotte sipped at her Campari as Davide talked with people he knew—and he seemed to know everyone. She smiled when gestured towards, and one of his friends looked at her and said, 'American teeth!'

'English, English,' Davide insisted and, putting his arm around her waist, ushered her away from the bar. 'We will go to some other place, somewhere more peaceful. It's better, no? And we must eat.'

He took her to a trattoria a few minutes' walk away, hurrying her along as if they had an appointment, while still seeming to show her off to every man they passed as if her looks were an achievement to which Davide laid no claim, but in which he took expansive pleasure. When he said her name, he pronounced the final 'e', ordinarily silent, as if it deserved its own special caress. His hand was hot on her waist.

At the trattoria, he ordered all their food: white beans in clay pots, plates of peppery spaghetti, flaky fish and potatoes and piles of wilted greens. Charlotte ate as if she hadn't already had dinner, and Davide was courteous and charming, holding her gaze, making sure their hands touched, talking about the hotel business, talking about Sister Mary Placid—'a good woman, but she always looks very tired'—and telling funny stories about a building he'd had an apartment in once, not far from the Vatican, which was ruled over by a bossy *portiere* and her half-feral cat. The *portiere* would assess the girls he brought home, shaking her head as he squeezed behind them into the building's minuscule lift.

All the while, he continued to make his gallant ventures into Charlotte's personal space, and she continued to allow them. She flushed as he smiled at her above a bowl of tiramisu, watching as she spooned the cream. She'd forgotten this feeling, this shared joke, when everything a couple said and did was permeated by the mutual knowledge that they were going to leave a place and sleep together. She and Davide seemed to float on a cloud of exquisite delay and silly, sexy understanding. If only her husband could see her now. The gingery scent of her new perfume drifted out, occasionally, from her wrists and neck.

After dinner, sipping glasses of limoncello poured from a bottle that had appeared at their table and been whisked away again, they were joined by a much younger man, barely twenty, introduced to Charlotte as Davide's nephew. They did look alike: the same squarish build, the same distinct top lip that seemed to vanish at the Cupid's bow, combed hair curling beneath their ears, slimming cut of shirt. The nephew spoke as if they'd been expecting him, apologised for his lateness, said there'd been an accident further along the street, a girl hit by a taxi, how badly he didn't know, and the street was jammed with onlookers, all of whom had advice to give, or were arguing with the taxi driver, or turning to each other to shake their heads and say, '*Poverina! Poverina!*'

But he was here now, and his name was also Davide, he held Charlotte's chair out for her when she went to sit down again, he called for the waiter to bring back the bottle of limoncello, and Charlotte saw that his similarity to his uncle was an act of homage: that young Davide wanted to be like old Davide in all things and all ways, and that old Davide was willing to teach him. Both Davides made the same gestures, told stories of the same length, held the same amount of eye contact; they weren't competing for her, she was understood to belong to old Davide, but she was nevertheless an opportunity for young Davide to hone his technique under the proud eye of his mentor. He ordered coffee and took charge of Charlotte's, offering sugar, asking if she enjoyed Italian coffee. She didn't like coffee at all, but she didn't say so; she drank her mouthful unsweetened, black and bitter, and felt it float on top of and then sink into the Campari and wine and limoncello. In a feverish moment, she imagined introducing young Davide to Tess; imagined a twinned sunlit future in Rome for herself and her daughter, each with their Davide.

The other girls were annoying Grace, alternating between simpering timidity and spurts of bravado that managed to be both coy and reckless; she wanted to shake them off. They behaved in the streets as if the whole dangerous gaze of Rome was on them, watching, disapproving, desiring, and they were all ready to be pursued by the judgement of God, or the disappointment of Sister Mary Placid, or the groups of glistening young men they encountered in every piazza. Eventually, they met a band of American college boys on a bridge, who flirted and bought them alcohol. By some inscrutable mechanism, each girl paired off with a boy; each couple strayed a short way from the next, sitting together on the low wall that ran along the side of the Tiber. Grace kissed her boy, as she was expected to, and felt an attentive pleasure at his breath on her face, at his bony body against hers, at the sweet grin he gave her when their glasses knocked together. But she was conscious at all times of the green flow of the river below her, of the lit domes above, of every bar and restaurant like an illuminated chapel waiting for her worship, and was ready to pull away even before Amanda Norton turned from the thick tongue of her partner and threw up on the pavement.

That brought an end to things for all of them, at Grace's insistence, even though Bridget Thomas was reluctant to be parted from her American.

'Amanda can't stop puking,' Grace argued. 'We have to take her back.'

'You take her,' Bridget said, but gave in when she realised Grace was the only one who knew the way to the hotel. And that was that: their Roman adventure was over, at least for tonight.

Grace took them as far as the corner of the hotel's street, then pointed at its doorway, which was lit by a pendulant orange lamp.

'What about you?' asked Amy Diouf.

'I'll come soon,' Grace said. She couldn't go inside yet. She wouldn't.

The girls looked at her and at each other and finally at Bridget, who lifted one shoulder in a shrug and walked towards the hotel. The others followed, except Monica Alvares and Laura Barr, whose faces were pleated with worry.

'What are you going to do?' asked Laura.

'You'll be careful, won't you?' asked Monica.

Grace gave them both the calm, condescending smile with which she saw teachers like Mary Placid reassure their most anxious students. Then she turned away, and was alone in Rome.

Old Davide was by Charlotte's side as they left the trattoria, his arm around her waist, and young Davide hung back, as if preparing to dematerialise. Charlotte felt the thrill of what came next. They stepped into the street and Davide turned her in one direction with a guiding hand, but she looked back, over her shoulder, and saw that there was something of a crowd the other way, presumably still gathered because of the girl who'd been hit by the taxi. It occurred to her, then, that she had a girl of her own, and was responsible for eight others, all of whom should be asleep in the hotel—what time was it, anyway?—but who were, still, girls who might have been hit by taxis.

'Just a minute,' she said, and stopped, looking briefly in her handbag at her pager, to see if anyone had summoned her. They hadn't. Still, she had to check, so she took Davide's hand and pulled him towards the crowd. He allowed himself to be pulled, but she saw a look pass between the Davides: surprise from the younger, along with alarm at the lesson gone awry; a stern, teacherly glare from the elder, accompanied by a quick shake of the head, all of which morphed into an expression of resigned good humour, so that her Davide became a man reconciled to being henpecked and adorable. *There is nothing*, his face seemed to say, *I would not do for a fuck*, but there was still, somehow, a kind of dignity in it, something happy and adaptable, as if he were a child who has just understood how to manipulate his mother into buying him a chocolate bar.

Young Davide mimicked his uncle, for a moment, in a submissive strut. Then he broke into a grin and cried, '*Ciao!* I have to go! I have an appointment! A pleasure to meet you, Charlotta! *Buona notte! Ciao!*' By the time Charlotte and old Davide reached the edge of the crowd, the nephew was gone.

Tess Gibson woke when the girls returned from their excursion. They came into the room in a huddle, as if they'd all passed through the door at exactly the same time; they turned on lamps and spoke in agitated whispers. Tess pulled the headphones from her ears. The first thing she saw was Amanda Norton looking queasy in a chair, attended to by Rosie Delahunt. Then she saw Monica Alvares and Laura Barr leaning out of the window, as if waiting for someone.

When Tess sat up in bed, Monica turned to her and said, 'Grace stayed out on her own. She wouldn't come back with us.' There was nothing gleeful about her obvious dismay, but it did fizz with a sort of excitement.

'What time is it?' Tess asked.

'Nearly one,' Laura said, tugging at the St Christopher medal she wore around her neck.

Monica nodded.

Tess looked to Bridget Thomas and said, 'You should have made her come.'

Bridget shrugged and climbed into bed, leaving Jenny Jessop to say, 'It was all Grace's idea, anyway.'

Now Tess forced herself to swim out of the glassy sea she had waded in since finding out about the divorce. It took some effort. Her first thought was that Grace was brave and independent; if anyone could be out in Rome by herself and almost certainly be fine, it was Grace. For Tess to raise the alarm, to tell her mother or Sister Mary Placid, would constitute a betrayal. It would be easy enough for her to take her headphones and nestle them into the tight drum of each ear, to lie down and press play and float back into the dream, where, surrounded by the music—the low drums and the layered guitar—she would feel at once both still and rushing, like a tide on the very point of turning. She hoped to reach, in this way, the condition of zero, in which her body and soul cancelled one another out and finally, finally silenced her heart; she'd not reached zero yet, never for more than a fraction of a second, but the promise was there, beyond everything. The music tugged at her, and the anonymous warmth of the bed. There would be loyalty in doing nothing.

But there was also the thought that something terrible might happen to Grace, who Tess admired and was a little intimidated by. Grace had a tendency to taunt disaster, as if she wanted its attention precisely because she was afraid she'd never be noteworthy enough to get it. In English class, when they'd studied the scene in which Lear calls down the storm on the heath—'Blow, winds, and crack your cheeks'—and everyone had laughed and accused each other of farting in Shakespearean language, Tess had thought of Grace, who seemed sometimes to scoff at the world's weather. But then, Grace had lived a life of safety: her parents were still together.

Which led to the thought that if something terrible did happen, Tess's mother might be held responsible; her mother for whom she felt such pity that she could barely look at her and so held herself at a distance, as if that might protect them both. Tess hadn't told anyone at school about the divorce, not even Grace. She swung her legs out from under the blankets and stood up, her feet cold on the tiled floors.

'Where are you going?' Amy Diouf asked from the next-door bed.

Tess's hand was on the doorknob.

'Are you going to Mummy?' Jenny asked in a childish sing-song. 'Are you going to *tell*?'

The girls all looked at Tess: Monica and Laura hopeful at the window; Amy, Jenny, and Bridget wary, already in bed; and even Amanda Norton and Rosie Delahunt, who now sat together on the chair, embracing, locked in a crisis of their own and still unsure of what stance to take on Grace.

'I'm going to the loo,' Tess said, and didn't wait to see whether or not they believed her.

Grace out alone at night was in love with Rome. She was immersed in the city but invisible to it, aware that no one who knew where she was cared, and no one who cared where she was knew. She only wanted to walk through the streets, some of which were full of traffic and people, the traffic nudging at the people and vice versa; other streets were empty, and lit by yellow lamps. It didn't really matter. It was all immense and radiant. Grace walked everywhere with a sense of things just out of sight: vast gardens, rats, lovers, sleeping priests, satellite televisions, water rushing through subterranean passages. She didn't need to see these things because she knew now that, one day, she would. She'd make sure of it. Walking through Rome, she felt a dazzling strength, a powerful upsurge of possibility. She'd been afraid of stasis, boredom, a life of humiliating diminishments; here in Rome she saw that this was, at least in part, within her control, and there came a flowering of hope and effort. She made plans: to take a gap year of her own, to work for six months in a pub or a shop and save every penny, then spend six months travelling, no matter what her parents said. Bangkok, Phnom Penh, Jakarta, Sydney. Unlike

Bridget Thomas, she didn't need her daddy to pay for her trip to Australia—she'd get there without anyone's help.

Grace found herself in a quiet neighbourhood and wanted to be back among the crowds, so she walked until she came to the river and followed it to the bridge on which they'd met the Americans. They were gone, but other boys stood there now, in clusters and pairs. Some of them looked with interest at Grace, and she looked back, but without heat; she felt, walking across the bridge, that boys like the one she'd kissed an hour ago were insignificant. She felt, as she neared the hotel, that there was something else waiting in the world for her, some man or woman she would find beautiful and exciting, and she would pour herself into the work of loving them, just as she planned to pour herself into the world.

So she was smiling as she stepped out in front of the taxi, and still smiling when a man behind her took her by the arm and pulled her back out of the taxi's path. She hadn't seen the taxi, but she saw it now, braking hard, and she saw the girl collide with the side of it, caught in the act of running across the road by the taxi's unanticipated stop. The girl fell backwards with a startled look on her face, and Grace was reminded, for a moment, of her mother's expression when she answered the call telling her that her father had died back in Hong Kong: an astonishment that looked almost like rapture, until something collapsed inside of it.

The girl sat on the ground, young and pretty, wearing a glittering miniskirt, and was surrounded at once by a crowd. The driver emerged from the taxi, people began shouting, the girl was helped to her feet. The man who'd pulled Grace from the taxi continued to pull her, although not insistently, until she was far enough towards the edge of the crowd that no one would suspect her of having been involved. She heard him say, 'Be careful, miss.' Then he disappeared; she never even saw what he looked like.

Grace climbed onto a low wall in order to get a better view. Her heart leaped in her chest, she felt fire along the surface of her skin, her breath was flimsy in the back of her nose. She saw the girl, an Italian girl, surrounded by friends who were both laughing and crying. The street had erupted with objections, eyewitness accounts, and sympathy. Grace heard women to her left saying, '*Poverina, poverina!*' Another woman spoke in Italian to her date and Grace, somehow, understood her to have said, 'He wasn't looking!' The date disagreed: 'She wasn't looking!' The dispute was genial, as if both parties were pleased to have come to different conclusions.

Grace stayed and watched until it was clear that the girl in the miniskirt was all right. Even then, Grace stayed, along with much of the crowd. It was as if the accident had created an energy to which they were irresistibly drawn. The driver wanted to leave, but the crowd wouldn't move out of the taxi's way; then the *carabinieri* arrived. Grace's heart and breathing calmed. She felt, now, an odd detachment from the scene for which she'd been the catalyst. Having recovered from the shock, she saw almost clinically how she might have handled it better. She also saw the version of Rome in which the girl had been seriously hurt; and she saw the Rome in which the man hadn't pulled her by the arm, in which she'd been hit and thrown by the taxi. She saw herself die, and she saw Sister Mary Placid preparing to make the phone call to her parents. She saw her mother's face, her mouth wide against the receiver. She saw the women saying, '*Poverina, poverina!*' and the man saying, '*She* wasn't looking.' And she saw Tess's mum—saw her really, standing in a sparkling blouse on this street in this Rome, the real one in which nothing truly awful had actually happened.

Mrs Gibson was drunk. That was clear to Grace immediately, although she couldn't have said why: maybe just that there was something exaggerated about the way Mrs Gibson stood on her tiptoes, leaning against the solid shoulder of a man as she tried to see what was going on. Grace was embarrassed for herself, for Tess, and for Tess's mother. Then she recognised the man: he was the owner of the hotel, and he was talking to people in the crowd, then talking to Mrs Gibson with soothing gestures. He put a hand on either side of her waist and tugged until her heels, presumably, touched the ground. Mrs Gibson appeared confused and worried. She lifted one hand and adjusted her hair, blonde and cut like Princess Diana's. The hotel man was growing impatient, Grace saw, but he was concealing this impatience by nodding and smiling, until finally Mrs Gibson seemed reassured. Then she stepped away from him and looked for something in her handbag. He allowed this with good humour, but soon drew her back to his side with a hand on her waist.

Grace didn't really know Mrs Gibson. She had never been to Tess's house; accepting an invitation would have meant having to reciprocate, which would be impossible. But Grace knew that Mrs Gibson was married, that she was Tess's mother, that she had never met this man before today, and that she was nice. She was trusting. She was perhaps too old and nice to understand that she might be in danger. His arm was around her shoulder now, as if she were a naughty child, and he began to steer her away from the crowd and down the street, in the direction of the hotel.

Grace remained calm. She wasn't afraid. She stepped down from the wall and followed them.

Tess, in the hallway of the hotel, half-hoped to encounter her mother, or Sister Mary Placid; but the hallway was empty, and she found herself running the few steps to her mother's room as if she were still a little girl frightened by nightmares, hurrying to her parents' bed but stopping in front of their bedroom door, hesitant, careful, turning the knob as slowly as possible, pushing at the door in silent increments, proceeding with the knowledge that the slightest noise would wake them, when waking them was exactly her goal. Once in the room, Tess had always been daunted by their sleeping forms: how unguarded they looked, somehow younger than during the day, and caught up in a complicated togetherness from which Tess was excluded. Then she would startle them out of sleep by hovering above them, crying in her white nightgown like the ghost of a Victorian girl, and her mother would say, 'Oh, Theresa,' and her father would chuckle blearily; he would turn over and go back to sleep, and her mother would take Tess to her room, say Hail Marys, hum to her, stroke her hair, sometimes with lulling patience, sometimes as if she were paying by the minute, and Tess vowed to herself each time that she would never wake her mother again, would never intrude on her privacy, no matter how gruesome the nightmare.

Here in Rome she opened her mother's door without hesitation. It didn't occur to her that her mother could have any privacy from Tess that wasn't also shared with Tess's father, and her father wasn't here; was, no doubt, in some vague location with vague Delia, which was why her mother was on this trip in the first place.

So when Tess stepped into the room, which was lit from the window by the orange lamp above the hotel door, and found it empty—no Mum sleeping, or cleaning off her make-up, or reading magazines in bed—she was shocked, and frightened, and felt a powerful homesickness, and could do nothing, for a moment, but stand in the shadowy middle of the room, breathing in a heavy, unfamiliar scent.

Grace followed, but at a distance; she let Mrs Gibson and the hotel man turn corners well before she did. She heard the man make a joke, and she heard Mrs Gibson laughing, but her laughter verged on delirious. Rosie Delahunt had laughed in a similar way when she saw that Amanda Norton had been sick: her laugh had been ready to flee, to scream, it had been scandalised and disbelieving and broken-hearted all at once.

Then Mrs Gibson and the hotel man both fell silent, and Grace came around a corner to see that Tess's mother had stopped and was looking in her handbag again, presumably searching for whatever she'd been trying to find earlier, when the man had interrupted her by drawing her to him by the waist. And look, he was stopping her again, with more overt impatience now, with clear intent: he stood directly in front of her and took the bag, it dangled from his hand like an abandoned kite, and he began to move forward, slowly, so that Mrs Gibson had no choice but to back away from him. He glared at Mrs Gibson, and she looked at him with unsmiling attention, as if she now had some sense of the trouble she was in, but was dazed by it, was hypnotised, and had no choice but to go where he led her, to walk backwards towards a darkened alcove. Her Princess Di hair quivered around the hotel man's head like a halo. Then they were in the alcove; the man dropped the handbag, took Mrs Gibson's wrists, and pressed her back into the deeper dark, so that they both disappeared.

Grace felt a clear, lucid fury that carried her over to the alcove and pulled at the hotel man's arm like he'd just stepped in front of a taxi.

'Get off her,' Grace cried. 'Get off.' Her voice was loud, with a growl in it.

A shriek from Mrs Gibson, a shout from the man; he went to defend himself, to push Grace away, speaking loudly, incredulously, in rapid Italian; then he seemed to recognise her, and he stepped back with his arms raised in surrender, saying, '*Va bene! Va bene!*' He stepped warily into the street, adjusted his belt, and looked for a moment towards Mrs Gibson, who was still hidden in the darkness of the alcove. Then he turned on the heels of his lustrous shoes and walked purposefully away in the direction of the hotel, as if followed by fiends he was pretending not to fear.

Grace shouted after him. 'That's right,' she called. 'Piss off, prick! Keep your creepy hands to yourself!'

She felt righteous, triumphant, as if she could march through the Forum at the head of an army, as if she could slay ten lions in the Colosseum. She turned to Tess's mother.

'Grace,' said Mrs Gibson. She sounded fragile and bewildered.

Grace reached into the alcove, found an elbow, and pulled Mrs Gibson into the light. She saw that Tess's mother was really quite good-looking, with her blouse crinkled and the dark lipstick blurred against her mouth. She seemed not to understand what had just happened to her; to be holding herself very still, as if it might be possible to return, via stillness, to the moment from which she'd just been rescued.

Grace bent to pick up the handbag, which had a pleasing weight, as mothers' handbags do: even compact ones like this, made of patent leather. She handed the bag to Mrs Gibson, who responded as if she'd been given a parcel of excruciating delicacy. There was something like dismay on her face. She turned the handbag over slowly in her hands.

Sister Mary Placid was jolted out of sleep a moment before she heard the pounding on her door, as if a bell had rung in warning from the highest point of some walled city. For that moment, she lay in her bed with the dark beating at her face. Then she heard the pounding, got up, put on her robe, and went to the door. She expected Laura Barr, hysterical with homesickness, or Bridget Thomas with a set of demands, but not Tess Gibson with a very red face, stammering, shaking, claiming that both her mother and Grace Reed were missing. The news felt, to Mary Placid, both entirely unforeseen and almost prophesied; she'd been leading these trips to Rome for years, and now she'd finally come upon her disaster. She was self-possessed in the face of inevitable surprise.

She held Tess by the shoulders and said, 'Wait for me at the top of the stairs. I'll be right out.'

Tess went. Mary Placid prayed as she dressed—*Virgin most powerful, Virgin most merciful*—and although she took no more than two minutes, the time felt long to her. She was worried about Grace, of course, and to a lesser extent about Charlotte Gibson, and was running through possible scenarios in her head about where they might be and what might be required of her. But she also couldn't help thinking that this situation, whatever its outcome, would probably be the end of her trips to Rome, which had always raised eyebrows. And that wasn't all: she also perceived a shift, a slowing, a turn in the direction of older age, of retirement from teaching, of silence. It was slight, but palpable. She tugged at the laces of her white trainers.

When she went into the corridor and hurried to the top of the stairs, she expected to see all the girls, frightened by the sounds of knocking and the news of Grace's disappearance. But there was only Tess Gibson, her back to Mary Placid, standing at the window that looked down over the front door of the *pensione*. Tess's body was rigid, her arms hidden from Mary Placid's sight. She was gazing at the street, where the light of an orange lamp made it look as if she must be holding a flame in her hands—a vestal fire. Mary Placid felt some part of herself leap out to Tess, as if they belonged to the same vigilant sisterhood, born to keep watch in the dark. She joined Tess at the window.

Looking out, she saw Grace Reed and Mrs Gibson walking down the street towards the hotel very slowly, almost dreamily, as if they were reluctant to return. Or, Mary Placid saw, it was Mrs Gibson who was reluctant to return, who seemed to stay as far as she could from Grace while still allowing the girl to hold a guiding hand to her elbow. Grace, the streetlamps flashing in her glasses, was leading Charlotte Gibson home.

For a moment, Mary Placid felt some hope that all of this might still be fixable, that there might be some way to keep the secrets of the night among themselves: herself, Tess, Grace, and Charlotte Gibson. But then she saw, even from a distance, that Charlotte was in some disarray and was walking with the tense deliberation of the very tipsy, and that she was allowing Grace's guidance, although it horrified her, because she thought it might disguise her shame. And then, as they drew closer still, Mary Placid saw sullen grief on Charlotte Gibson's face, as well as deep embarrassment and a weary, almost noble acquiescence; on Grace's face, she saw the easy scorn of the very young, who can't yet imagine the ways in which the world will bend them. Both Grace and Charlotte felt, Mary Placid could see, responsible for the other, and resented it. But Charlotte, being a grown-up, was concealing her resentment by an act of submission: allowing Grace to hold her by the elbow.

When Grace and Charlotte reached the door of the hotel, they looked up with eerie synchronicity to where Tess and Mary Placid stood at the window, looking down. Mary Placid heard Tess make a slight, childish sound when she saw her mother's startled face bathed in orange light, and the nun couldn't help but watch it, too: the ways in which it mourned and hoped, the plea that sprang from it, the privacy and love. It came unbidden: *Mother most amiable, Mother most admirable.* Tess stared down at her mother, who stared back up. The window, in the lamplight, seemed to melt. And mother and daughter might have stood there forever, transfixed, except that Grace made a sudden, peevish movement: she scowled, took Mrs Gibson more firmly by the arm, and dragged her inside, through the door.

It was the decisive audacity of this gesture—the scowl, the grasping of the arm, the pull—that Sister Mary Placid found herself remembering eighteen months later, when she learned that Grace Reed had been attacked while backpacking in Australia, and that she had escaped being dragged into the man's car by scratching and kicking at him. When, some years after that, Grace flew back to Sydney to be the key witness in the trial against her attacker, Sister Mary Placid had already retired from teaching and disappeared into the convent. She turned out to be more suited to the cloister than she'd expected. From within the convent, she could still hear the noises of the school—the whistles of the netball umpires, the hymns from chapel, the bells and shouts—but they felt distant to her, as if they belonged to events that had taken place years ago; the sounds were only now reaching her, belatedly, like the light of stars.

She spent her days in prayer—*gate of heaven, morning star*—but at night, if she found it hard to fall asleep, she still walked between Piazza Navona and Piazza Colonna, back and forth, under a November moon. She looked in at the fountain of the four rivers, the curtain of ivy hanging in via di Sant'Eustachio, the play centurions on Piazza del Popolo, the real guards with their machine guns outside the Parlamento, and the high marble spiral of the column of Marcus Aurelius, with its bronze St Paul on top. Back and forth in the night. And she stopped, when she remembered to, in via dei Sediari, where the patient woman sat in her wicker chair, weaving, weaving, weaving the cane.

FAT SUIT

(2024)

When Noah wakes up, Wylie still hasn't leaked the divorce to the press. This is a good thing. Today will be Noah's first day filming in the fat suit. This is a bad thing.

Before she left him, Wylie urged him to accept this role. She said, You need to be taken seriously. She said, You need people to think of you as more than just a comic actor. His agent disagreed. His agent wanted him to get absolutely fucking ripped and cast as a superhero, and warned him that there were certain parts for which he'd never even be considered once he'd played a serial killer. Wylie said, Tell that to Sir Anthony Hopkins.

Noah's worn the fat suit once before, in a costume fitting. He expected to feel uncomfortable, ridiculous, maybe depressed. He didn't expect to feel as if he were being buried inside the body of his dead father. So there's a certain amount of dread today, in the car on the way to unit base.

Once Wylie convinced Noah to take the serial killer role, his agent said, At least the accent will be on point. His last role, as a rom-com lead's goofy wingman, had required a Southern accent. As one critic remarked, both Southerners and Australians do tend to twang, but not in remotely the same way.

His father saying, Speak up. His father saying, Don't mumble.

Noah suspects Wylie pushed him towards the role so that he'd have to spend months filming in Australia. Which would make it easier for her to call him from their house in LA and tell him their marriage was over. Which she did, almost as soon as he arrived in Sydney. That was five weeks ago.

The director has asked Noah to sound even more Australian than he really does for the role.

It's also possible that Wylie thought it would be good for Noah to be in Sydney, where his mother and brother live, when he received the call. It's possible that, when she called to tell him she was leaving, she didn't want him to be alone.

Not long after filming started, working on a short scene in which Noah had to fill a truck with petrol at a service station, the director accused him of walking like he was in a sitcom. The director reminded him of some of the ways they'd talked about inhabiting the mindset of the serial killer. Pretend your wife left you, the director said. Pretend you're unloved.

Once Wylie announces the divorce, people are going to say, as his agent did, Six years is good for Hollywood! They're going to say, as his manager did, At least there are no children! But there are children: Hugo, 11, and Wren, 9. From Wylie's first marriage. He loves those kids.

He'll spend most of the six-part limited series as a young-ish, rangy guy who coaxes hitchhikers into his truck with his disarming intensity. The fat suit only features in the final episode, when the killer's been in jail for decades. The suit provides the padding that's natural to age.

Hugo, 11.

The driver taking him to unit base this morning is called Dave. Dave is Noah's regular driver, and they often talk about what it's like to raise eleven-year-old boys. This is something they have in common. The relevant boys—Dave's son, Noah's stepson—are obsessed with the same obscure British comedian. They could both watch YouTube clips of this comedian for hours. Dave says, Maybe he should raise my kid!

The serial killer Noah's playing is—was—a real man. Noah had heard of him before he took the part, of course. Every Australian has heard of him. Most Americans haven't. Wylie hadn't. Noah tried to explain: This is like playing Ted Bundy. This is like playing Jack the Ripper. Wylie said, Good! A complex, brave, meaty part! He knows she considers Australia, and everything in it, smaller than anything in the US or Europe. Unconsciously, of course. Smaller serial killers, smaller murders, smaller grief.

His father saying, I didn't raise a coward.

Wren, 9.

Wren is obsessed with sea creatures in general, and specifically with whales. Did you know that sperm whales are the world's loudest animals? Noah knows, because Wren told him.

Noah was about Hugo's age when the serial killer was caught, tried, and condemned to twelve consecutive life sentences. The announcement of the killer's guilty verdict was one of the few times in Noah's childhood that he ever heard his father swear. His father sat in front of the television, watching the news, and said, May he rot, the bastard. Noah and his brother looked around for their mother, but she was making dinner. There was no one to reprimand his father or remind Noah and his brother that it was wrong to swear.

Dave swears at the wheel and interrupts his complaints about the British comedian in order to complain about Sydney traffic. This is something Dave has in common with Noah's father, who used to talk about Sydney traffic for hours—angrily, lovingly.

———

His father saying, Do they just hand out licences to anyone these days?

Wylie is currently promoting a movie in which she plays a smart, sexy international art thief who juggles her life of crime with the challenges of being a single mom. She gets all the other school moms—and one gay school dad—involved in a heist. But it's not a conventional heist movie—it's a surprisingly moving dramedy. When Wylie accepted the part, she told Noah that being cast as a mom used to be the kiss of death, but now it's edgy and relatable. She said, We've entered the era of the Sexy Mom.

Wren struggles with Big Feelings. A few months ago, on the advice of her psychologist, she started classifying the strength of her Feelings by whale sizes. The Biggest Feelings are blue whales, then down to right whales, then humpbacks, then minkes, and, finally, belugas. Although belugas are only Small Feelings, they should still be acknowledged.

Arriving at unit base, getting out of the car, saying goodbye to Dave, and walking to his trailer, Noah realizes that if both boys are obsessed—one in Sydney, one in Los Angeles—then the British comedian may not be so obscure after all. He may only be obscure to middle-aged men.

He doesn't mind the other aspects of being aged up for the last episode. He can watch the make-up and prosthetics and wig go on, and he knows they'll come off. But the fat suit feels permanent. He's afraid that, if the wind changes, he'll spend the rest of his life playing the part of his father.

Online, Noah's marriage is often referred to by the compound nickname Nylie. Sometimes Wyloah. Noah's name is actually Shane.

His father saying, What's wrong with the name we gave you?

One of Noah's favourite things about Wren's list is that it measures both Good and Bad Feelings. A blue whale can mean terror, but it can also mean overwhelming joy.

The costume assistant, Holly, has already hung the fat suit in his trailer. Noah is hours from having to touch it; he'll go to make-up first. For now, he sits in his trailer, drinking a cappuccino, trying not to look at the suit.

Noah knows he'll be asked, in interviews, how he prepared himself for the role. He might talk about focusing on the physicality as a way of managing the horror. He might talk about the lift of the chin, the impatient tremor in the right leg, the exact force of the spit into the dirt.

He hasn't had any communication with Hugo or Wren since Wylie ended things. They haven't answered their phones or responded to his emails. He suspects there are only so many times a man can contact his soon-to-be-ex-stepchildren without appearing to stalk them.

He might mention watching the video of a talk given by the killer's one survivor, a woman who now works in victim advocacy. During the talk, she held her arms out in front of her and said, The first time he hit me, he looked at his hands as if he found them funny. This woman is working as a consultant on the limited series. It's been agreed that she and Noah will never meet while he's in costume.

His father saying, Keep your hands to yourself. His father saying, You're too old to hold my hand.

He'll never actually have to say lines while wearing the fat suit. The episode will show him doing ordinary things in his prison greens: eating dinner, reading a letter, struggling to sleep in his cot, having a chest X-ray, watching footage of the World Trade Center collapse. The idea, according to the director, is to show the painful dailiness of the killer's life, and at the same time to contrast it with the lost lives of each of his victims.

Before Noah left LA for Sydney, Wren was working on exercises to help her brain with something called 'crossing the midline'. Her occupational therapist suggested that this, among other things, could provide support for Wren as she coped with Big Feelings. Every morning, Noah, Wylie, and Wren stood by the pool touching their left toes with their right hands, then their right toes with their left hands. As they stretched and touched, they often recited Wren's list of whales.

Noah, in his trailer, looks on his phone for news of himself online. He looks even though his manager has promised to be in touch the minute anything divorce-related surfaces. There's no news. Only photos of him with Wylie, of him with Hugo and Wren, of the four of them together. He puts his phone away.

Blue whale, right whale, humpback, minke, beluga.

He can't help looking at the fat suit. It's made of foam, spandex, and bags of beads that reproduce the drag and sway of age. It looks like the rough draft of a torso. It looks like an art installation, an obscene one, involving dolls. It stops at the knee and elbow: Frankenstein's wetsuit.

Despite the sperm whale's noisiness, Wren didn't include it on her list of Feelings. The word *sperm* made Hugo giggle, which made Wren giggle. They had the same reaction whenever Wylie read her horoscope aloud and referred to Uranus, the planet of surprise.

His father saying, What's so funny?

Wylie has said she doesn't want news of the divorce to hijack press about the art-thief movie, but the movie isn't gaining much traction. Noah knows, Wylie knows, various agents and managers and publicists and producers know, that news of the divorce will drive attention to the film. Which is why he wakes every day expecting Wylie to have leaked it to the press.

He never saw his father naked. His father's decline was sudden, and Noah couldn't get away from LA because he was mid-shoot on season six of his hit sitcom, in which he played the part of a bumbling airline pilot. His brother told him, later, about sponging their father's naked body.

The pouchy breasts of the fat suit are unbearable.

His father rarely referred to the fact that Noah lived in LA. Except to ask about the traffic. His father's glee, hearing about the LA traffic.

Noah is collected from his trailer by a runner whose name is either Paxton or Braxton. As they head towards the make-up truck, he hears news of his movement relayed to the rest of the crew on their walkie-talkies. *Number one to make-up.* The whole two-minute walk is narrated, though not by Paxton, who is showing Noah the vintage Mexican biker ring he bought on eBay. Sometimes, getting out of bed to piss at night, Noah can hear a faint, staticky voice saying, *Number one is ten-one.* The chunky silver ring flashes on Braxton's finger.

His father rarely referred to Noah's acting career. As if it were equivalent to a drug addiction, or joining a cult—too shameful to mention. His mother said, You have to understand, he's proud of you. He just doesn't want anyone to look at him and say, He thinks he's better than we are, because his boy's on TV.

———

When the survivor first learned that Noah had been cast as the killer, she objected. She was worried the audience, used to his airline antics, would find him silly, even endearing. The director reassured her. He said, The audience won't even recognise him. The transformation will be so complete.

The few times his father did refer to Noah's acting career, it was with genial contempt. His father saying, Anyone would think your shit didn't stink.

In the make-up trailer, Diane complains about her next-door neighbour, who recently installed incredibly bright motion-sensitive lights in their carport. The lights shine directly at Diane's bedroom window, and they come on at the slightest of pretexts: possums, the changing shadows produced by a passing car, a gust of wind. Diane, who's hardly slept, is less gentle about putting on Noah's wig than she might be. It tugs and snaps. He watches himself in the mirror, going grey, commiserating with Diane. He sees the way his forehead creases in sympathy. Diane grips it with her powerful fingers and says, Keep still!

The British comedian is surprisingly open about Big Feelings. Not long before leaving LA, Noah sat with Hugo slumped against his shoulder, and they watched the comedian on YouTube. The comedian talked a lot about bodily fluids, but also about grief. He had a bit about needing to take a shit at a funeral, which was funny and filthy until it became touching.

When it finished, Noah closed his eyes and rested his cheek on the top of Hugo's head. His father had been dead for nearly four years.

Wren couldn't decide between two options for the smallest Feeling on her list: belugas or narwhals. Hugo talked her into belugas. Narwhals are too pointy, he argued. Wren said it probably didn't matter, since none of her Feelings were beluga-sized anyway. Hugo said, What about right now, sitting next to me on the couch, wrapped in a blanket? Just sorta nice? Isn't this small enough to be a beluga? Wren thought for a moment. Then she said, No, this is a minke.

Noah did make it home in time to see his father die. He went straight from the airport—where people stopped him to take photos and called him Captain and asked why he wasn't in uniform—to the hospital. Shortly after his arrival, his mother and brother stepped out of the room for a quick trip to the hospital cafe, leaving him alone with his father, and that's when his father died. Noah was deeply embarrassed by the cinematic timing. It's often the way, said the nurses. They wait. He felt as if he'd robbed his mother and brother of a moment they'd earned, but they wouldn't hear of it. His brother said, He was only holding on until you got here. His mother said, We expected this to happen. It's often the way.

It takes two hours for Jay, the make-up artist, to age Noah's face, and Noah finds himself conscious of his breathing. He tries to synchronise it with Jay's, but this leaves him short of breath. Jay competes in triathlons. Jay keeps a very nervous Flemish Giant rabbit as a pet, and sometimes he brings it to work with him. The rabbit spends most of the day sleeping in a large tote bag placed discreetly in a corner of the make-up truck. If things get too loud in the truck, Jay shushes everybody. The rabbit must be present and asleep today, because someone laughs and Jay hisses an immediate, *Shh!* In the chair, Noah watches his nose spread and his crow's feet deepen, and holds his breath.

To think of his mother and brother leaving the hospital room, going to the cafe, expecting it to happen.

His parents didn't come to the wedding. It was small and sudden, and held in a fairly inaccessible part of Costa Rica. Noah flew home to see them not long after, and took Hugo with him. His father taught Hugo how to play chess. Wylie and Wren joined them for a long weekend at the end of the trip. His mother kept saying, All this way for a long weekend! She was scandalised.

Paxton appears in the mirror with another cappuccino, and a straw. He looks at Noah's ripening face, grimaces, grins, and leaves the truck.

The image of those two heads, one young and one old, bending over the chessboard. His father looking at Hugo and saying, That was good thinking. His father saying, You've got a good head on your shoulders.

In the corner of the make-up truck, the tote bag trembles.

During that Sydney trip, they all went to the aquarium. Wylie's PA had called ahead, so they didn't have to wait in the long queue. The queue, however, was where visitors had their photos taken, in groups, to commemorate the day. At the end of the visit, people bought these photos at inflated prices. Since they'd missed the queue, the official aquarium photographer sought out Noah and his family, took their portrait, and gave it to them for free. His father bristled at the special treatment their group received. Noah saw his mother squeeze his father's hand and whisper, Try to enjoy it.

Once, at a party, Noah listened to an actress talk about how hard she'd worked to keep some precious part of her life safe from her children. Afterwards, he expressed his disapproval to Wylie. He thought a parent should give everything to a child. Wylie said, Never say that again. Never even think it. You can only think it because you're rich and not a woman. Noah, objecting, said he'd happily lay his life at Hugo and Wren's feet. Wylie said, No one will ever ask you to.

It was at the Sydney Aquarium that Wren started her love affair with sea creatures.

The runner who comes to take him back to his trailer is called Kai. They're shy, and rarely speak—at least, not to Noah. Noah has been told by others that Kai is a big fan. They majored in media studies and once wrote an essay about the male gaze in Noah's sitcom. Kai never looks directly at Noah's face.

———

After the aquarium, Noah's mother made her famous lamb roast. His father shared his views on immigration at the dinner table. Getting ready for bed that night, Wylie described his father as the salt of the earth. He was a retired insurance claims adjuster. It's just that Wylie's father is the heir to an electronics fortune.

Kai leaves him at the door of his trailer, still not looking at his face. The costume assistant is in the trailer now, and calls him in.

His father saying, At least it was an honest day's work.

It occurs to him that if he and Wylie had made children, those children would be dual citizens: both Australian and American. Hugo and Wren are just American.

The fat suit is still hanging in the trailer.

The death itself wasn't dramatic. His father was already unconscious when Noah arrived from the airport, and he never woke up. Noah sat by the side of the hospital bed and counted the liver spots on his father's hand. The hand was alive; then it wasn't. Noah remembers thinking it looked crooked.

The costume assistant, Holly, sees him looking at the fat suit and says, At least you're not filming with birds today. At least that cockatoo can't crap all over you. The killer kept cockatoos as pets. It's noteworthy, apparently, how many murderers turn out to have kept birds as pets.

Noah didn't hold his father's hand as he died. There was an IV pulling the skin tight at his father's thin wrist, and Noah didn't want to bump it.

Holly has just come off an action movie set in ancient Egypt. She was attached to second unit, working with a troop of stunt horsemen who travel the world appearing in TV shows and movies in which men need to ride horses and shoot arrows at the same time. The stunt horsemen, who are the best in the world at riding horses and shooting arrows at the same time, are all Mongolian, with one Argentinian exception.

When Holly suggests to Noah that he use the toilet in his trailer before getting into the fat suit, he's reminded of the comedian's bit about needing to shit at a funeral. Holly gives him gloves to wear over his hands, which have also been aged with make-up.

Wren loves killer whales but wouldn't allow them on her list of Feelings, because they're not actually whales. They're dolphins. Hugo said, Same difference. Wren laid her head on the table, exhausted. Wren said, I'm sick of your bullshit.

He uses the toilet. Afterwards, when he peels the gloves off his hands, he's surprised by how old they look. How fleshy and tired. He tilts them to take in different angles. He looks at them as if he finds them funny.

Wylie saying, I'm sick of your bullshit.

———

As she removes the fat suit from its hanger, Holly talks about the affair she had with one of the Mongolian horsemen. She doesn't know how to pronounce his name. Like the rest of the crew, she called him Bobby at his request. He's known all over the world as Bobby. The sounds 'bo' and 'ee' are both more or less present in his actual name.

Noah liked watching Hugo watch the comedian. Hugo had seen the clips so many times he often mouthed the punchlines, then fell back laughing as if he'd cracked himself up. Noah watched Hugo experience a joy that seemed both casual and true. Maybe that Feeling could be classified as a killer whale.

Wylie saying, You're not as funny as you think you are.

Holly tells him about an incident on the set of the Egyptian movie. They were filming outside, and Bobby spotted a cockatoo pecking at the grass beneath a tree. In full costume, Bobby crept up on the cockatoo with such stealth that he managed to pluck a long white feather from its tail.

Noah wonders if his father would have commented on this serial killer role. It might have made his father feel as if he could finally admit to having a famous son. No one could accuse him of being proud if he saw a murderer on screen and said, Look, that's my boy.

Noah strips, preparing to step into the fat suit. He thinks of the hatred on his father's face as he sat in front of the nightly news, hearing the guilty verdict. His father saying, May he rot, the bastard. Then his father standing up and turning off the television, saying, What a coward. Noah and his brother were still open-mouthed at the fact that they'd heard their father swear. They looked at each other with wide eyes, trying not to giggle. They didn't know yet that *coward* was, to their father, a far greater insult than *bastard*.

His father would have considered it cowardly to sneak up on a bird and take a feather from its tail.

Before she left the room for a quick trip to the hospital cafe, his mother said, Talk to him. He may still be able to hear you.

Wylie saying, Why don't you ever actually hear what I tell you?

He didn't hold his father's hand, but he did touch it. He rested his fingers on his father's fingers.

He steps into the fat suit. Holly holds it at the shoulders and says, Come on, Elvis, wiggle for me. Wiggle your hips. He wiggles his hips, and the fat suit shifts. Holly lets go of the shoulders, and the suit drops. He remembered it as being heavier. He thinks of the fragrant, yielding beanbags Wylie heats up in the microwave and rests on her neck or forehead when she has a headache. Little hot weights.

Wylie saying, I can't take you seriously.

———

He'd like to consult Wren on her taxonomy of Feelings. Blue whale, right whale, humpback, minke, beluga. What he feels right now: is this a humpback or a right whale?

Holly coaxes his different parts into the fat suit. She adjusts his thighs, buttocks, his pecs, the muscles of his upper arms. He's reminded of Wylie putting on a bra—the way she'll lift each breast inside its cup and settle it into place. Holly zips up the back of the fat suit. Noah doesn't look at himself in the mirror.

This Feeling is probably right in the middle of the list of whales. It's probably a humpback.

He's since thought of all the things he might have said to his dying father; all the Big Feelings he might have expressed. What he did was describe, in detail, the traffic between Sydney Airport and the hospital.

Holly asks, How does it feel? Move for me. He tries to touch his left toes with his right hand and his right toes with his left hand. He can do it, more or less. He feels a foreign thickness at his middle.

Maybe he thought his father would be so outraged by the state of Sydney traffic that he would open his eyes, sit up, and live. But his lips paled, his hand was crooked. It's often the way.

Wylie saying, Can't you see I'm exhausted?

———

Newly married, newly a father, saying goodbye to his parents in a private lounge at Sydney Airport. His father shaking Noah's hand, pulling him in to slap at his shoulder blade. The gruff love of Australian men. And, with surprising discretion, passing Noah two folded twenty-dollar notes. His father saying, Buy the kids something nice.

Now Holly dresses him in his prison costume. He's zipped and tucked and snapped, then made to turn. He's straightened and brushed. He doesn't look at himself in the mirror. Holly's walkie-talkie crackles to say the costume designer is on her way to the trailer.

This Feeling may be bigger than a right whale. It may be a right whale and a humpback, swimming together.

Noah's brother found a small version of the aquarium portrait in their father's wallet after he died.

Holly says, Look! She's showing him a long, white cockatoo feather. He doesn't know where she plucked it from. He feels the irrational urge to check his tail.

Wylie saying, I do love you. It's just that this marriage has run its course.

Kai is at the door of the trailer with the news that the designer was on her way but is now going to meet them on set. The walkie-talkie crackles to say the same. Holly tucks the feather into the holster where she keeps her scissors.

On the back of the aquarium portrait, his father had written the children's names and their ages.

Kai is here to take Noah to set. When Noah turns towards them, he sees that they're looking directly at his face. Their forehead is creased in sympathy. He knows what this means, knows instantly, but still checks his phone. He's missed several calls from his manager. The phone vibrates as he holds it—his manager again. He puts the phone away.

Blue whale, now.

Kai holds the door open, still looking directly at his face. In a moment, Noah will have to step through that door and walk among a hundred people who've just found out his marriage has run its course.

Blue whale, blue whale.

Noah turns to the mirror. He sees that he has his father's gut and pouchy breasts, the slope of his shoulders and the slight hump of his back. He has his father.

Blue whale, right whale.

———

He looks at his hands and sees his father's. Imagines them writing on the back of the photo.

Hugo, 11.

Wren, 9.

Blue whale, right whale, humpback, minke, beluga. All of them, swimming together.

Holly watches, waiting for him to move.

Also sperm whale, narwhal, orca.

Kai holds the door, still looking at his face.

His hand in his father's hand. The gruff love. He remembered it as being heavier.

Also horse, dolphin, lamb, rabbit, possum. The cockatoo of surprise.

Hand in hand, Noah and his father step towards the door. Hand in hand, they pass through it.

PODCAST

(2028)

[INTRO MUSIC]

LUKE: [Singsong voice] Hey.

SARA: [Singsong voice] Hey.

LUKE: Hey to all our Little Misses and our Near Misses and what was the other new name?

SARA: Oh yeah, I don't like that one.

LUKE: But what was it?

SARA: Miss Bitches? Bitch Misses?

LUKE: Something like that. Why don't you like it? Are you trying to tell me you're not a bitch?

SARA: [Gasps] How very dare you? [Laughs] No, no, I'm a total bitch.

LUKE: Uh-huh.

SARA: No, it's trying too hard. Don't you think? It's like, hey, we're such bad bitches, listen to our murder-adjacent, comedy-adjacent podcast and we can all be edgy bitches together. Like we're so feminist for being obsessed with true crime . . .

LUKE: We *are*, though.

SARA: . . . and also, I never know with 'bitch'. Like, are we still reclaiming it or are we using it ironically? Am I only ironically a bitch? Why haven't I figured this out by now?

LUKE: I for one am a *sincere* bitch. No irony whatsoever.

SARA: And I love that for you.

LUKE: We should get started, though. I'm maybe in trouble . . .

SARA: Why? Why are you in trouble?

LUKE: Because I am literally in *Hawaii*, on my *honeymoon*, and I get this message from you saying we absolutely *have* to record this week, because there's *huge* news, and we're so special and important that *everyone* wants to hear our take on this *huge news*. And *my husband* is not impressed.

SARA: So you're just in trouble with Nate. Little Misses, I'm rolling my eyes *hard*.

LUKE: I'm *on my honeymoon*. So this better be the hugest news of all time.

SARA: It's pretty huge.

LUKE: I have a half-hour max, otherwise I'm getting a divorce, so let's just get the intro done and get into it.

SARA: Okay, okay. This is Sara.

LUKE: And this is Luke.

BOTH: And you're listening to the *Miss Demeanor* podcast.

SARA: I bring the Demeanor.

LUKE: And I bring the Miss.

SARA: Actually, as of last week, you bring the Mrs. We're going to have to change the name of the podcast to *Mrs Demeanor*.

LUKE: Never! I still identify as a Miss.

SARA: [Laughs] How does Nate feel about that?

LUKE: [Sighs] Nate has a lot of feelings about a lot of things.

SARA: He really does. He's a regular feelings factory. Just pumping out feelings like CO_2.

LUKE: [Sarcastically] Ha ha. Anyway, we can't talk about him while we're recording.

SARA: Oh, right, right, he 'values his privacy'. Otherwise you would *definitely* have made a fortune selling your wedding photos to *Entertainment Weekly*. [As if reading a headline] Moderately successful podcast host marries personal trainer who isn't even on Instagram! Exclusive pics!

LUKE: Maybe not a fortune. At least enough to cover a month's worth of meal kit subscriptions, though. But yes, he—

BOTH: —values his privacy.

SARA: Then he should quit looking like he's always in hiding. He gives off this vibe, like he's an undercover European prince on vacation in Vegas—no one's actually going to recognise him, but he still wears sunglasses inside, and hovers in corners and uses a false name, and he acts so suspicious that people just stare at him anyway.

LUKE: [Laughs] Strangers do get kind of obsessed with Nate.

SARA: Because he's so jacked. It's not natural. It's not! He looks like a bodyguard. It's like he's a prince disguised as his own bodyguard.

LUKE: Halloween costume idea noted! But he's sulking in the next room.

SARA: What, you're in, like, a bungalow? Nice. It looks fancy.

LUKE: I'm so fucking fancy. Seriously, he's given me exactly thirty minutes of our honeymoon to talk to you about murder.

SARA: The pressure!

LUKE: You said it was important, and it better be.

SARA: [Loudly] Have you even *looked at* social media in the last twenty-four hours?

LUKE: Shhh! I'm serious, he's really annoyed about it.

SARA: Why can't he just read a book for thirty minutes? That sounds like a really good time to me.

LUKE: He's not a big reader.

SARA: Doesn't he read a whole lot of queer *Lord of the Rings* fan fiction?

LUKE: Fuck! Sara! I told you that in confidence! He doesn't know I know about that!

SARA: Now everyone knows about that.

LUKE: We can edit it out.

SARA: There's no 'we'. *I* edit this podcast.

LUKE: Anyway, I think it's adorable. It's really wholesome, you know?

SARA: It's porn.

LUKE: Yeah, wholesome porn. He doesn't like being sad, so he only reads the ones where he knows the characters are going to end up together.

SARA: Isn't that kind of heteronormative?

LUKE: How can it be heteronormative if it's two men? Or a man and a dragon, or whatever.

SARA: Either way, I can't believe you married a man who doesn't get it.

LUKE: Doesn't get what? The true crime thing? I can't believe he married *me*. It's not like 'true crime obsessive' is at the top of everyone's dating list.

SARA: It should be.

LUKE: People are all, like, how many dates until I have to tell him I have kids or I voted Republican or whatever? How many dates until *I* have to tell him everything I know about Ted Bundy?

SARA: That doesn't *make* you Ted Bundy. It makes you *less* likely to be Ted Bundy.

LUKE: I know that, you know that, all the Little Misses know that. *He* doesn't know that.

SARA: He still married you.

LUKE: Oh my gosh, can we talk about the wedding? I really want to talk about the wedding. We need to talk about the DJ with the green hair who tried to hit on you.

SARA: Not if you only have a half-hour.

LUKE: All business, as usual.

SARA: It's big business, I promise. It's Biga business.

LUKE: [Disbelieving] No.

SARA: Yes.

LUKE: Big Biga business.

SARA: BBB.

LUKE: How much Biga business can there be? Didn't he die, like, ten years ago?

SARA: Yeah, in 2020. Eight years.

LUKE: Did he die of Covid?

SARA: I don't think so. Do you want to hear this business or not?

LUKE: Sorry, sorry, very much yes to hearing this business. Tell me everything.

SARA: Okay. So for those of you who don't know, we're talking about Paul Biga, the Australian serial killer.

LUKE: Oh, the Little Misses know. Um, Netflix documentary with that one hot detective? Also, *Hunter on the Highway*, revelatory Noah Daley TV show in which he suddenly reveals himself to be capable of acting sinister as fuck?

SARA: Okay, okay. But just in case: Paul Biga was that guy who picked people up off the highway south of Sydney, mostly young travellers. He killed twelve people between 1990 and 1997. He was a total monster, held them up at gunpoint, drove them into the forest, shot them, stabbed them, assault, all the worst stuff. Just the worst. A taxi driver, which I find super creepy—this is the guy who's getting you home on a Saturday night when you're drunk. Though he was always driving his own truck for the murders. *But* they caught him when they pulled him over for speeding in his taxi and found an unlicensed gun, and things unravelled from there.

LUKE: They were looking out for taxi drivers, weren't they? The police? [Pause] Okay, for everyone listening, Sara just nodded, because apparently she still hasn't figured out that podcasts are an audio medium.

SARA: Shush, you. Okay, he was arrested in 1998, died in jail in 2020. If you want more details, I covered the whole case on a big double episode back in 2022, episodes forty-five and forty-six. That was by popular demand—we got so many requests from Aussie Little Misses.

LUKE: That episode was epic. We did that whole riff about his haircut. What did we call it?

SARA: Hamster Overlord.

LUKE: [Laughing] Hamster Overlord. But give me the news. I need the news, I'm dying.

SARA: Okay, so: they found . . . another . . . body.

LUKE: Oh my gosh, oh my gosh. Where?

SARA: Barrow State Forest, where all the others were.

LUKE: I didn't think Australia even had forests.

SARA: What, you think there are no trees in Australia? Or none really close together?

LUKE: No, but they call it 'the bush', don't they?

SARA: Barrow State Bush?

LUKE: It's like they're talking about one single shrub. Like, 'In this state we love this one bush in particular. We must protect The Bush at all costs!'

SARA: How do they choose The Bush?

LUKE: Maybe there's an election.

SARA: Yeah, with a long, drawn-out campaign, and everyone's so jaded about it, they're just like [poor Australian accent] 'It's only about which bush raised the most money, mate.'

LUKE: [copying poor Australian accent] 'It's just a popularity contest these days, mate.'

SARA: Isn't that the definition of an election?

LUKE: But one year there's this dark horse bush, comes out of nowhere, takes the lead, wins in a landslide. Maybe a literal landslide, like it just sails down a hill in a cloud of dust and glory.

SARA: Wins the popular vote in a literal landslide, loses the electoral college.

LUKE: Fucking typical. Poor The Bush.

SARA: Stop saying 'The Bush', it's getting kind of vaginal. And stop distracting me. You're the one with the time limit.

LUKE: Okay, sorry, sorry. I'm here, I'm listening. They found another body.

SARA: [Reading] *A group of orienteers found human remains in Barrow State Forest on Wednesday afternoon.*

LUKE: What are orienteers?

SARA: We don't have time for that.

LUKE: Are they what I think they are? Like Boy Scouts? Grown-up Boy Scouts? Creepy.

SARA: [Reading] *The discovery was made approximately two kilometres—that's about 1.2 miles—from the area of the forest in which the bodies of serial killer Paul Biga's victims were found in 1997.*

LUKE: Why would anyone even *go* there? For *fun*?

SARA: You wouldn't go?

LUKE: I *would*, but not for fun. Maybe I should have suggested it to Nate for our honeymoon.

SARA: I'd definitely go. I don't know why I feel so much kind of ownership of this case.

LUKE: It's because you dated that Australian guy for six months, right before you met Justin.

SARA: Five months.

LUKE: And that makes you an expert on Australia.

SARA: That does make me an expert.

LUKE: Even though you've never been there.

SARA: I've never been there less than *you've* never been there.

LUKE: Exactly.

[Sound of a dog panting into the microphone.]

SARA: Wait, Siegfried is here. How did you get in here? I thought I closed the door.

LUKE: Hi, Siggie! Hi, baby! Siggieface! Has he lost weight?

SARA: He's gained. No, Siggie. Lie down. Good boy. Yeah, he's gained. We think he has sleep apnea. We tried to find him one of those CPAP masks—you know, the ones you sleep in? But they don't make them small enough, so then Justin wanted to make one out of a baby snorkel. Turns out baby snorkels don't exist either.

LUKE: Oh my gosh, can you imagine, a snorkelling baby.

SARA: It seemed like a good idea at the time. [Baby voice] Who's my good sweet boy? Who's my sweet snort-snorer?

LUKE: He's perfect.

SARA: Of course he is. Okay, so I'll summarise. These three orienteering guys are running around in this, like, haunted forest and it starts raining really hard, so they go shelter in this kind of shallow cave.

LUKE: Sounds suspiciously like 'shallow grave'. Also, who goes into random caves? Unless you're in a horror movie. What do you expect to find in there?

SARA: Human remains.

LUKE: Exactly. Fuck, I'm glad I'm not in a horror movie. So fucking exhausting.

SARA: It's not really a cave, though, it's just like part of the hillside got washed away in heavy rain—but there's a chunk of rock left behind. Here, what does the article call it . . . [reads] *a rocky overhang uncovered by recent torrential rains.*

LUKE: That's better. Not a cave. It's still giving horror movie.

SARA: So they're standing there under this rocky overhang thing, and one of them notices something weird-looking in the soil, and he pulls it out, and he's not sure, but he thinks it could be a human femur.

LUKE: Fuck, can you imagine?

SARA: And one of the other guys sees the edge of another piece of bone. They know not to move anything, and they know they have to call the police, but they don't have cell phones.

LUKE: Okay, *that* I don't believe.

SARA: Apparently you don't take cell phones orienteering. It's cheating.

LUKE: So cheat! Who chooses to walk around with a compass like some fucking pirate when satellite positioning technology is a thing?

SARA: I don't know, who still listens to vinyl when digital music is a thing?

LUKE: Hey, don't judge me, I like the aural artefacts. It's like listening to time as well as music.

SARA: Whatever. So they make a note of the cave on their orienteering map and then they have to wait for it to stop raining so hard.

LUKE: Holy shit. They're just waiting there in a cave with human bones in it. In a murder cave.

SARA: Right. Waiting, waiting. Finally, the rain gets lighter and they head out, they're gonna walk out to their cars and call the police. But they *get lost*.

LUKE: [Snorts] World's worst orienteers.

SARA: I know. I feel really bad for them. This wasn't the day they had planned.

LUKE: Maybe it was. Maybe you only go orienteering because you want to find dead bodies.

SARA: Have I already talked on here about the time I met a professional Etruscan tomb raider?

LUKE: Yes.

SARA: I mean, he was Italian, but he raided Etruscan tombs.

LUKE: Yes.

SARA: I've told all my stories. It's depressing. Okay, so these guys are lost, and they come across this little hut.

LUKE: Made of gingerbread?

SARA: It's like a ranger's hut. And there's this electrician guy in there working on some wires or whatever he's doing—

LUKE: Suspicious.

SARA: Why suspicious?

LUKE: An electrician in the middle of a murder forest?

SARA: I don't think the hut's in the middle of anything. It's near the road. Anyway, the electrician has a phone and they use it to call the police. But the police are sceptical, because apparently they get calls from this area all the time, and it's always people thinking they've found another Biga victim. But as far as they know there *are* no other victims—just the twelve he went to jail for.

LUKE: Wait, wait, but what about Blondie?

SARA: Exactly. For those of you who don't know—I mean, you all know, you're Little Misses—Paul Biga had one survivor that we know of, one incredible badass woman called Grace Reed who got away. *She's* not Blondie, though; she's got black hair, she's an eighteen-year-old English backpacker travelling in Australia, she's waiting for a bus in 1996, he stops and offers her a ride, she says no, he tries to get her into his truck . . .

LUKE: And she fucking *fights* him. She scratches at his eyes, which we all know we're supposed to do but it's so hard to, like we have this in-built disgust mechanism that means we won't touch eyes. But she just *went for it*, just full on *gouged*, and with *nails*. I love Grace Reed. They should make an action figure. I'd buy ten.

SARA: No: no murder toys. No murder as entertainment.

LUKE: This isn't a toy. It's a tribute.

SARA: Yeah, yeah. We're going to get strongly worded emails about that. So, when Grace Reed starts to fight, Biga says, 'You're even worse than Blondie.' God, I hate quoting him, it makes me sick to my stomach. I'm not doing it anymore. But we know from what he went on to say that Blondie was female.

LUKE: I just always imagine her as Debbie Harry. I can't help it. But none of Biga's known victims were blonde, right?

SARA: Not until—

LUKE: Oh right, right, there were blondes later: the Swiss couple—or were they German? But they went missing *after* Grace Reed, so he couldn't have been talking about them. Are you telling me they've found Blondie? It's got to be her. Poor Blondie.

SARA: Just wait. So—the local police are used to getting these calls and going to check them out, and it's always just animal bones. No one's really expecting to find anything. First of all, no one's ever been able to connect Biga to any other murders. Also, this whole area was thoroughly searched in 1997, after the first bodies were found. *Also*, if this *is* Blondie, those bones would have to have survived at least thirty-three years without decomposing.

LUKE: When did Grace Reed get away?

SARA: '96.

LUKE: Bones can last that long, right?

SARA: It depends how they're buried, what kind of soil they're buried in. [The sound of a dog's snoring.] Shh, Siggie.

LUKE: So maybe they were buried pretty deep.

SARA: The others weren't. [Pause] What?

[Pause]

LUKE: He's moving. Nate's moving around. Whoa, that was a sigh. Did you hear that? How much longer do we have?

SARA: Twelve minutes–ish.

LUKE: [Loudly] Thirteen more minutes! [Pause] Nothing. Maybe I should just go.

SARA: Just let me talk. He'll be fine. Okay, the police come to the hut, the orienteers lead them to the cave, and they find the incomplete skeleton of a young woman.

LUKE: Oof.

SARA: She was buried in the hillside, but the rain washed her out.

LUKE: That's so . . .

SARA: I know.

LUKE: It's so lonely.

SARA: I know. Let's talk about Blondie for a minute. There are a few possibilities, but only two really good candidates: two different light-haired women of around the right age who went missing in the area before 1996. And there's a specific window, remember, because Biga moved back to the area in 1989, when his wife left him. He moved back in with his dad.

LUKE: I always forget he was married.

SARA: Yeah, but only for a couple years. Creepy. Imagine being her.

LUKE: [Suddenly stricken, low voice] What if Nate turns out to be a serial killer? Maybe that's why he's so private?

SARA: He's not a serial killer.

LUKE: I bet that's what Paul Biga's wife said.

SARA: Nate isn't a serial killer. He listens to NPR.

LUKE: He has a name for his toothbrush.

SARA: He's really polite to chatbots because he doesn't want to hurt their feelings.

LUKE: He turns our mattress every six months.

SARA: *That's* kind of suspicious.

LUKE: What if he listens to this? He won't listen to this. Cut all that out. Love you, baby.

SARA: No more tangents. Stay focused.

LUKE: I'm focused. Blondie.

SARA: Blondie. We have two main candidates. First possibility is Jennifer Rutledge, Jenny Rutledge. She was a twenty-seven-year-old Australian elementary school teacher, last seen broken down by the side of the highway about a hundred miles south of Barrow State Forest in early 1990. A hundred kilometres, sorry. Her body's never been found.

LUKE: Didn't someone confess to that murder?

SARA: Yeah, some complete piece of shit called Mark Macintosh, but he withdrew his confession later. He confessed to other murders he couldn't have committed, too. But he could have killed her—he was in the area.

LUKE: It's like Biga, though. Side of a highway, car broken down.

SARA: Right. The second good candidate for Blondie is Angela Harris. She was twenty-one, English, college student, backpacking around Australia with friends. She was last seen in a campground south of Sydney in December 1989. She went to the toilet block and never came back. Body also never found.

LUKE: So this could be either Jenny Rutledge or Angela Harris.

SARA: It's possible. Apparently it's harder to tell the age of the bones on sight, because they didn't see them in their burial position.

LUKE: I wonder why he buried her deeper than the others?

SARA: If this really is Jennifer or Angela, she's his first victim.

LUKE: First victim? That's huge. So he's more careful with the first one? He gets sloppy later?

SARA: Which is how they catch him.

LUKE: And why they don't find her in '97.

SARA: So they'll date the bones and match dental records and do all that stuff, then maybe we'll know.

LUKE: Imagine being their parents and waiting to hear.

SARA: I don't even know if their parents are still alive. That always kills me, when they solve a cold case but the victim's parents aren't around to see it.

LUKE: She might not even be one of Biga's victims. She might have nothing to do with him at all.

SARA: Well, listen to this. They found something else with her.

LUKE: What?

SARA: A Christmas decoration.

LUKE: [Loudly] What?

[A muffled sound]

LUKE: Okay, so the door to our bungalow just slammed, which is kind of an achievement because it's made of bamboo and a curtain, and right now I can see Nate stomping away to the pool with his goggles on.

SARA: We've been talking for exactly twenty-five minutes. I get five more minutes. He gets the whole rest of your life.

LUKE: Shit. Marriage is hard.

SARA: You're so torn right now. I can see it—you want to know about the Christmas decoration, and you want to go after Nate. Look at you! You're sitting up really straight and peering out the window. You're like Siegfried when he's waiting for Justin to get home. [Dopey voice] Where's my daddy? Where's my big, pretty, incognito daddy? [Dog's happy bark] Good boy, Sig. Go back to sleep.

LUKE: Ah! Tell me about Christmas! And hurry it up! You've got four and a half minutes.

SARA: Okay, so among everything that got washed out by the rain, all the bones and everything, they found this bit of plastic holly, with spiky leaves and red berries, like you'd stick in a fruitcake or something.

LUKE: Okay, that's weird. It's not necessarily connected, though. Right? Maybe there just happened to be some plastic holly lying around?

SARA: Decades-old plastic holly? In the middle of a forest?

LUKE: Wait, I remember the episode when you covered this case. You said a ton of people were leaving flowers in the forest—flowers and messages and balloons, stuff like that. You know, honouring the victims, mourning. Wasn't there so much stuff they had to ask people to stop? So maybe it's not that weird to find old plastic flowers in this particular forest.

SARA: But why holly? Why Christmas flowers?

LUKE: That I don't know.

SARA: Well, listen to this. Jenny Rutledge was last seen on February 25, 1989.

LUKE: Okay . . .

SARA: But Angela Harris disappeared on December 23, 1989.

LUKE: Oh shit.

SARA: She was camping with her friends over the holiday.

LUKE: Camping in December?

SARA: Australia, remember? Christmas is in summer.

LUKE: Which blows my mind. Okay, so it's Angela then. It's got to be. I mean, allegedly. I mean, that's my wildly uninformed and not-legally-binding speculation.

SARA: But why the holly? Did she just have it on her? Did he bury it with her deliberately?

LUKE: He didn't bury them with anything, did he? The other ones? I've got two minutes . . .

SARA: Nope. He took everything, burned most of it, kept some trophies.

LUKE: But she was his first.

SARA: Don't put it like that. Remember, we don't use language that sexualises murder.

LUKE: Right, right, sorry. What I mean is, if this was his first murder and he was taking more care, maybe he wanted to bury something with her. As a kind of token. Like a memorial.

SARA: Like funeral flowers? That's so fucked up.

LUKE: Everything he did was so fucked up.

SARA: We need to know if there were holiday decorations up at the campground. Maybe there was a party and she picked up this bit of plastic holly and stuck it in her hair, or something.

LUKE: Hear that, detectives of Reddit? Do your thing. Listen, I've really got to go.

SARA: Are we on the same page, though? It's probably Angela Harris?

[Pause]

LUKE: [Subdued voice, as if no longer recording] Nate's going to ask if this was worth it.

SARA: What'll you say?

[Pause]

LUKE: What can I say? This is my job. This is my weird job. I don't know—can we justify it to anyone? Edit this out. Let's sign off. [Lively voice] You've been listening to *Miss Demeanor*. Goodnight, and—

SARA: We still need to honour the victim.

LUKE: We don't know who the victim was.

SARA: So you don't think it's Angela?

LUKE: I don't know. It probably is. Does it matter what I think?

SARA: Well, we should honour all of Biga's victims again.

LUKE: Can you do that? I've really got to go. We'll do the sign-off and we can edit it later?

SARA: Okay, okay. [Sarcastically] Happy honeymoon!

LUKE: Fuck you. I mean that in the most loving possible way.

SARA: I love you, too. Hey, congratulations. I mean it. I'm so happy for you. You deserve all the good things.

LUKE: Don't, you'll make me cry. Let's get this done.

SARA: Say your line, then.

LUKE: Okay, good night—

SARA: —and good luck.

BOTH: And be on your best behaviour. Bye!

[The sound of headphone cables knocking against a microphone]

SARA: Okay, Luke's gone. I am so not editing this later. But here on *Miss Demeanor*, we like to name the victims in the cases we're talking about, because we know how in true crime we tend to hear the murderers' names over and over again, and it all becomes about them. We're not interested in glorifying serial killers. So here are the names of the twelve people who died because Paul Biga was a demon from hell.

Patricia O'Connor.

William Herron.

Juliet Herron.

Benoît Dupont.

Victoria Lee.

Lauren Greenaway.

David Sciacci.

Miranda Ford.

Leila Patel.

Daniel Bielefeld.

Sabina Rengel.

And Josephine Teague.

And possibly number thirteen: maybe Angela Harris.

It's a lot of names. Every one of them was a whole world, full of love and curiosity, and every one of these worlds touched hundreds of others. This is our flower laid out for each of you. We don't know what else to do, so we do this.

And to the Little Misses: we love you. I love you, Luke loves you, Siegfried loves you. Even Nate probably loves you. He really loves Luke, I can tell you that. He cried all through the wedding. [Sound of a phone vibrating] [Reading] *All fine*. That's from Luke. Lots of emojis. So love wins again. Love trumps death.

[Pause]

You've been listening to *Miss Demeanor*. Find us on socials at 'littlemissdemeanor', all platforms, 'demeanor' spelled the red-blooded American way: no 'u'. Subscribe to our Substack, check out our merch store, blah blah blah . . . I hate signing off on my own. Okay. Okay, bye. Good night and good luck and be on your best behaviour. Goodnight, goodnight, goodnight . . .

[OUTRO MUSIC]

THE WAKE

(2020)

vy and Joan were woken so early by cockatoos screaming outside their bedroom window that it made sense to rise properly, shower, and prepare for their daily swim. This done, they left their flat, went down their building's three flights of stairs, out of the front door, and into the quaking morning. The cockatoos still wailed in the treetops. Looking up, Ivy found exactly what she'd expected to: a possum, electrocuted, strung at the top of a telegraph pole.

'I knew it!' she said. 'Nothing makes them panic like a dead possum.'

But Joan had already turned towards the sea; her whole sleek body was angled in that downhill direction.

'I'm going for forty laps today,' she said and, swinging her goggles and swimming cap in one hand, nudged the low gate open with her hip and passed into the street. She wore navy shorts with an elastic waistband over her navy swimsuit, and the dark grey of her hair was navy, almost, in this pinkish gentle early light.

Ivy followed her.

Their building was only three streets from the water, three streets typical of a not-quite-fashionable Sydney beachside suburb: red-brick bungalows with terracotta roofs, blocks of Deco and sixties flats bearing fanciful names in white iron-work, stubby frangipanis and bottlebrush trees furred with fine blossom. High-kneed, ponytailed girls ran by in slick leggings. Towards the bottom of the hill, a car rounded the corner, and Ivy was displeased, because this time of day didn't belong to cars. The corner shop wasn't quite open yet; the newspapers had only just been delivered. They would, of course, be full of articles about the new virus, which began in China and had reached Europe and America but hadn't yet arrived here. Perhaps it never would. Ivy waved to the owner of the corner shop, who was lugging the tied bundles of papers inside. A minute more, and she and Joan had reached the water.

This was what it meant to live in a coastal city: just a quick sloping walk from your front doorstep to the whole wide spread of the sea, with the rectangle of the ocean pool alongside it, built into the rocks and with light waves washing in. The morning was calm, no seaweed on the beach, a few surfers, and the tide just turning. Ivy stopped for a moment, overcome, as usual, by an embarrassing exultation. There was such a fine balance to the morning—it was almost dangerous. It would be so easy to fail in the face of this beauty, to abandon some obedient, genial, generous part of herself and become, as a result, a person capable only of standing still and looking at the sea.

Joan would never think this way. Joan was sensible and busy, even in retirement. She'd gone ahead; Ivy could see her already greeting the volunteer at the turnstiles. It was a Wednesday in March, so the volunteer was Margaret, who'd been a biochemist. Margaret's cropped white hair looked as if she were wearing a permanent swimming cap. She knew not to demand payment or identification, because Ivy and Joan had annual passes, were here every morning, were part of the flotilla of middle-aged and older women who years ago had claimed this pool, staffed its gates, watered its potted shrubs, and established its sensible rules. It would be Joan's turn at the gates the following morning, and Ivy's the morning after that.

Ivy hurried over to the turnstiles. Greeting Margaret, she looked down at the pool and saw that someone was already swimming. This irritated her, just as the car had; she liked Joan to be the first in.

Margaret nodded towards the early swimmer. 'It's a man,' she said.

This phenomenon—a man at the pool, midweek, right at opening—was rare enough to be a novelty.

'And,' Margaret continued, raising her tabby eyebrows, 'you'll never guess who.'

'Who?'

Margaret, protective of her mystery, gave a sly smile and shook her head. She had one foot perched on the bar of her stool and the other swinging freely beside it. Her strong legs were clad in green shorts and dotted, like her arms and forehead, with the faint silvery scar tissue of removed carcinomas. Ivy was similarly marked, and so was Joan. This was the price you paid for Sydney: skin cancers that you hoped were minor and went to have frozen off by a dermatologist every few months. The Pride and Aboriginal flags stirred lazily above their heads, ringing faintly at their flagpoles, as Ivy passed through the turnstiles.

Joan, beside the pool now, had dropped her towel on a bench, pulled off her shorts, kicked off her thongs, and was snapping the swimming cap over her hair. Ivy watched her take the deep breath she always did before putting on her goggles, as if they might affect her breathing. A few strides, one of her long, shallow dives, and Joan was in the pool.

Ivy sat on the bench, fussing with her cap and puffing from the walk, intending to put off her ordeal for a few minutes more. Ivy loved the water and she loved Joan, but she hated this regulated swimming, with a cap and goggles, and laps to count. She always chose the lane nearest the sea, the one the serious swimmers shunned, where the water was choppy and the waves sometimes reared up and flew in and drew back out, and no one could swim straight against the suck and force of the sea. In this lane, Ivy could persist with a slow, frog-legged, crawling stroke, head above the water, while Joan shot back and forth. Ivy waved at Hamish, the teenage lifeguard, who was already in position on his aerial chair. Behind him, a bank of pale blue cloud was lifting out of the sea, and the sky above it was the faintest purple, eyelid-coloured.

Ivy saw that the man in the pool, the earliest swimmer, was very good. He had a long body and an excellent stroke. But he seemed to register that Joan had joined him: his body dropped, his head lifted out of the water, he looked across the lanes at Joan and then up at the benches where Ivy sat, and his goggles reflected the bruised sky. He was at the shallow end of the pool, nearly at the end of his lane, and he began to wade towards the ladder, lifting and ducking under the floating lane markers as he went.

Ivy watched as he rose out of the water. He was in very good shape, although not a particularly young man: tall, with a cumulonimbus of muscle above the mid-section, a mass of shoulder that tapered to nothing at the waist. He shook his long feet and pulled off his goggles and swimming cap. There was something marsupial about him, something partially aquatic. He walked as if his limbs were heavier than other people's, and as he passed in front of Ivy's bench she saw how white his legs were, and how boldly the dark hairs lay against them. Ivy liked being reminded that humans were hairy. There was a sense of comfort in belonging, so cosily, to the animal kingdom.

'Lovely morning,' she said, beaming up at the swimmer.

He looked down at her with a tight smile and said, 'Yes, it is.' He moved away, then stopped, turned, and said, 'I assume you're planning to shower before swimming.'

'Oh,' Ivy said.

The man lifted one sculpted arm and, still gripping his cap and goggles, pointed at the large sign that laid out the rules for use of the pool. He said, 'I noticed your friend didn't shower.'

Ivy looked at the water through which Joan was making her efficient way.

'My wife,' she said. She waved towards the hill behind the beach. 'We live just up there. We shower before we come.'

The man stood above her, the impressive bulk of his arms now crossed.

'Still,' he said.

They looked at one another for a long moment. Then his chest heaved with an incredulous sigh, he shook his head, he turned and disappeared into the beige stucco of the men's changing rooms, leaving a dull, wet trail on the concrete.

Ivy peered at the sign, which did indeed instruct guests to wash before swimming. But she knew this already: Ivy, who'd been a graphic designer, had painted it herself, years ago. She remembered there being controversy about the shower-before-swimming decree, back when the rules were being ratified at the inaugural meeting of the Friends of the Pool. Joan, in par-ticular, had expressed contempt for it, pointing out that this was an *ocean* pool, without a *filtration system*, open to the *tides*, and that no one *washed* before swimming at the *beach*; but someone had suggested a show of hands, and Ivy, conscious as she some-times was of being her own person, had voted against Joan and in support of showering. The shower vote passed. Joan had be-rated Ivy about it on the way home from the meeting, but only briefly; since then, neither of them had ever showered before entering the pool.

Ivy remained on the bench, waiting for the self-righteous swimmer to re-emerge; when he did, she intended to confront him. She would stand before him, all five foot two of her, and chide him for his arrogance, stomping into the pool and as-suming that he, a stranger, knew better than the women who were its lifeblood. Ivy stood up when he appeared, sheathed now in the lacquered spandex of a cyclist, but she was too slow—Hamish had abandoned his lifeguard post, approached the swimmer, and was now holding out his phone, taking a

photo of the two of them together. They parted at the turnstiles, where the swimmer exchanged a few words with Margaret before passing through and out into the morning. Margaret
noticed Ivy and offered an exaggerated thumbs-up before pivoting away on her stool, still swinging that silvery leg.

Hamish, passing on his way back to his lifeguard station,
grinned and said, 'Can you believe it? He said he'd be back
tomorrow.'

Hamish showed Ivy the photo on his phone, and with a
shock she recognised the interloper: he was Gavin Watson,
Olympic swimmer, somehow made more real by appearing
on a screen. Ivy remembered the nail-biting excitement of his
100-metre gold-medal win in Athens, with the whole nation—
the whole world—watching; she remembered the way he'd
emerged, victorious, from the pool, and simply nodded, as if he
agreed with the result.

His celebrity produced in Ivy a heady flutter, but that soon
gave way to further indignation: in fact, Gavin Watson's fame
made his scolding her about the shower rule even more disgrace-
ful. She wanted to express her outrage to Joan immediately—
to complain and also, perhaps, to marvel a little—but Joan was
still a sleek stripe in the water. The stripe was more than just
her body: it was both her body and the trough of water that
followed behind her and showed where she'd been, like the tail
of a comet. When Joan tilted her head to breathe she made, as
usual, a distinctive sound, halfway between a gulp and a cry,
then plunged her face back into the pool. Ivy, feeling an uncomfortable tug between the showers and the water, decided
not to swim today. She waited on the bench for the sun to rise

properly, the sky to turn its bright, clean blue, the pool to fill up with swimmers, and Joan to finish her fortieth lap.

On the way home, Joan went into the corner shop for the newspaper—she was almost perversely faithful to its printed form—and came out a few minutes later with the folded *Herald* wedged under her arm. As they walked up the hill, Ivy said, 'You know what annoys me the most?'

'What?' Joan said, walking ahead, so that Ivy could see the knotted, blue backs of Joan's knees.

'It didn't even *occur* to him that I might be a regular,' Ivy said. 'As if he's the king of swimming! As if all pools belong to him! He didn't think *even once* that I might know the pool better than he does. Imagine if I'd turned around and said, "I painted that sign myself! I painted it while you were still in nappies!"'

Joan didn't answer, not even to point out that the sign was only about ten years old, but Ivy knew this display of indifference to be unconscious habit, a protective mechanism born of Joan's decades as a woman in the police force. To show a particular interest in something was, for Joan, to show weakness. Most people considered her inscrutable, intimidating; but most people had never watched her come apart in bed, legs quaking, back bowing, her rigid face jolted by pleasure into a gulping and gasping that Ivy thought of every time Joan surfaced for air in the pool.

'His legs were hairy,' Ivy continued. 'Don't swimmers shave their legs? Of course, he's retired. He'd be in his forties, wouldn't he? And he'll be back tomorrow, according to Hamish. So do we shower before swimming, or not?'

'We do whatever we like,' Joan said.

But Ivy was troubled. She could see that the rule was silly, but also that it was the rule. She spent the rest of the walk home consumed by the dilemma, but resisted saying, 'To shower, or not to shower? That is the question.' Why was she so bothered? She was very conscious, walking up the hill, of the strain and sweat of her body, which insisted on continual motion, as if that were its reason for being.

They reached their building and Joan, ducking branches, said, 'If they don't come and trim this hibiscus soon, I'll do it myself.'

Ivy looked for the dead possum and saw that it still dangled from the top of the telegraph pole, but that the cockatoos had gone. She followed Joan through the gate.

'Why would Gavin Watson be swimming in our pool?' she asked, glancing back over her shoulder as if he might be marching his unlikely self up the hill behind them.

'Why wouldn't he?' Joan said. Just as she was about to reach for the handle of the front door, she stopped, took the newspaper—still folded in half—from beneath her arm, and held it out to Ivy. Ivy accepted the offering but kept her eyes on the odd expression on Joan's face. Out of that odd expression, Joan said, 'Biga's dead.' Then she opened the front door, entered the building, and began to climb the terrazzo stairs two at a time, heading for their flat on the third floor.

Ivy looked down and saw the headline: SERIAL KILLER PAUL

BIGA DEAD AT 57. And below it, the top of a man's head: sparse hair, creased forehead, two dark eyebrows rising over the horizon of the paper's folded rim. Her first thought, still standing at the front door, was that Joan had known Paul Biga was dead since she went into the corner store to buy the *Herald* and had said nothing about it. Joan had let Ivy go on about Gavin Watson, of all people, and all this time she'd known Paul Biga was dead and hadn't breathed a word. Ivy's spasm of loneliness lasted only a moment. Really, it made sense that Joan might want some time alone with the news: the Biga case had, after all, been the most high-profile of her career, and certainly the most stressful.

Only then did it properly occur to Ivy that Paul Biga, a man who had caused the unimaginable suffering of many people, was dead, and that this was a good thing. The families—think of the rejoicing of the families! Then a delicate, superstitious part of her felt uneasy, as if it might be bad luck to be pleased by anyone's death, even that of a murderer, and she squinted up at the dead possum with a shudder of frightened pity.

Ivy went inside, climbed the stairs—one at a time—and found Joan in the kitchen of their flat preparing to slice grapefruit, as she did every morning. Behind her, the sea dazzled at the window, and the sky, above it, was its habitually magnificent blue.

Joan rested the knife against the grapefruit and pressed down on it, cutting into the firm, flushed skin.

'What killed him?' Ivy asked.

'Don't know,' Joan said. 'Didn't read it.'

'Do you want me to?'

Joan shrugged. 'Suit yourself,' she said, wiping the knife on a paper towel.

Ivy sat on a bar stool and unfolded the newspaper across the kitchen island. The face on the first page was unrecognisable, with its pinched mouth and fleshy cheeks—when had Biga got so old? She scanned the article. It was full of things she already knew: the Polish father, the failed marriage, the taxi driving, the birds, and of course the bodies in the forest, the investigation, manhunt, arrest, and trial. Where was the information she needed, the cause of death? She grew annoyed, then realised it was right there in the opening sentence.

'Cardiac arrest,' Ivy said.

Joan snorted. She had sprinkled the cut grapefruit with sugar; now she pushed it, tipsy on its plate, across the island, along with a serrated spoon. Ivy began the sour daily task of eating her grapefruit. She hated it even with the sugar and the ceremonial spoon, even when she took care with the spoon to separate the plump flesh from the bitter membrane. Joan began cutting her own grapefruit into neat, unsweetened segments. Before she'd finished, her phone began to ring.

The first member of the task force to call was Jim Haslehurst, who had, early in the Biga investigation, dismissed Joan's idea that the killer was a taxi driver, and orchestrated a series of taxi-related pranks when she stuck to her theory. The second was Ken Byron, who used to leave his warrant requests on Joan's desk, expecting her to correct the spelling. The third was Warren Grady, who'd once drunkenly offered to cure Joan of her gayness, then cried about his divorce. Joan took each call standing in the kitchen, still wearing her swimsuit and navy shorts. She continued to cut grapefruit as she listened. She nodded, she laughed occasionally, she said, 'Uh-huh.'

Ivy sat at the breakfast bar, prodded her grapefruit, and flipped through the newspaper, skipping any mention of the virus. She was eavesdropping, of course, but Joan had perfected the art of revealing nothing on the telephone. For years, their phone would ring in the middle of the night and Joan would answer, speaking only in urgent monosyllables. Now, sitting at the breakfast counter, Ivy felt her fingertips grow grubby with newsprint.

'Will do,' Joan said into the phone. 'Gotta go, someone else is ringing.'

Then she greeted a new caller, who Ivy managed to identify as Aldo Mediano. Aldo had once arrived to collect Joan in the early morning, fidgety with a new lead and expecting Ivy to babysit his two-year-old.

On page five of the newspaper, Ivy found a photo of Gavin Watson wearing an ill-fitting suit and shaking the hand of a man in a wheelchair. The suit appeared to be in the act of wrestling itself off his improbable torso; like all athletes in ordinary clothes, he looked like a member of another species trying to pass itself off as human. Gavin had been at a charity swimming event in the UK, apparently, though it had been cancelled part way through because of the virus, and he and his wife had managed to get a seat on one of the last flights from Heathrow to Sydney. He would have landed just this morning. A surge of irritation washed through Ivy: this man, fresh from London, strutting about the pool as if he owned the place. It was Joan's turn to be in charge of the turnstiles tomorrow morning. What if she just didn't let him in?

More calls for Joan: Jim Haslehurst again, then Don Clark, who had recently come out as gay after years of jovial homophobia. That rounded out the Biga taskforce: the other key member, a discreet man with a passion for bridge, had thrown himself off the Gap years ago.

Then a call came on Ivy's phone: it was Margaret, still on duty at the pool.

'Oh, Ivy, thank goodness,' Margaret said, sounding flustered. 'Is Joan there? I've been trying to call.'

Ivy carried Margaret's rattled voice out of the kitchen and into the bedroom. 'Joan's on the phone,' she said, standing by the window and looking down at the compact car park behind their building, which was reached by a driveway so long and narrow they referred to it as the birth canal.

'I don't want to bother her,' Margaret said. 'It's just that something urgent's come up at the pool.'

Ivy watched her reflection sigh in the window. 'Joan's busy,' she said. 'You must have seen the news.'

'Well, exactly,' said Margaret. 'That's just it.'

'Margaret,' Ivy said, protective and unyielding. Poor, harmless, baffled Margaret. 'Now isn't the time. You're on the pool board. You'll just have to deal with it yourself.'

And she hung up—a dramatic gesture she rarely made, but when she did she always felt a sharp current go buzzing through her veins, was startled by her own rudeness, and also wanted to giggle. She saw on the screen of her phone that she'd received a text from her great-niece, Bella, who identified as something called a 'murderino' and was constantly pestering Joan for stories to send to her favourite true crime podcast. Bella only listened to US-based podcasts, and seemed to feel that she would be a better US citizen than most actual Americans. She was informed, judicious, and usefully outraged. If asked, she wouldn't have been able to name the current Australian treasurer. Her message simply read: !!

Ivy put her phone away without responding and looked out of the window again. She remembered a late night she'd come to stand in this exact spot, having been woken by the sound of Joan's car coming down the birth canal. Joan had left home forty-eight hours or so earlier, intimating that there was about to be an arrest in the Barrow State case; Ivy had lived through each of those hours with increasing dread. The next morning, all of Australia knew Paul Biga's name, but that night, standing at the window, Ivy didn't. Joan was conscientious about confidentiality; far more so than the other detectives, whose wives were confessional at barbecues.

That night, when Biga was still a secret, Ivy had watched Joan park then gone back to bed, intending to feign sleep. After nearly an hour had passed, she returned to the window and saw that Joan was still sitting in the dark of the car. Ivy returned to bed and fell asleep listening for the sound of a step on the stairs, a key in the door; when she woke, it was to the noises of Joan getting out of the shower. The sun was up, the day was beginning, it was time to go down to the pool.

'We got him,' Joan had said matter-of-factly, while combing her hair. And Ivy wondered, then, what ritual Joan must have had to perform in the safety and solitude of the car in order to emerge undamaged from the Barrow State manhunt. Perhaps 'undamaged' wasn't quite the word. Pre-retirement, and especially during the Biga case, Joan sometimes used to drink too much, lose patience with Ivy, accuse her of oversensitivity, snap, criticise, dislike talking about anything emotional; but Ivy, then as now, thought of Joan's job and shook her head and said to herself, No wonder, no wonder.

Another message, this time from Margaret: *pls ring, truly urgent.*

Ivy went out to the kitchen, where Joan seemed to have finished her calls.

'How are they?' Ivy asked. 'The boys?'

'We're getting together tomorrow morning,' Joan said, and licked grapefruit juice from her fingers. 'We're holding a wake.'

Ivy folded the paper—backwards, so that the sporting pages were visible and not Biga's face—and placed it on top of the microwave, where ephemera tended to gather. 'A wake?'

Joan looked at Ivy in such a way that she knew she had become a particular version of herself: prissily disapproving, hard-of-hearing, and extravagantly nonchalant. The horror and happiness of being so known!

'It's a joke, Ives,' Joan said. 'Not a real wake.'

Ivy couldn't help herself; she pursed her lips. She disliked the idea of a joke wake. She disliked the idea of Joan disappearing into this crowd of male detectives. During the search at Barrow State Forest, Joan would call sometimes from a payphone in the Munnaburra Hotel, when she knew Ivy would be home from work. She said nothing about the search or the upsetting things she must have seen. Instead, she delivered instructions on paying bills, watering plants, hiring plumbers. In the background, Ivy would hear the drunken roars of Joan's colleagues, calling her back to the bar. It wasn't that Ivy was jealous of the men, or that she distrusted Joan. If Ivy lacked faith in anyone, it was herself. Her capacity for love had been tested and tested, had always held firm, but what if it failed? Even now, after all this time, the possibility frightened her.

Her phone dinged again.

'Grady's in AA,' Joan said, rinsing her plate. 'So no booze, no going out at night. We're doing a brunch, and we're doing it dry.'

Ivy's phone rang: Margaret, presumably. She didn't answer. The call jogged her memory, though, and she said, 'You're on turnstile duty tomorrow morning.'

'You'll have to do it for it me,' Joan said. She was standing with her back turned, at the sink.

Ivy was piqued, for a moment, that Joan hadn't asked, had just assumed. She picked up her grapefruit spoon without speaking.

Joan turned, but Ivy refused to look at her. Why bother? She would be holding her tongue up against the root of her left incisor, as if digging at some stubborn scrap of food; her eyes would be half-lidded; her face would be expressive of deadpan disbelief.

'Turnstile duty,' Joan said. 'Really? You think that's a priority? You expect me to stay home, the only woman on the task force, and police the turnstiles?'

Ivy felt herself tremble. She felt the years when moments

like this had sprung up frequently, and with the same sudden force: Ivy would say or do something stupid, and Joan would tell her so, at length.

Now Joan walked to the breakfast bar, spread her arms out, and leaned over it, so that her face wasn't far from Ivy's. Which meant, of course, that Ivy was obliged to look at her, and when she did, she saw that Joan had a speck of grapefruit stuck high on one cheek: a thready sac of fruit. It became possible, then, not to hear what Joan was saying, not to be buried beneath the rhetorical questions of Joan's scorn, because Ivy could watch the slow, glimmering passage of the blob of grapefruit down Joan's cheek.

'I fail to see,' Joan said, and it quivered.

'Might it be possible, just this one time,' she said, and it looked on the verge of taking flight.

'Is it too much to ask,' she said, as it made its snail's way both out and down, towards the ear, along the track that a tear might run if Joan cried while lying flat on her back. If Joan cried.

'Is it beyond comprehension,' she said, as it became involved in the darkening down of her hairline.

When, at last, the piece of grapefruit fell from Joan's face and onto the counter, Ivy was disappointed, the way she often was by meteor showers. She pushed at it with the middle finger of her right hand. It was still contained in a membrane of its own, which Ivy used her fingernail to burst. She imagined, for a moment, a life without Joan in it, without grapefruit and daily lap swimming. This Joan-less life might feel, at first, still and safe; then it would break, widen, became blank and unbearable.

Ivy ducked her head. 'Of course I'll do the turnstiles,' she said. 'Of course you should go to your wake. I never said you shouldn't.'

'You didn't have to,' Joan muttered, turning away towards the sink.

Ivy examined the back of Joan's swimsuit, the slightly wedged tuck of her navy shorts. She looked scrawny and strong and lovely. Because Ivy had given in, there would be only a brief period of sulky silence, in which Joan would achieve useful things, bustling with such purpose through the flat that her retirement silverware would clatter in the sideboard. Joan would go to the wake tomorrow morning feeling blameless, and Ivy would go to turnstile duty feeling embarrassed, aggrieved, and grateful.

But Ivy's phone chimed, and Joan huffed and said, 'Who's so desperate to get in touch with you?'

Ivy took her phone from her pocket and looked at it, although she knew who it was. Margaret, of course, pleading: *Urgent!!! must talk re Gavin Watson.* That was the entire message, but it was enough for Ivy to understand why Margaret was in such a tizz at the pool, and she said, 'Gavin Watson has put in a complaint, but I've told Margaret that the board will just have to manage it without you.'

'Gavin Watson,' Joan repeated.

'So I suppose it's just as well I'm on the turnstiles tomorrow,' Ivy said, finally turning her phone to silent. 'No need to decide.'

'Decide what?'

'To shower or not to shower. That is the question.'

'Are you telling me,' Joan said, and Ivy looked without

thinking for the grapefruit on her cheek; it wasn't there, and Joan continued, 'that Gavin Watson put in an *official complaint* because I didn't *shower* before getting in the pool this morning?'

Now she began another genre of argument, in which she wouldn't go to the wake, she'd come to the pool to deny Gavin Watson entry and tell him exactly where to stick his shower. As Joan described exactly what she would say to Gavin Watson, he took on new, inexcusable forms. He was like the mosaics of dolphins Ivy had once been startled by in a documentary about ancient Rome: half-man, half-fish, all furious muscle, wearing an expression of pure malevolence. He grew larger than he had been, sloping through the pool with the bevelled shoulders of a Disney prince. He was inexcusable—Joan didn't say this, but Ivy knew it as Joan cursed him—because he needed and wanted nothing; because he had won his gold and broken his records, and now he was living in the long afterward, beyond the end of all things, without desire, and had chosen despite this sublime purity to put in a complaint about the showering.

Joan threw her hands in the air. 'They're all the same!' she cried, meaning Gavin Watson, meaning Aldo Mediano, Jim Haslehurst, Ken Byron, Warren Grady, Don Clark, and also, in this rage of hers, meaning Paul Biga, although Ivy knew that was unfair—that Biga was something else. Ivy sat silently as Joan swore to protect her from all of them, until she reached a point at which Ivy was understood to be doing Joan a favour by forcing her to miss the wake and come, instead, to the pool.

And now it was time for Ivy to insist that Joan go to the wake, that she had as much right to be there as anybody. And Joan would protest, and acquiesce, until she was understood to be doing Ivy a favour by going to the wake; and finally they would reach an agreement: Joan would come with Ivy to the pool, she would be there to open the gates and confront Gavin Watson, and then she would go to the wake, leaving Ivy at the turnstiles. Ivy spoke her lines, feeling their inevitable motion.

'You have as much right to be there as anybody,' she said. 'More!'

And Joan said, 'This isn't about any one individual. We were all on the task force.'

And Ivy said, 'You were worth at least two of any of those individuals. Who was right about the taxi? Who spent hour after hour on the taxi logs? Was it Aldo? Was it Grady? Was it *Haslehurst*?'

Until Joan confessed: it was not.

Ergo, she must go to the wake!

Joan agreed. Then she collapsed, exhausted, with her head in Ivy's lap, and Ivy stroked her hair, and she talked about the day they met: Joan the rookie policewoman and Ivy the free-lance signwriter. They were both smoking outside a church hall at someone's wedding, a wedding Ivy had very nearly not at-tended except that she'd bought a new pair of red shoes and had wanted to show them off, and she knew Joan liked to hear her talk about this near miss, about the brief break in rain dur-ing the reception that meant they both went in those few min-utes to smoke, about all the ways in which they so easily might not have met, which led, naturally, into a reflection on the won-der that they had. They met at this wedding, and they met again and again until they never parted, and here they were on a grey faux-suede couch in Sydney's eastern suburbs, ex-smokers now, married since it had been legal, in a world full of viruses and murderers and Gavin Watson.

Joan put her phone on airplane mode. They spent the rest of their day in mundane activities: chores, reading, a glass of wine on the balcony, a show about house renovations. They went to bed early. Joan set the alarm. Then she turned and took Ivy in her arms.

The next morning was quiet: no cockatoos. The possum, too, had vanished. Joan and Ivy went down the hill even earlier than they had yesterday; the papers hadn't yet been delivered to the corner shop. The plan, as formulated the night before, was that Joan would stay with Ivy until Gavin Watson arrived; then she would go to the wake. As they walked, Joan didn't hurry ahead. She slowed her steps, stayed by Ivy's side, might even have been said to stroll. They reached the gates of the pool together; together, they saw the printed notice: POOL CLOSED DUE TO COVID-19.

Joan called Margaret. Ivy walked away a few paces as Joan on the phone demanded answers, as she listened, as she began to make noises of assent. Ivy looked out across the beach, which struck her as deserted. There was a low-tide hush on the sea.

'It's Gavin Watson,' Joan said, suddenly at Ivy's side. 'He got in touch yesterday morning: he thought we should know his wife's tested positive for coronavirus. He was negative, but the board still decided to close the pool. Better safe than sorry.'

So the virus was here. Ivy realised, then, that she had been standing by the window for weeks, waiting to hear the virus come down the driveway.

'Oh no,' she said, and Joan nodded. She was kind enough to say nothing about the showers.

'No need for turnstiles, then,' Ivy said. 'You should get to the wake.'

Joan was silent for a moment. Then she said, 'You know what this means? This will bury him. The virus is bigger news than he is. The bastard's dead, and no one's going to give him a second thought.'

For one ugly moment, Ivy thought Joan meant Gavin Watson was dead; then she remembered the aged face of Paul Biga. She reached out to take her wife's hand.

'Everything he did,' Joan said. 'Not a second thought.'

It was impossible to tell from her face whether she was pleased or angry; impossible for anyone but Ivy, who saw that Joan could not herself decide what legacy she wanted for her monster. To bury him, yes—finally and in silence—but also to scream his filthy name.

Ivy held Joan's hand tighter and pulled her towards the pool entrance. She unlocked the gate, went through, ushered Joan in, locked the gate, and ducked beneath the turnstiles. The surface of the water was taut and silky, waiting for Joan to break it. Ivy nudged her. Joan stripped off her shoes and shorts and towel, but she didn't dive; instead, she sat on the edge of the pool and slid in, and Ivy watched the ripples float out from her moving hands. Then Joan went under. Then she surfaced with an ecstatic gulp.

Neither of them had showered, not even at home.

'Aren't you coming in?' Joan asked.

But Ivy was caught by the side of the pool, caught by the fineness of the morning, by the sign she'd painted herself, by the notice she'd ignored and the rule she'd broken, by the possibility of sickness and death and burial. She looked around her—at the pool, the turnstiles, the empty beach and sea and sky—as if she were about to leave them all for a long journey, perhaps forever, and needed to commit each part of them to memory.

LUCY

(1950)

One night in late summer, two of Lucy's brothers take her to the park to show her what men and women do together. Their cousin comes, too. Lucy is eight and has never before been invited to leave the house with her brothers after dark. She's frightened, but that's not unusual; she's often frightened. The park is brighter than she expected it to be, perhaps because the moon is almost full. The boys—brothers Peter and Danny, cousin Colin, who are all older—lead her to the big boulder with dirty words painted on, and they hide behind this boulder in order to watch what men and women do together. No southerly wind has blown in to relieve the heat of the day, and the cicadas are so loud Lucy feels as if itchy swarms of them are hiding in her damp hair. She scratches at her scalp and stays quiet, as instructed, and she waits. Lucy doesn't know exactly what she's waiting for, only that it's secret and monstrous, but also funny, and coming for her whether she likes it or not.

Eventually, a man and woman come stumbling through the dark and fall to the grass in front of the boulder. They look, to Lucy, like a single, many-legged creature, which squirms on the ground, groaning and hissing, laughing occasionally, and finally, after a shout that may come from either the man or the woman, growing still. Behind the boulder, the boys grin. The couple stands; the woman takes out a compact and tilts it to the moon, checking her make-up. She's only a girl, really, with a wide, worried face, concentrating on the application of her lipstick as if something vital depends on it—at least, this is how Lucy will remember her, much later, as Lucy herself stands in the moonlight, correcting the smudges of her own bitten mouth. The man begins to walk away through the park, and the girl, seeing this, snaps the compact shut and hurries after him.

Behind the boulder, the boys snort and spit. They dig bony elbows into one another's bony ribs.

'D'you see now?' they ask Lucy, but she doesn't see. The park, which she'd thought she knew well, is too strange, like a place she's never been before and will never visit again. She can make out the lights of houses through the trees, but they seem very far away.

The next couple to arrive are quieter. They're pressed up against the trunk of a tree, and all Lucy can see is the dim flash of a man's bare backside moving in the gloom. His trousers hang just below his hips; they look as if they should slide to the ground, but never do. A mosquito lands on Lucy's arm, and she slaps it instinctively. The boys hush her; her cousin pulls her hands behind her back, holding them so she won't do it again. The couple don't seem to notice. The man's pale backside continues to move with regularity, into and out of the darkness of the tree, accompanied by the faint tinkling of his belt buckle. This goes on for some time, until murmured discussion leads to a shift in positions: the gleaming arse is replaced by the back of the woman's head, which resumes the in-and-out motions.

'Get a load of that,' Peter whispers, but anxiously, as if he's just testing the phrase. Danny cups his own crotch and hops about on silent feet. Colin, whose less-assured status as cousin seems to require an additional assertion of authority, holds Lucy's wrists tighter until whatever is happening at the tree is over.

The couple walk away, and Lucy hears the man say, 'A bit of bullshit, eh,' but softly, as if it were an endearment. The woman laughs.

Once they're gone, Colin releases Lucy, and she rubs at the ache in her shoulders.

'We'd better get her home,' Peter says.

'Give it another minute,' Danny says. He's sweating—Lucy can see the shine of it on his forehead. They wait in silence for what seems like hours. Bored, Lucy sits cross-legged in the grass and begins to pick at the scabs on her knees. When mosquitoes land on her arms, she shakes them off.

Finally, Colin says, 'If it gets too late, all we'll see is queers.'

The boys cut through the bush, along the track they've created by coming and going from their house to the park and the bus stop and the shop. Lucy follows them, stomping her feet to frighten snakes and wondering if she's behaved well, and if she'll be invited to sneak out with them again. She didn't enjoy herself, but that doesn't matter; what matters is to be invited.

When Lucy and the boys reach home, the house is dark, and Robbo is smoking on the front verandah. He's the oldest brother, fifteen. He sits on a milk crate with his long legs stretched out in front of him, tapping his shoeless feet. He sees the boys and takes a deep, final drag of his smoke, then flicks it into the grass.

'Where've you little shits been?' he asks, in the listless way he has that manages to communicate both contempt and indifference.

'Give us a fag?' Danny, ever hopeful, dances up to Robbo's feet. And Robbo might hand over a cigarette, he really might; he's given to moments of occasional charity, which appear as suddenly as his temper and are almost as overwhelming. But then he sees Lucy and swears, kicking out at Danny's ducking head. The boys scatter when Robbo springs off the verandah. He squats at Lucy's feet.

'Where'd they take you?' he asks. 'What'd they do?'

She recognises tobacco and beer on his breath. The smell reminds her of their father, who died six months ago and whose brother, Hal, recently moved in to take over the market garden.

'Well?' Robbo says.

Lucy closes up the back of her nose as if she's about to jump into the river, and says, 'Nothing. We were only walking around.'

He looks at her without speaking, as if waiting for her to stumble and reveal the truth. She keeps her face still and her eyelids heavy.

'All right,' he says. 'Bugger off to bed. And I better not catch you out at night again.'

From inside the house comes the sound of Uncle Hal shepherding all the phlegm in the world to the back of his throat, ready to expel it into a tissue.

1951

Uncle Hal and Colin sleep out on the back verandah for about a year; then Uncle Hal moves into Mum's bedroom. Lucy never sees him kiss Mum, or even touch her with anything like tenderness, but he does make appreciative remarks about her figure and look around as if daring the boys to object. Danny makes fun of him behind his back, much to Colin's outrage. Peter becomes withdrawn and watchful at the dinner table. Lucy hears Uncle Hal's comments about her mother's legs and chest and feels a keen, swollen shame about her own small body.

Only Robbo stands up to Hal, on the rare nights Robbo's home for tea. One night in September, when Robbo and Hal begin to shout across the table, Peter tugs Lucy's arm so she'll follow him outside, and they crouch with Danny and Colin beneath the kitchen window. Lucy can't quite catch the words of the argument; it's as if Robbo and Uncle Hal are speaking Polish or Croatian. Still, she feels as though she can hear the spittle flying from Uncle Hal's mouth, and also every snarling inhalation Robbo makes through his twice-broken nose.

There's no sound out of Mum, not even when a glass shatters, or when someone shakes the table so that everything on it jumps and tumbles. But she's at Robbo's side as he slams out of the house; she walks him down the drive to the road, linking her arms with his the way girls do with their friends at school.

Robbo will go off now to sleep the night at a mate's or in his car or in the bush. Peter releases a noise of disgust and slinks away into the garden. Danny punches Colin in the arm, says, 'Your dad's a real piece of shit,' and then the two of them are grappling in the dirt. Mum runs up from the road, and Uncle Hal comes out bellowing, loosening his belt. Lucy waits a moment to see if Robbo will return; when he doesn't, she goes inside to start clearing the table. Soon afterwards, Danny and Colin, thoroughly strapped, are marched through the kitchen by Uncle Hal. Peter sneaks by later, just as Lucy finishes the dishes.

The next morning, the boys are up early as ever to work in the garden before school. When, itchy with lime powder, they come back to the house, Uncle Hal takes change from his trouser pocket, jingles it in his hand, and throws it into the grass as if scattering seed. As Peter, Danny, and Colin scramble for the money, Uncle Hal presses a coin into Lucy's palm—presses it hard, as if he wants it to sink into her flesh. Mum fries sausages and brings them bursting to the table on a glossy plate.

A few days later, Robbo and some of his mates break into a service station at North Ryde and go into hiding out bush. Uncle Hal waits for the police to arrive at the house, as they always do when anything is burgled or burned or beaten in the area, and rats Robbo out in a loud, clear voice. Lucy hears him from the kitchen, where Mum sits stony-faced at the table. Immediately after Uncle Hal tells the police exactly where they'll find Robbo, Lucy detects something like anger and love and sadness on Mum's face, but then it's gone again, as though it were a cloud that passed for an instant in front of the sun.

1952

Lucy falls on the school's asphalt playground and breaks her arm; waiting in the sick bay with two scratching girls, she catches chicken pox. The long days at home alone with her mother—Lucy daubed in calamine lotion, scraping at her cast-bound pox with a knitting needle—are some of the happiest of her life. One afternoon at the kitchen table, Mum drinks two beers and asks Lucy how she'd feel if they left the market garden, the house, and Uncle Hal. When Lucy asks where they'd go, Mum only laughs, considers the empty bottles of beer, and taps the neck of one so that it topples onto the table and rocks back and forth in its own amber shadow.

Lucy, recovered, returns to school. Uncle Hal wins an award for his beetroots at the Royal Easter Show. Colin, newly obsessed with flight, has plans to join the air force, and Mum conceals from Uncle Hal how often Danny is playing truant. Peter spends a lot of time making strange, stifled noises out in the dunny. No one ever mentions Robbo, who's in some sort of prison farm in Emu Plains.

Mum starts to brush her hair in the mornings and hum to herself as she mops the floors. She seems happy, and Lucy doesn't know why until Mrs Blasevic comes from next door to smile with her crowded mouth on the blessing of a new baby.

1953

Danny brings home the yellow Pontiac Chieftain well before he's legally allowed to drive it. That wouldn't deter him, but the car is missing an engine, among other things, so it rests on bricks in the front yard for months as the necessary parts are acquired. Lucy, eleven now, knows better than to ask where from. She's never actually seen the boys steal a car, race it, aim it at letterboxes and fences and cats, bounce it over paddocks shooting at rabbits and roos with Uncle Hal's guns, roll it down to the river, or set it on fire. She has, however, seen the burnt-out cars smothered in lantana, which seems to grow up overnight to conceal them, and she knows which items in the house are the spoils of these goings-on. Some belong to her now: a white purse with a tube of apricot lipstick and the stub of a bus ticket inside; a pretty chain she could attach to a pair of glasses, if she wore glasses; a pocket knife with a mother-of-pearl handle. She sometimes finds these gifts on her bed, and knows not to acknowledge their existence.

The Pontiac is ready around the same time Robbo gets out of Emu Plains Prison Farm. Danny stands proudly beside the big yellow car as his eldest brother strolls up the driveway, carrying a knapsack and followed by a wiry boy who looks to be about Danny's age. The heads of both Robbo and this boy are so close-shaven it's as if they've simply rubbed dirt into their bare scalps.

Lucy sits on the edge of the verandah, swinging her legs. Mum comes through the front door. She stands beside Lucy, wiping her hands on her apron long after they must be dry. Uncle Hal is out in the truck, delivering the beans that the boys started picking at four this morning.

Robbo raps on the dazzling bonnet of the Pontiac. 'This car is a magnet,' he says. 'You know what for?'

'Pussy,' Danny says, grinning.

Robbo ignores him, turning to the wiry boy.

'Cops?' offers the boy.

Robbo shakes his head. 'Bugs,' he says. 'Creepy-crawlies. They love yellow cars. Drive this thing at any speed, and it'll end up fucking filthy with insect guts. Only an absolute bloody idiot would drive a yellow car.'

Then he walks to the verandah and catches one of Lucy's kicking feet in his hand. He's wider than she remembers.

'How's my little chook?' he asks, smiling, but not looking directly at her face, which makes him seem shy.

Lucy scrunches one eye closed and says, 'All right.'

Robbo drops her foot. He looks up at Mum and asks, 'Is he here?'

Mum shakes her head.

The wiry boy steps forward and introduces himself as Keith. He's a smooth one, this Keith, despite his big ears and freckles. He compliments Mum on her looks, on the house, on the smell of roasting beef that seeps from the windows, and asks her permission to stay a day or two, just till they've got their heads screwed back on.

Lucy watches him beam and twinkle. He reminds her of Donald O'Connor, the bloke in *Singin' in the Rain* who isn't Gene Kelly. Mum, powerless before charm of this kind, invites him in.

'Just a day or two,' repeats Robbo. 'Then we'll be out of your hair.'

Mum says, 'As long as you need. You know that.'

From inside the house, the baby emits the scrawny cry he only produces at the end of his midday sleep; his night-time cries—shrieks of panic—wake everyone and send Uncle Hal crashing through the kitchen and out the back door to smoke in the truck, just to get a bit of bloody peace. Mum often lacks patience at night, especially when Uncle Hal is angry, so Lucy has begun getting up to look after the baby, to hold him and walk back and forth. She's sick of his pinched, inconsolable face.

'S'pose I'd better meet this new brother of mine,' Robbo says, and he climbs the steps to the verandah, where he kisses Mum on the cheek. Keith, following, turns his head, looks Lucy in the eye, and winks.

Once Mum, Keith, and Robbo have gone in, Danny—still standing by the Pontiac—hawks up a wad of spit and ejects it with some force into the grass.

1954

On starting high school, Lucy acquires a best friend: a girl called Sylvia, whose father works at the flour mill and whose mother has red-dyed hair. Sylvia is short and blonde. One of her eyes turns out when she's tired, but she refuses to wear glasses. She's a great flirt. Lucy is aware that Sylvia has befriended her in order to gain access to her older brothers, but that doesn't matter; she's grateful for the way Sylvia pets and bosses her, for every note passed in class with her name on it, for Sylvia's head on her shoulder while they watch the after-school footy game down at the oval. It seems to Lucy as if this game never had a beginning and will never reach an end, and that her brothers are playing it even as they work in the garden, sit at the dinner table, and do whatever they can to stay out of Uncle Hal's way.

Colin is bad at football, and Danny is decent, but Peter's a natural. He moves as if he lives two seconds further into the future than anyone else. Every time he scores a try, he'll shake the sweat from his hair so that it flies in droplets, any one of which Sylvia would apparently be happy to taste. Lucy watches Sylvia watch Peter as he flicks his wet head back, his Adam's apple rolling in his bullish neck. He's got much larger in the past year—taller, broader—and looks more and more like Robbo, who hasn't been heard from since announcing, last Christmas, that he and Keith were heading out west to work as jackaroos.

When Peter joins a junior footy club with the promise of a premiership career, he vanishes from the local oval. Lucy assumes the after-school game will fall flat and that Sylvia's attention will drift. But Peter's absence seems to release the other players: free of the burden of true excellence, they roar and butt across the grass, they preen and swagger, and if Danny goes down in a tackle, his knees smeared with dirt and blood, Sylvia is ready to leap up, to leave Lucy, to run breathlessly to his side.

1955

Mum says she wants to bake a sponge cake, needs baking powder, and sends Lucy to the shop with the baby. He can walk, but not well, so Lucy puts him in the pram and studies him as she pushes it along the bush path. His resemblance to Uncle Hal isn't striking—he takes, everyone agrees, after his mother—but Lucy looks for the Hal in him all the same, ignoring the blue eyes and the rumpled pucker of the top lip, and focusing instead on the puffy nose, the steep, meaty forehead, the obvious effort involved in moving such a cumbersome head. She's wiped every part of his body, worn his vomit, swallowed his sneezes, and been too slow, while changing his nappies, to stem the sudden fountain of his urine. In the privacy of her thoughts, she calls him the Goblin. Everywhere else, he's Charlie.

At the shop, Lucy buys baking powder and cigarettes—the other item on Mum's list, and the real reason for the trip. Collecting the change, Lucy notices two women looking at her and then at one another, tutting.

'So young,' says one, who's grown plump around her wedding ring.

The other says, 'Getting younger all the time,' and squints at the label on a tin of peaches. It's not until Lucy leaves the shop that she understands: those women think *she* is the mother of this sturdy child, that she not only pushed it out of her body but allowed a man to put it there in the first place. The Goblin is delighted by the furious way she takes the bush path. With every forceful jolt, he seems to rise higher in the pram, as if ascending under the steam of his overinflated head. She vows never to have a baby.

When they reach home, Mum takes Charlie and the ciggies and asks Lucy to leave the baking powder on the kitchen table. She doesn't bake the cake.

1956

Lucy is fifteen and hears that Robbo and Keith are back from the bush, tanned and hairy. But Robbo won't come home while Uncle Hal is on the scene, and Uncle Hal is always on the scene, dirt lodged deep in his nails and his knuckles, the lilac veins in his calves growing knottier by the day.

One scorching Saturday morning, with Hal and Colin away as usual making deliveries, Lucy hears an unfamiliar car pull up to the house. When its driver lays into the horn, she runs onto the verandah and sees a green Beetle, with Robbo at the wheel; after one last jubilant honk, he calls, 'Get dressed—we're going to the beach!'

'We' includes Keith, who leans from the passenger window, green-eyed, no longer wiry, his head shaggy with curls, a cigarette tucked behind one ear. He holds out one hand, and Lucy, without thinking, walks down the steps and takes it. He pulls her close to the car and says, 'What d'you think you're up to, being so sweet?'

Sylvia emerges, flushed and buttery, from the room Danny shares with Peter, and invites herself along; Danny, following as always at her heels, resigns himself to the trip. Peter is off with his footy mates. Mum shifts Charlie on her hip and peers down the road, as if Uncle Hal might materialise at that very moment. Robbo tries to convince Mum to come; Keith volunteers his seat, and Lucy feels a deep, tidal tug at his suggestion that she sit on his lap in the back. Mum refuses. Uncle Hal's been blaming her, recently, for the fact that Charlie hasn't yet started to talk.

It's so hot that, as Lucy gathers her things, the flies seem to collide with the sticky slopes of her arms, cling for an instant, then roll away. Several find their way into the car and set out with them on the excursion, staggering between Robbo and Keith up front, and butting against Lucy, Danny, and Sylvia in the back. Danny, relegated to the status of passenger, is gloomy throughout the drive. Sylvia leans forward from the middle seat, laughing so close to Robbo's ear that her breath ruffles the hair above it. Lucy makes a concerted effort not to think about Uncle Hal, or Mum, or Charlie's face smeared with food and snot. The windows are mostly down, the hot air pours in, and the flies, exhausted, lie sizzling against the glass.

At the beach, Keith chooses Lucy: he snaps out her towel and lays it on the sand; he reclines beside her with his head pillowed on his coppery arms; he buys her a cone of slightly gritty chocolate ice cream; he coaxes her into the water, where he dives under and pulls at her feet. At first, unaccustomed to this kind of attention, Lucy is bewildered and embarrassed. She reassures herself that it has come through no fault or flirtation of her own.

Later, though, when she sees that Sylvia is jealous of Keith's showy devotion, a sense of powerful cleverness expands inside her. It feels connected, somehow, to the waves and the weather, as if she might today have some say in the direction of both. Sylvia, in response, redoubles her efforts to beguile Robbo, which continue to fail. Danny, fuming, strides into the surf, slapping at its surface as he goes, and stays out beyond the breakers, his small, dark, furious head rising with every swell.

Keith doesn't take Lucy quite so far. Pressed against him in the churning water, she feels a hand at her waist; it dips lower, running first over one cheek and then the other, before returning to her waist, which it squeezes.

By the time they leave the beach, Sylvia and Danny are in the silent stage of a vicious fight, and Robbo is drunk. Keith drives, with Sylvia in the front seat. Lucy sits between her brothers in the back, where it feels as if a strange, sleepy enchantment has been cast over the three of them: Danny in his mute grievance, Robbo in his slurred contentment, and Lucy in the stupefying spell of their mixed moods. Noise, light, and happiness live in the front of the car, where Keith and Syl laugh about the veterinary student who—running with a makeshift torch fashioned from a chair leg, a pudding can, and a pair of kerosene-soaked undies—managed to convince a crowd, a police escort, and the lord mayor of Sydney that he was bearing the Olympic flame. About ten minutes from home, Syl—in the course of a casual gesture—places a hand on Keith's knee and leaves it there.

Lucy, seeing the muscles of his thigh twitch, shakes off her stupidity and leans forward from the back seat.

'Keith, whose car are we driving?' she asks.

Sylvia laughs and withdraws her hand.

'Who knows?' he says, and he smiles gleefully, conspiratorially—a smile that is not, Lucy sees, for anyone but Robbo, whose eyes Keith is meeting in the rear-view mirror.

1957

Sylvia is pregnant. Her father throws her out, so she moves into Danny's room, and Peter—who's rarely home—joins Colin on the verandah. Danny and Sylvia are very private about their room: they spend whole afternoons in there with the radio on, and no one is welcome unless invited. After each of their many fights, Danny emerges looking haughty but oddly slippery in the face, as if he's just been greeted by an over-friendly dog. When they're not fighting, Sylvia sends him out for the peaches she craves. She spends hours lying on the bed reading magazines and leaves saucers of sucked peach pits outside the door, which Lucy collects before the ants can find them. When Sylvia does appear, she seems to sail through the house without touching anything. Her pregnancy infuses her with a languid radiance over which Mrs Blasevic from next door can't help but fawn, despite her disapproval. Even Uncle Hal is gallant, calling her Syl, opening doors and pulling out chairs, as if she's too precious to risk the use of her own hands.

Sylvia and Danny marry in June. Sylvia's family don't attend, and Lucy, dressed in sickly pink, is the only bridesmaid. Charlie, five now, is ring bearer, and Peter a distracted best man, indifferent to anything that isn't footy; he's due to make his first-grade debut with Souths next season. Colin sulks. Robbo, who drives trucks these days and has no fixed address, preferring to rely on the temporary goodwill of a series of mates up and down the east coast, sends a telegram to toast the happy couple. Peter reads it aloud at the reception, lingering on Robbo's statement of disbelief that any woman would be willing to marry Danny. Danny reddens, so caught between agreeing with and being offended by his brother's message that he can do nothing but grin lopsidedly. Uncle Hal and Mum both look very smart, and Lucy finds herself feeling proud of them.

Sylvia's baby, another boy, is born in November. He's a redhead, as if Sylvia's mother's hair-dyeing has had biological consequences. His name is Norman, but they call him Nonnie, and aside from his ginger hair, he resembles the prime minister: the same pouchy jaw and upswept eyebrows. Sylvia loves him so much that she's reluctant to let anyone else hold him; as a result, Lucy isn't expected to care for him as she was for Charlie. Instead, she's free to simply like this baby. She likes his rosy skin, his greedy mouth, and the curt little adult gestures he makes with his fisted hands. She likes watching his miniature moods gust through him like weather. Most of all, she likes playing almost no part in the management of those moods.

Sylvia, convinced that Nonnie will catch the Asian flu, gets Danny to quit his job at the flour mill—too many foreign workers, she says. An uncle of hers offers him work in Grafton, and they move north not long before Christmas. Once they've gone, Lucy expects the house to feel empty, but it doesn't. Mum seems hardly to notice; she never took to Sylvia and is occupied now by Charlie's belated yet endless chatter. Colin and Peter both vie for the vacant room until Hal, proud of Peter's sporting prowess, decides in his favour, and the matter is settled. Colin, wounded, stays on the verandah. The room soon acquires Peter's steady musk of sweat, grass, and wet tin; he's taken a job as a garbageman, because the early-morning shifts leave time for training. Lucy still finds herself keeping an eye out for peach pits in the hallway.

1958

The road outside the house is busier than ever with traffic, and Uncle Hal hires a crew of Italians to build a farm shop on the strip of land alongside. Lucy, seventeen now, has finished school and, without knowing what else to do, is willing to be installed behind the counter, which is as good a place as any to wait for the husband who will take her far away from it. Uncle Hal begins growing gladioli to sell, setting out the gaudy blooms in buckets to attract passing cars. Once the shop has been established, he gives Colin the responsibility for its running. Colin struts about like a princeling, ordering Lucy to polish this and sweep that, and scolding her for being cold with the customers.

'They'll spend more if you smile,' he says, pressing at her cheeks with his index fingers to force the upward curvature of her mouth.

Then he falls for a Croatian girl with dark, curling hair and a tiny waist, and Lucy rarely sees him at the shop. When he does show up, he brings Marija with him and takes her into the storeroom. Twenty minutes or so will pass, and he'll emerge looking dazed, then go to smoke in his car. Marija always appears a few minutes later, not a hair out of place.

One day, Lucy compliments her on being so put together.

'What do you think we're doing back there?' Marija asks. 'I'm not stupid enough to let him stick it in me.'

Lucy shrugs and pushes her tongue hard into her cheek.

'No, no,' Marija says, and laughs. '*He* does *me*, with these.' She wiggles her fingers.

Not long after, Marija's brothers put it about that Colin is a dead man. He disappears overnight. The brothers come to the house looking for him, all of them muscled and dark-haired in white T-shirts, smelling of tinned peas, so eerily similar it's as if they've been replicated in the canning factory where they work. Uncle Hal stands at the front door with his .22 and tells them that Colin left last week to be a ski instructor in the Middle East.

1959

Now that Uncle Hal has run out of sons to employ in the garden, he hires immigrants. They're unreliable, he says, but in such endless supply they can easily be replaced. At six every morning, he drives to Chatswood station and collects any men he finds waiting there. His departure always wakes Lucy, and by the time he returns with a clutch of workers bouncing in the tray of the truck, she's dressed. The men look pale and grim, and each sits staring ahead as if alone. Later in the day, though, when the sun is higher, they joke together in Polish or Hungarian as they weed the onions or fertilise the spinach. Sometimes they sing. Most bring their own lunches, but sometimes they come into the farm shop to buy a drink or a sandwich, and they're unfailingly polite. Lucy gets to know a few regulars: the sandwiches they prefer, the names of their sweethearts. Still, she holds herself aloof from them. Hal has never liked to see her talk to men.

One of these regulars, who calls himself John, comes into the shop almost every day. He's at least ten years older than Lucy, with thinning hair and a permanent squint. The hair is a shame: it was clearly once a gorgeous thicket. He invariably buys an egg sandwich. Their exchanges are brief, and he's painstakingly courteous towards her, as if he has studied gentlemanly manners and is intent on their demonstration. When he's not in front of her, Lucy never thinks of him. She thinks, instead, of being married. Her husband takes the vague, devoted, glimmering shape of Elvis Presley, only because Elvis is so continually offered to her imagination. She spends most of her time picturing the home she'll make and manage—its tidy privacy.

One day in spring, John appears at the shop's front window with his left hand wrapped in a bloodied handkerchief: he has, apparently, crushed the tip of his finger with a hammer, and Hal is bringing the truck around to take him to hospital. Lucy goes out to him. She moves buckets of gladioli off the bench and manoeuvres him to sit; then, she sits beside him. For five minutes, she catalogues every foolish way she, too, has injured herself in the course of her life, including the arm she broke at age ten on the school playground. John, whose lips have gone white, listens intently, holding his bloody hand aloft like a candle. Then Hal arrives, his face as red as the beets he grows. When John tries to climb into the bed of the truck, Hal honks the horn and shouts at him to come up front. As they drive away, it occurs to Lucy that she's never before seen her uncle allow a worker to sit beside him.

She assumes John is gone for good, but he's back less than a week later, with his left index finger neatly bandaged. He resumes his visits to the shop, as reticent and courteous as ever, as partial to egg sandwiches, except that now, on occasion, he refers to Lucy as his nurse.

1960

Keith turns up at the shop one afternoon and starts calling Lucy 'the Mona Lisa of Mona Vale Road'. He bothers her at the counter, kissing her cheek and begging her to come out with him. She expects Hal, and therefore her mother, to disapprove, but they're busy these days—expanding the garden, renovating the house—and they surprise her: yes, she can go alone with Keith to the pictures, to the beach, to Peter's games, and by extension to the park at night, where she checks behind the boulder for crouching children. The innocent thought of Keith's hand against her bottom four years ago makes her blush, then makes her laugh, then vanishes altogether in the wincing muddle of her first time. Her second time, she's yielding. Her third, demanding. Lucy, on her back, meets each thrust. The moon is full above the park. The boulder, scrubbed of its ancient obscenities, glitters with mica.

'Fuck,' Keith says, loudly; then again, but quietly, 'Fuck'; then he comes inside her, though he's promised not to. In that moment, Lucy feels a hilarious pleasure in having given herself up, just this once, to chance; it might be the only accident of her narrow, decided life. Later, however, she'll come to think of her whole life as an exercise in chance, and she the victim of many accidents: the accident of those parents, of that uncle, of those brothers, of that husband and that son. But for now, tonight in the park with Keith—who's still glazed with bliss, fumbling through apologies, manhandling his slippery prick, straightening her clothes but hopelessly, as if he's forgotten how skirts and buttons work—tonight, Lucy feels for the first time older than he is, as if she were the one who once sweet-talked him into the water and pressed against him in the surf's shaggy foam. They vow, of course, never to let it happen again, but ten days later, when her period arrives, Lucy is almost disappointed.

The weather turns cold. Keith, now always armed with protection (he calls them rubber soldiers), is strangely coy about where he actually lives, so they make do with the cramped confines of whatever car he's currently driving. They park in secluded spots all over Sydney—bushy, hidden places, which Keith somehow knows about. There are no more trips to the pictures or the beach; it feels as if there's time for nothing but their urgent back-seat encounters, which usually begin with Lucy kneeling between Keith's thighs and end with his frantic, exultant face collapsing into the space between her neck and shoulder.

Before dropping her home, he likes to pull over half a mile down Mona Vale Road and double-check that her clothes, hair, and make-up are all in order. One night, she asks if he does it because he's afraid of Hal.

'That maggot?' Keith scoffs.

An intimate mood has come over them, as it tends to, afterwards in the sultry car.

'It's Robbo,' he says, and gives her earlobe a tug. 'Robbo would kill me. He'd gut me like a fish and watch me bleed out.'

Keith tucks a strand of Lucy's hair behind her ear. Then, with a small squeal of the tyres, he pulls back onto the road, so that an approaching car is forced to slow.

1961

There's a glut of vegetables on the market, and Hal chooses to plough his back into the ground rather than let them go at a loss. Other farmers dump theirs at sea. Subdued in after-dinner

lamplight, he talks about selling up and moving to the Shoal-
haven, where Colin lives these days. The land down there is
cheap. Lucy waits for someone to mention that the house and
garden actually belong to Mum; but who's going to say it, apart
from herself? She's the only one of her father's children left at
home: Robbo is driving for the mines at Mount Isa; Danny is in
Grafton; Peter's moved closer to the Souths ground at Redfern.
Hal relies entirely on men like John Biga, who's remained loyal
despite the crushed finger, and on Lucy, who's still in the shop.
Charlie, Mum says, isn't old enough to work yet.

There was a time when the routine of dusting the counter,
arranging shelves, and making sandwiches pleased Lucy, because she thought of it as a rehearsal for being Keith's wife. But
Keith has disappeared. He stopped visiting weeks ago, without
word, and now her days are made up entirely of the shop and
the house. When she's in the shop, she longs for the house;
in the house, only the shop seems tolerable. It takes her three
minutes to walk between them, and it's in those three minutes
that something like life is lived, because she gets to feel the sun
on her face, or exchange pleasantries with John, or scold the
myna birds as they chase kookaburras from the clothesline.

Early one evening, Sylvia shows up at the house. She's carrying Nonnie, who is three years old and looks more than ever
like a tiny politician: tense, apologetic, and waggish in turns as
he squirms on Lucy's lap. His red hair swirls around his crown
like a drawn storm on a weather map. He talks a great deal
about a dog with fleas, then falls asleep. Lucy sits with him
on the verandah while Mum and Sylvia argue in the kitchen.

Danny has kicked Sylvia out of their place in Grafton, and she has nowhere else to go.

'I've never,' she declares from the kitchen, 'I have never in my life even looked twice at another man.'

Charlie stands at Lucy's side. He's nine now, and veers between sweetness and casual cruelty. At this moment, he's sweet, leaning against her leg and gazing at Nonnie's sleeping form.

In the kitchen, Mum pleads with Syl. She says, 'You can't expect me to side against my own son.'

Charlie studies Nonnie. 'Is he my cousin?'

'He's your nephew,' Lucy says. 'You're his uncle.'

Charlie nods, thinking this through. Then a look of shrewd elation crosses his face. 'I can boss him,' he says.

Lucy holds Nonnie tighter. 'You can't,' she says. 'He's a baby.'

But Charlie gallops away singing, 'I can boss him,' rotating one arm above his head as if readying a lasso.

Sylvia comes slamming out of the kitchen. 'Your mum can be such a bitch,' she says, gathering Nonnie into her arms. 'She doesn't want us here. Her own grandson.'

Nonnie blinks, yawns, and snuggles against his mother's chest.

'What did she say?' Lucy asks, although she knows exactly what Mum said: no. It's unlike Mum to say no, and Lucy feels both pride in her mother's firmness and pity for her friend. Still, it's been many years since Sylvia passed secret notes and lay her head on Lucy's shoulder.

Sylvia ignores the question. 'You know what I'll do?' she says to Nonnie, jogging him so that his tipsy head jiggles. 'I'll wait for Hal. Hal will want me here. Yes, he will, baby boy, he'll want me here. Won't he? Won't he? Yes, he will.'

Yes, Lucy thinks, he probably will, and Mum will give in to him, as she always does. Then Hal will pull out the flashy manners he reserves for pretty young women: he'll treat Syl like a queen, he'll make insinuations and find excuses to touch her, he'll ingratiate himself with Nonnie and laugh at his own son's slight lisp, and all the while Mum will be there, washing Hal's shirts and cooking his chops.

John Biga walks past the verandah. He has his own car now and often works late. He calls goodnight as he goes, tips his hat, and Charlie returns a *yeehaw* from out by the clothesline.

'Who's that?' Sylvia asks, appraising.

'He works for Hal,' Lucy says. 'He's very old-fashioned. Syl, did Keith ever come to Grafton?'

'Keith who?' Sylvia leans in close to Nonnie's face and kisses him on the mouth.

'Robbo's old friend.'

'Oh!' Sylvia cries, as if addressing Nonnie's nose. 'Yeah, a few weeks back. They were around for Danny's birthday.'

Lucy notices Sylvia's 'they'.

'Did he have a girl with him?'

'No, it was just him and Robbo. But get this . . .' Sylvia gives Lucy a sly, pleased look over the top of Nonnie's head. 'You can't breathe a word of this to anyone, but Danny swears he saw the two of them—you know—going at it. Out the back garden. Keith was against the shed, Robbo was kneeling and . . . well, sucking. Slurp, slurp, slurp. It was dark, but Danny swears it.'

Lucy feels suddenly as if words and bodies have nothing to do with one another. In fact, she no longer believes in bodies at all: not Keith's, not her brother's, and least of all her own, which sits shivering on the verandah, though the evening isn't cold. Lucy has nothing to do with her body, just as its shivering has nothing to do with the temperature of the air, or with the sweep of John Biga's departing headlights, or with the brave way Charlie yells, 'Daddy!' as Hal comes striding into view, grinning madly. Sylvia, passing Nonnie to Lucy, stands up to greet Hal, smoothing her skirt and shaking out her yellow hair.

1962

John Biga asks Lucy to marry him in January. This isn't completely unexpected: he's been preparing to leave Hal and set up on his own, and he's always been attentive to her in his stiff, courtly way. The proposal itself has a rigidity to it, as if it's a plank of wood he's been instructed to hold perfectly flat. They're sitting together on the bench outside the shop, just as they did when he crushed his finger. He keeps his eyes on the ground and talks, almost apologetically, of the injustices of Soviet Poland, the immigrant indignities of Australia. His Polish name, apparently, is Jan.

Lucy, looking at the smooth stub of his shortened finger, wonders if he knows any women in Australia other than herself. He describes at length a cat his mother would feed at the kitchen door, although his father had forbidden pets, and Lucy can't help but think of him, too, as a kind of stray: shy, grateful, less shiny than he might have been under different circumstances. She's noticed him, though, be hard on the other workers in a quiet, forbidding manner that seems more effective than Hal's bluster, and once or twice he's watched Sylvia saunter off and muttered a word beneath his breath that Lucy knows, without speaking Polish, means 'whore'.

Lucy asks him if she might have some time to think about her answer, and he agrees—he isn't leaving immediately. He seems to interpret her reluctance to refuse him outright as an act of pity. This would infuriate a man like Hal, but not John, who appears to take that pity and make space for it among all the other disappointments of his life. Lucy is almost sure she won't marry him.

In February, a letter comes from Mount Isa saying that Robbo has been badly beaten, that he was found unconscious early one morning in a public park, that his injuries suggest multiple attackers, and that while he's expected to 'pull through', he'll always need 'a certain level of care that is best provided by family'. It's signed by a union rep.

That evening, at tea, Hal says, 'What the hell was he doing in a park so late at night?'

Sylvia shoots Lucy a meaningful look, and Lucy recognises in herself a stubborn refusal to accept the fact of Robbo and Keith in the Grafton dark. She now feels that refusal falling away.

Mum says, 'We'll have him here.' She speaks offhandedly, barely glancing at Hal, although it's clear that her whole being is intent on him. There's something withered about her, Lucy thinks. But every now and then, she unfurls herself.

Hal nods sagely above his sausages. 'He can help Lucy in the shop,' he says, his brow furrowed as if with concern. 'He can give change. If he can still count to ten, that is.'

Mum's chair squeals against the lino as she pushes it back, throws down her knife and fork, stands, and leaves the kitchen. Hal laughs, Charlie echoes him, and Hal swats out at his son, cuffing the back of his head. Then Sylvia leans across the table and places her hand on Hal's forearm. She has gained weight, is prettier than ever, and careful, Lucy knows, to dance just out of his reach. Watching the two of them, she finds herself recalling the Polish word for whore.

Charlie is crying. Nonnie stares at him with stricken awe. Sylvia speaks in soothing whispers, stroking Hal's arm.

Lucy is disgusted by all of it, and mostly by what she recognises as the stinginess of her own heart, which twists at the thought of Robbo and his 'certain level of care'. Already she can see him at the table, drooling, with a stunned and stupid face. Danny won't visit; Colin's useless; Peter, the footy star, pretends the family doesn't exist. Keith is gone for good. Lucy will, she knows, be left to wipe and feed Robbo, to dress him as she did Charlie, to comb his hair and kiss the top of his head, even when the smell of it turns her stomach. She sees herself years from now, still in this kitchen, loving Robbo, fretting over him, and sunk in steady hatred.

Across the window, across the table, comes the bright bubble of John Biga's headlights. He's leaving for the day. He might leave forever. What a thought: to leave forever. Lucy stands and runs to the verandah, where she calls his name and waves her arms above her head. He's almost at the road, and she doesn't think he's seen her. But he stops the car, opens the window, leans out, and looks back at her, uncertain. Then she's down the steps, across the lawn. His head withdraws from the window. She runs, afraid he'll drive away. He doesn't. He waits. The passenger door swings open, as if by magic.

ACKNOWLEDGEMENTS

These stories were written with the generous support of residencies from the Australia Council for the Arts and the Santa Maddalena Foundation, for which I'm very grateful.

I'm also grateful for the support of my colleagues and students at the University of Sydney and the University of California, Berkeley. I think especially of Lyn Hejinian.

I'd like to thank the publications in which several of these stories first appeared, and the editors who worked with me on them: Deborah Treisman at *The New Yorker* ('Demolition' and 'Hostel'), Michael Ray at *Zoetrope: All-Story* ('Tourists' and 'Lucy'), and Emily Stokes at *The Paris Review* ('Hostess').

Enduring thanks to the marvellous Stephanie Cabot and everyone at Susanna Lea Associates.

In the US, I'm thankful for everyone at Farrar, Straus and Giroux, especially Mitzi Angel, Milo Walls, Emma Chuck, and Janine Barlow.

ACKNOWLEDGEMENTS

In Australia, thank you to everyone at Allen & Unwin, especially Jane Palfreyman, Angela Handley, and Ali Lavau. And in the UK, thank you to everyone at Sceptre, especially Federico Adorno and Carole Welch.

Ahoy-hoy to Karen Kilgariff and Georgia Hardstark, whose existence helped me write this book.

Thank you to my brilliant early readers, Fatima Kola and Namwali Serpell.

I'm indebted to the friendship, generosity, and critical eye of Michelle de Kretser, who took every word of this book seriously, and to whom it is dedicated.

Thanks to Giamaica Jones, who continues to be the world's most perfect snort-snorer, and to Emma Jones, who saw every word, thought, doubt, and joy before anyone else. Three stars!

And finally, love and thanks to these dear ones: Ian, Lyn, Katrina, Evan, Bonita, Rowan, Anneka, Archie, and Jemima McFarlane. I'm so lucky.

A NOTE ABOUT THE AUTHOR

Fiona McFarlane is the author of *The Night Guest* (2013); *The High Places* (2016), which won the International Dylan Thomas Prize; and *The Sun Walks Down* (2023). Her short fiction has been published in *The New Yorker*, *Zoetrope: All-Story*, and *The Paris Review*. She teaches at the University of California, Berkeley.